# A CASE OF ROBBERY ON THE RIVIERA

A Freddy Pilkington-Soames Adventure 6

CLARA BENSON

## A Case of Robbery on the Riviera

It's fair to say that Freddy Pilkington-Soames is not having a good day. His grandmother is threatening to marry a lounge lizard, his old friend has lost her lover, a racehorse has been kidnapped, a priceless diamond has gone missing, and everybody seems to think he should sort it all out.

(Oh, and there's a dead body on the terrace.)

Now Freddy's on the sunny French Riviera, caught in the crossfire of a feud between an audacious thief he's locked horns with before and a murderous gang who will stop at nothing to get what they want. He'd keep his head down if he could, but there are questions that need answering. Who took the diamond? Who is double-crossing whom? And is his grandmother's intended quite all he seems?

(And where *did* that dead body go?)

A political scandal at the highest level is looming and the future of an international conference hangs in the balance, and once again it's up to Freddy to save the day—in more ways than one.

---

ISBN: 978-1-913355-15-9



clarabenson.com

Cover by Shayne Rutherford
WickedGoodBookCovers.com

# A Case of Robbery on the Riviera

## Author's Note

This book can be read on its own as a standalone mystery adventure, but it also forms the continuation of a story thread which began in the Angela Marchmont Mysteries and carried on through the earlier Freddy Pilkington-Soames Adventures. As such, reference is made to events that took place in previous books, so you may enjoy this one more (and will avoid inevitable spoilers) if you are familiar with the back story and characters before you start reading!

# Chapter One

IF THERE WAS one thing Freddy Pilkington-Soames regretted more than anything else in his life, it was having given his mother a key to his flat. He had done it in a moment of inattention, and had realized immediately afterwards that nothing good could come of it, but by that time it was too late, and short of throwing her to the ground and wrestling the thing back off her there was nothing he could do to remedy his mistake. It had occasionally occurred to him to have the lock changed, but he knew that would cause more trouble than it was worth, because Cynthia would want to know why, and then would insist on being given the key to the new lock. No, the deed was done: the genie had been let out of the bottle, and nothing would induce it to go back in again. As a result, whenever he was at home these days he felt obliged to keep a wary eye on the door, especially if he was doing anything of which he knew his mother would disapprove.

One Saturday morning in September Freddy was sleeping the sleep of the righteous: the sleep of a man who has had a hard week at work, and has rewarded himself for it with a night of merrymaking and conviviality with friends at several of his favourite hostelries. It had been a first-rate evening, during which libations had been offered in abundance to Dionysus, and many hilarious things had been said and done. Then, after the god had been duly toasted to everyone's satisfaction and the night was drawing towards the dawn, Freddy had made his way unsteadily back to his flat and toppled into bed, with the vague intention of remaining there for the whole weekend.

But it was not to be: it seemed that he had barely closed his eyes when the familiar slam of a door intruded into his consciousness, followed by the sound of a voice calling his name. Freddy's eyes flickered open, then closed again. Whoever it was could go away. He was available to nobody. A minute afterwards his bedroom door was flung open and someone came in, already talking. Through the heavy sleep-clouds in his mind Freddy recognized the voice of his mother. She stopped halfway through whatever it was she had been saying, and exclaimed:

'Good heavens! What on earth are you doing still in bed at this time?'

Freddy stirred.

'Mmph?' he replied, with difficulty.

There came the rattle of curtains being thrown open. The daylight blazed in through the window directly onto Freddy's face, and he uttered a sound of protest and pulled the blanket over his head. Cynthia pulled it down again and stood over him, wearing an expression Freddy had long ago learned to fear.

'There's no time for this sort of nonsense. I need your help!' she said.

Freddy emitted a silent groan, and hoped briefly that the manifestation before him was merely part of a mildly unpleasant dream. Cynthia went on:

'Your grandmother wants a divorce and we can't have that! What will people think?'

Freddy groped desperately for his mental faculties, which

he suspected were hiding behind the ringing headache that was rapidly developing in the harsh glare of the morning light.

'Divorce? From whom?'

'From your grandfather, of course!'

Freddy woke up a little.

'From Nugs? But I thought he'd divorced her years ago, when she ran off for the fifth time and it became obvious there was no future in the thing. Although personally I should have thought he might have taken the hint after the second or third escape attempt.'

'Don't be flippant. It's no laughing matter.'

'Believe me, I'm not laughing. Quite the contrary, in fact.'

The pain in his head had begun to intensify. Freddy groped for his watch and squinted at it blearily. The hands said a quarter to eight. It seemed an odd sort of time for family news to arrive.

'Did you find this out just now?' he asked.

'No, yesterday afternoon. I was with Father when the telegram arrived from your Great-Aunt Ernestine. A good thing too, or I'm sure he'd have kept the news to himself.'

'Yesterday afternoon? Couldn't you have told me then, instead of waiting until the crack of dawn to burst into the place and start haranguing me while I'm half-asleep?'

'What are you talking about? I've been up for hours. But never mind that. You don't understand. Your grandmother is threatening to marry a *lounge lizard*, and we must do something to stop it!'

'She's threatening to marry a what?'

'A lounge lizard. At least, that's what Aunt Ernestine called him, although you know she and Mother don't see eye to eye, so it's always possible she's exaggerating. He calls himself the Comte de Langlois—although I don't see how it can be a real title, since the French sent all their aristocrats to the guillotine years ago—and Aunt Ernestine says Mother has quite lost her head over him. Anyway, you must speak to your grandfather. He's refusing to listen to reason. He says if she wants a divorce she's welcome to one and she can marry as many lounge lizards as she likes.'

'Sounds very sensible to me. I wish them all joy. Let me know if they throw a party afterwards—for the wedding *or* the divorce.'

Freddy turned over and closed his eyes. Perhaps his mother would go away now. Instead, she merely came around to the other side of the bed and went on talking.

'You're not listening. They mustn't get a divorce, I simply won't allow it! What would Mrs. Belcher say? And Edith Murgatroyd. She's been dying to do me a bad turn ever since her daughter ran off with that married Argentinian polo player twice her age—I dare say you remember the scandal—and I wrote in the *Clarion* that it was probably the result of the girl's having come from a broken home. *Which* is almost certainly true, since no child could have lived with Edith and Harold throwing china at one another day in day out without getting a *little* disturbed in the head. At any rate, Edith will be crowing from here to Hurlingham if she finds out about this.'

Freddy screwed up his eyes more tightly, trying to ward off the barrage of words, but it was no good, as she merely raised her voice, as though she thought his eardrums were situated behind his eyelids. He opened them again.

'But what am I supposed to do about it?' he asked, realizing as he did so that this was a mistake, as it never did to allow any sort of opening where his mother was concerned. As he had feared, she pounced.

'Why, you must go out to Villefranche with your grandfather and help him talk her out of it, of course!' she replied, as though the answer were obvious.

'But why can't he go by himself?'

'What? After that awkward business last year, when we put him on a train to Brighton and two days later got a telegram from that dreadful woman in Ipswich asking us to come and fetch him? I shouldn't trust him to go as far as Clapham on his own.'

This was a fair point.

'Well, then, why can't you go?'

'Oh, darling, you know Mother and I aren't exactly on speaking terms at the moment. Besides, even if we were she never listens to a word I say.'

'If she won't listen to you then she certainly won't listen to me.'

'Nonsense. She's always had a soft spot for you.'

An excuse came to him.

'I can't go—Gertie has invited me up to Fives for the weekend,' he lied, then glanced at his watch again. 'Good Lord, is that the time? I'm going to miss the train.'

He sat up hurriedly, a move which proved to be a mistake, for it caused his head to spin wildly. But it had been a pointless enterprise anyway, because Cynthia was not fooled in the slightest.

'Don't tell lies!' she exclaimed. 'I happen to know Gertie is in Deauville with her mother at present, and won't be going up to Scotland until October at the earliest.'

Freddy grimaced. He ought to have remembered his mother knew where everyone was at any given moment: she was, after all, the author—to use the term loosely—of the *Clarion*'s society column. Still, even if Gertie could not come to his rescue, Freddy was certainly not going to France. The Riviera was very pleasant at this time of year, but he had enough sense to give the place a wide berth, since his grandmother and his Great-Aunt Ernestine lived there together in a state of mutual and more or less open hostility. If he did as his mother said, he would undoubtedly be drawn into an unedifying family row in which everybody would behave badly and he would somehow get the blame for it all. Besides, the last thing he wanted was to travel with his grandfather, who had an eye for the ladies and not infrequently needed reminding in the most forceful terms that they did not necessarily have an eye for *him*. How could Freddy get out of it? Suddenly he remembered he had a job. A job was a perfectly reasonable excuse not to go gallivanting abroad.

'Look here, Mother,' he said. 'I'd love to go, but you know we're short-handed at the moment, what with half the office coming down with German measles, and old Bickerstaffe simply won't be able to spare me.'

Cynthia huffed, but could not deny the truth of this.

'You're both as bad as each other! First Father refuses to go, and now you. How am I to get anything done?'

'Nugs refused? Then why did you come here and ask me?'

'Because I thought you might be able to persuade him.'

'Sorry, there's nothing doing, I'm afraid.'

Cynthia knew when she was temporarily beaten, especially since her son was showing signs of drifting off to sleep again.

'Very well,' she said. 'But don't think I've finished with you.'

On that ominous note, she departed. The door slammed loudly behind her, and Freddy winced. He felt rather pleased with himself for his success in having dodged an unpleasant task. His mother would no doubt direct pointed remarks at him for the next week or two, but that was a state of affairs so common that he barely noticed it any more. The important thing was that he would not have to go to France and embroil himself in affairs which did not concern him and could bring no benefit to himself. He lay, enjoying the silence caused by Cynthia's departure, and at length felt himself falling gently back into a comfortable doze.

Ten minutes later the doorbell rang shrilly, rousing him with a start. He might have ignored it, but the ringing was followed by a knocking and a voice outside the door which informed him of the arrival of a telegram. Muttering epithets to himself, Freddy rose, took delivery of the envelope and opened it. It had been sent from Nice, and was reply paid. His first thought was that his Great-Aunt Ernestine must have taken it upon herself to try and persuade him to come and talk to his grandmother. But the message was from quite a different person. Freddy stared at it in astonishment, all thought of sleep now forgotten.

> *In a spot of bother* (it said). *Could do with your help. Please come. Angela.*

Freddy looked at the envelope and read the telegram again. The address given was a hotel in Villefranche-sur-Mer, but other than that there was no clue as to what it might mean.

'Good Lord!' he said.

## Chapter Two

'You're looking well for a chap with German measles,' remarked Nugs maliciously.

'There was nothing else for it,' said Freddy. 'Bickerstaffe would never have given me the time off. I only hope he doesn't try and call me at home, or I expect I'll be in for the boot.'

The train was speeding through Kent on its way to Dover, leaving behind it the chill grey drizzle of the city as it bore them towards the English Channel and a promise of blue skies and warm sunshine. Freddy's grandfather, Nugs (or Lord Lucian Wareham as he was known in polite society, to which he was occasionally admitted), was dressed in his smartest travelling clothes in the style of twenty years ago, and was as restless as a small child, getting up and sitting down, opening and shutting the window, and giving the conductor a hard time of it. Freddy was doing his best to ignore him, but he was so fidgety it was almost impossible.

'Why don't we head off somewhere else?' Nugs suggested at last. 'We might slip off the train in Paris and go and have some fun. There was a night-club I used to frequent back in the eighties—a cabaret, they call it now. Plenty of drinks and pretty girls wearing a few frills and not much else.' His eyes were wistful. 'There was one girl, now: Odette, her name was. Eyes like limpid pools and a smile that could light up a whole room. Beautifully soft skin. I wonder what she's like now. Old and fat with more grandchildren than teeth, I expect.'

He gazed down sadly at his own burgeoning frontage.

'Can't be done,' replied Freddy. 'Mother telegraphed to let them know we're coming.'

'Did she?'

'Of course she did. You don't think she'd risk letting us loose in France to whisk off wherever the wind takes us, do you?'

'But I don't want to go. Lord knows I don't fancy speaking to your grandmother, and Ernestine looks at me perpetually as though I were something one might tread in on a long country walk.'

'They're expecting us now. We'll go there, you can let Baba talk, then we'll come back and tell Mother you tried and failed to persuade her out of the divorce. Unless you *do* want to persuade her out of it, of course?'

'Ha!' barked Nugs. 'I shouldn't even try. Good riddance, I say! I wonder who's the poor chump she's got her hooks into now. Well, he's welcome to her. The woman has been nothing but trouble since the day I met her. But I still don't see why I have to drag myself all the way out to the Riviera, when I might just as well have sent her a letter with my blessing.' He adopted a wheedling tone. 'Couldn't we just—'

'No!'

'You're a disappointment, that's what you are. That I should live to see any grandson of mine be so henpecked by his own mother! It's a disgrace.'

'Then why are you here with me?' inquired Freddy pointedly. 'Who henpecked you?'

Nugs glared at him and turned to look out of the window.

'All right,' he said at last. 'But don't think I'm staying in that ghastly villa with them. We'll go to a hotel.'

Freddy was inclined to agree, given the delicate state of affairs subsisting between Great-Aunt Ernestine and his grandmother, Cecily Wareham (known to all as Baba), who occupied opposite wings of a moderately large villa in the hills above Villefranche. Baba had moved into the place shortly after the war, and had lived there quite happily until Great-Aunt Ernestine, upon attaining the status of Dowager Duchess in 1920, had announced that she intended to make the villa her home, and that Baba must move out—which Baba had refused absolutely to do. The house belonged to Freddy's cousin Cedric, the current Duke of Purbeck, who had a horror of squabbling women. When appealed to as adjudicator he had declined to intervene, merely announcing that the two of them were welcome either to stay in the villa or to throw each other off the Grande Corniche, he didn't much care which, just so long as they left him out of it. So Great-Aunt Ernestine and Baba had come to an uneasy truce, and had shared the house, bristling at one another from opposite ends of it, ever since. Freddy suspected the arrival of himself and Nugs was almost certain to upset the fragile equilibrium that had developed over the years.

'Very well, then,' he said. 'I know of a hotel, as a matter of fact. We'll get rooms there.'

'Oh? Which one?'

'It's called the Bellevue. A friend of mine is staying there and I promised to meet her.'

Nugs leered.

'A friend, eh? What about that girl of yours? I don't suppose you've told *her* about it, have you?'

'Take your mind out of the gutter. Not that kind of friend. Her name is Angela Marchmont, and it's all perfectly above the board.'

'Angela Marchmont? Don't know the woman. Who is she?'

'She used to be a sort of amateur detective, but she gave it up and went to America. I don't know why she's come back.'

'Marchmont ... Marchmont. Where have I heard the name before?' Nugs's face cleared, as his memory served up the required information. 'Ah, yes, she's the hussy who blew her husband's head off in a fit of pique, isn't she? It was in all the papers a year or two ago.'

'She didn't blow his head off. And I shouldn't bring the subject up if I were you, or she's liable to freeze you with a deathly stare. She's in some kind of trouble and I said I'd help her, that's all.'

'Hmph. All these women with their problems. Why can't they leave us alone?'

Nugs settled down, muttering, to read his paper. Freddy, on the contrary, was very curious to see his old friend again. It was over a year since she had taken herself off to America, and he wondered what had induced her to return. Most people had by now forgotten the scandal which had seen Angela Marchmont tried and sensationally acquitted of the murder of her husband, but it would have been easy enough to whip up interest in her case again, and for that reason Freddy had not mentioned anything about the telegram to his mother, who would have had no qualms about resurrecting the story for her newspaper column, and might even have insisted upon accompanying him to France.

The journey passed smoothly, with only one attempt by Nugs to sneak off the train at Paris, which was easily foiled, and the two of them arrived at their destination next day shortly before lunch. The Hotel Bellevue was a modern building set in a favourable position, perched up on the cliffs, with a large East-facing terrace overlooking the harbour of Villefranche and magnificent views over the bay and Cap Ferrat on the other side. Its discreet luxury attracted the sort of clientele who shunned ostentation and the attention of the public in favour of a quiet retreat and efficient service, and it was a favoured haunt of those 'in the know'. At high season the hotel would have been full, but the winter sojourners had not yet begun to arrive in their masses, and so Freddy and Nugs had no difficulty in securing rooms. Once the formalities had been completed and their luggage disposed of to a nearby porter, Freddy inquired after Mrs. Marchmont and was informed that she was to be found on the terrace, of which they could see a tantalizing glimpse through the large windows of the dining-room to their left. There was no resisting the lure of that view, and Freddy and Nugs needed no further urging. Once outside it was impossible not to pause to absorb the warmth, admire the vista before them and feel the cares of London ebbing away—for what hope did misery or anxiety have against such a determined onslaught of pure pleasure on the senses? The sun cast its rays lavishly onto a calm sea that reflected the deep blue of the sky, and the red roofs peeping out through the trees on the hillside across the bay seemed to doze in the late summer glow, while boats bobbed gently on the ocean and seagulls wheeled overhead. The blues were bluer, and the greens were greener, and the warmth was warmer, and even the people seemed brighter and cleaner to look at, as though something of the place had rubbed off on them. Freddy began to be pleased he had come after all.

He glanced around, looking for Angela, and saw a familiar dark-haired figure sitting at a table and gazing out at the view. Her face spread into a wide smile when she caught sight of him, and she stood up as they approached.

'Freddy, darling, I'm so pleased you've come,' she said. 'In fact, I shall kiss you!'

She did so, then stepped back so they could assess one another properly. She was dressed in a light, elegant summer frock and a smart sun hat of a style which manifested a certain American influence, and she looked much happier than when he had seen her last.

'Hallo, Angela. You're looking marvellous as usual,' said Freddy.

'You're too kind. I shall return the compliment and say you're handsomer than ever,' she replied.

Having established to their mutual satisfaction that neither of them should be ashamed to be seen with the other in public, they beamed at one another silently in the manner of two friends who have not met in some time, have much news to exchange, and are not quite sure what to say first. Nugs had brightened and was hovering hopefully.

'Ah yes,' said Freddy. 'Angela, this is my grandfather, Lord Lucian Wareham.'

'Charmed,' purred Nugs, as indeed he was. He bowed over Angela's hand with great courtly display and she accepted the attention graciously.

'Is it too early for lunch, do you suppose?' said Freddy.

They all agreed it was not too early for lunch, and the waiter was summoned. Conversation was necessarily of a general nature during the meal, given the presence of a third party, but at last Nugs, who had been too agitated to sleep on the train, decided that in order to restore himself to his full faculties for the coming interview with his wife, which promised to be a trying one, he really ought to have a nap. He therefore rose and departed, with many flowery salutations to his new acquaintance. Angela watched him go and directed a questioning look at Freddy.

'I had no choice but to bring him. I'll explain it all later if you think you can bear to listen. But never mind that old goat, what about you? Why are you here, and wherefore the mysterious telegram? I take it you didn't just lure me down here to chat about the weather and the stock market crash.'

'No, nothing like that. Something rather more personal, I'm afraid, which is why I asked you in particular.' A look of slight embarrassment crossed her face, and she eyed him sideways as if deliberating whether to tell him, then evidently realized that since she had summoned him all the way to the South of France she had little choice in the matter. She gave a resigned sigh. 'Freddy, I've lost Edgar.'

'What do you mean, you've lost him?'

'Just that. He's disappeared and I don't know where he is.'

Freddy was conscious of a faint pang of dismay. He was very fond of Angela, but the idea of having been brought all the way down here merely to act as confidant in a tangled affair of the heart did not fill him with joy. The man in question, Edgar Valencourt, was a former criminal—supposedly retired, but a shady character nonetheless—and Freddy had never been wholly convinced that Angela could be happy with him. If he had gone missing, the obvious conclusion was that he had had enough of the respectable life and had decided to make a bolt for it.

'I say, Angela, I'm sorry to hear that,' he said. 'But what can I do about it?'

'Why, I want to find him, of course, and I need your help.'

Her jaw was set firmly, and Freddy saw there was to be no escape: he was to be drawn into it whether he liked it or not.

'Suppose you explain,' he said.

'I don't know exactly what happened. He came out to New York with me last year as you know, then went up to Saratoga and bought a stud that was about to go under after the crash. There was a lot to do to make it a going concern, and his leg was still bothering him after he got shot, but I made him go and have it seen to so he'd be strong enough to manage the work, and the doctors did something frightfully clever and made it almost perfectly well again. He'd been quite content throwing all his efforts into the horses, and he'd just bought a stallion called Nightshade that had won dozens of races and promised well, and I stayed mostly in New York because of Barbara, and visited as often as I could, and it had all been going splendidly, until now.'

Her brow wrinkled worriedly, and she continued:

'A few weeks ago he came over to France to look at some thoroughbreds at a stable just outside Perpignan. He wanted to go because the people who owned the place had been friends of his mother's when she was alive, and had been kind to her. I wasn't keen on his making the trip, because—well, because the French police wanted rather badly to arrest him at one time, but he said there was nothing to worry about, as there was no reason anybody should connect a reputable buyer of horses with a man everyone thinks is dead. He wasn't using his old name any more, the people at the stable didn't know him by sight, and he promised to keep his head down and do nothing to draw attention to himself.

'So he went to Perpignan and everything seemed to be going well. He wired me every day to say he was safe, as I'd asked, and I stopped fretting—that is, until his head groom called me from Saratoga to say he'd been trying to get in touch with Edgar urgently for days, and did I know where he was?

'Of course I telegraphed him straightaway but he didn't reply, which was odd, so I got his hotel in Perpignan on the telephone, and to my surprise they told me he'd stayed only two nights and then left. I told them that was impossible, because he'd been wiring me every day from the hotel, but they refused to budge. He'd gone after two nights and that was that.

'Well, I dare say you can imagine my consternation. I saw there was no time to lose, so I took the first passage across to France, went straight to Perpignan and spoke to them at the hotel. They weren't at all helpful, but I wasn't going to be put off, so I made the most tremendous nuisance of myself and demanded to speak to everyone who'd so much as exchanged a word with Edgar while he was there.

'One of the clerks had a particularly shifty look about him, and I was convinced he knew something he wasn't telling. I got the information out of him in the end, but not without threats and bribery. He told me that on the morning of the day Edgar left, two rough-looking men had come to the hotel and asked for him by the name he was using. They'd waited for him until he came back that evening, and the clerk had seen them all talking together in the street outside. Then Edgar came in and told the man he was checking out in the next hour. He packed his things and left with the two rough men, and as he was paying the bill he gave the clerk a whole sheaf of telegram forms already written out, asked him to send one every day, and tipped him handsomely for his pains.' Her face darkened. 'Those were the telegrams I'd been receiving. The wretched man thought I'd never suspect a thing, and he was right—if it hadn't been for that call from Saratoga I'd have been quite convinced he was still in Perpignan. Fortunately for me, the clerk had overheard one of the men remark as they left that if they made good time they'd be in Nice by midnight. Whether that was just a stop on the way to somewhere else I have no idea, but it was the only clue I had—apart from the fact that one of the men he went away with wore an eye-patch, according to the clerk. But that's not much help if I don't know where they went.'

She twisted a napkin and stared broodingly out to sea.

'So now here I am, chasing shadows across France to no good purpose, and with no idea of whether I'll ever see Edgar again.'

# Chapter Three

THEY SAT a few moments in silence, then Freddy said, very gently:

'Was it wise of you to come here, old thing? Are you sure he hasn't just decided to do a bunk?'

'I won't say the thought hadn't crossed my mind,' admitted Angela. 'But there was nothing to suggest he intended it. On the contrary, he seemed very happy where he was. He said—well, never mind what he said.' She turned a little pink, then brought herself up short and looked at him defensively. 'And don't give me that pitying look. I know he's deceived me a hundred times before. I'm not a complete idiot. But there are one or two things that don't make sense. I asked the hotel clerk very particularly how Edgar looked when he said he was leaving—I mean, was he happy or sad? He shrugged in that irritating way the French have, and affected not to have noticed one way or the other, but eventually I wormed it out of him that he thought Edgar was more cross and preoccupied than anything else. That doesn't sound like someone who's thrilled at the thought of his impending freedom from a troublesome female, does it? And how did the men know the name he was using? He's been calling himself

Merivale, but only since he arrived in America. How did they know whom to ask for at the hotel?'

'He might have told them himself.'

'Perhaps,' she replied unwillingly. 'But then there's the question of the telegrams. Why did he bother with them? What was the use in wasting all that money to keep me in the dark, if he really had decided to make a run for it there and then? He must have been intending to come back, and the telegrams were merely to stop me finding out whatever he was doing in the meantime.'

'I suppose that makes sense,' agreed Freddy. 'But if you're sure he was planning to return, why follow him all the way here? Why didn't you wait until he got back to the States and confront him then? Wouldn't that have been easier?'

'Because he's in trouble, I can feel it,' replied Angela.

Freddy was not convinced, and his face said as much.

'What sort of trouble? And incidentally, why are you in Villefranche rather than Nice, if that's where they were heading?'

'I started in Nice, and asked at about fifty hotels, but the place is so crowded one can't hear oneself think,' she said. 'If he's there I'll never find him. Besides, I've found a clue. Look at this.'

She delved into her little handbag and brought out a folded page torn from an English newspaper of a few days earlier. Freddy took it.

'"Contrary to widely circulated reports, the Grand Duke Nicholas has not gone to Bavaria",' he read. 'That's a relief. I've barely slept a wink in days worrying about it.'

'Not that, this.' She indicated a paragraph tucked away in the corner. Freddy followed the direction of her finger.

'"Mrs. Jessie Weeks, the wife of Mr. R. G. Weeks, is to spend the next month at the Hotel Bellevue in Villefranche with her daughter, Miss Garnet Weeks, while her husband attends the reparations conference in The Hague. Mrs. and

Miss Weeks are to be accompanied by Mr. Jacques Fournier, the son of the French Prime Minister." R. G. Weeks? Ah, yes, he's the American fellow who's been doing all that sterling work, trying to broker an agreement between nations and get the Germans to stump up the cash they owe for obliterating half of France during the war. Some kind of rich industrialist, isn't he?'

'Yes. But read the rest of it.'

Freddy looked back at the paper.

'"Mrs. Weeks is well known for her love of fine jewels, and is the owner of the fabulous Mariensee diamond, which her husband presented to her last year on the occasion of their wedding anniversary. The diamond is said to be one of the most valuable jewels in the world, and is almost without price." Well? What of it?'

'Don't be obtuse, Freddy. You know Edgar's past. He never saw a pretty bauble he didn't like, and if she's brought this one with her it will be like dangling a piece of cheese in front of a mouse.'

'Do you think he's planning to steal it?'

'No—yes—I don't know,' replied Angela. She looked deeply worried. 'I don't know what to think. He's been so good, and I really thought he'd left it all behind, but I get very nervous whenever I hear about precious stones in connection with Edgar. What if he's fallen in with some of his old associates and been tempted in a moment of madness? Everyone knows that Jessie Weeks is here, and in which hotel. This will be child's play to him.'

'But you don't even know he's in Villefranche. Or do you?'

'No. He's certainly not at this hotel, at any rate. I was waiting for you to arrive before I started asking at the others.'

'Then perhaps he's not in the area at all. Perhaps it's as you said, and they merely stopped here on the way to somewhere else.'

'I wish I could believe it,' said Angela, 'but it all seems like far too much of a coincidence.'

The whole situation was sounding increasingly disagreeable, and Freddy's heart sank. At best, the thing promised to be a wild-goose chase, while at worst it looked as though he might be called upon to prevent the theft of a priceless jewel by the lover of an otherwise eminently sensible woman who had an incurable blind spot where this particular man was concerned. Still, there was a glimmer of hope: it was quite possible Angela was mistaken in her supposition that Valencourt had the Mariensee diamond in his sights. There was no certainty even that he was on the Riviera at present. Perhaps he had merely decided to disappear for a week or two for reasons of his own, and then return. If so, he had been fairly caught out, but that was a personal dispute in which Freddy could not be called upon to participate. In the meantime, it would be uncivil of him to object to helping his friend in her search.

'Very well, then,' he said. 'You may depend on me to use all the low cunning and base machinations I've learned to employ in my time at the *Clarion* to help in the search for this chap of yours. We'll inquire at every hotel in the area, and if we can't find him we'll speak to Mrs. Weeks and tell her to keep a close eye on her jewels. I mean to say, that's good advice at any time, whether the place is crawling with thieves or not.' He glanced at his watch. 'But we'll start tomorrow, if you don't mind. 'This evening I have family business to attend to. Not that I relish the prospect, but my mother has spies everywhere and if I don't do as I'm told I'll never hear the last of it.'

'You're a darling, Freddy. I knew I could rely on you. There's no-one else I can tell, and if it is bad news then I know you won't crow.' He looked at her questioningly, and she continued: 'I can see what you're thinking: I'm a silly woman who can't see the obvious when it's right in front of her nose. I'm quite aware I'm most likely making a fool of myself.'

'Then why not cut your losses and go home?'

'Because it wouldn't be right. I made a promise to try and keep him straight, so try I shall. If he is up to something illegal, then I shall do my best to stop him before he does it.'

'But what if he isn't up to something illegal?' asked Freddy.

'You mean what if he's simply tired of me?' She narrowed her eyes dangerously. 'Then he shall tell me so to my face. If he thinks he can duck out without facing the consequences he's very much mistaken.'

Freddy could not help being amused at her differing attitudes to Valencourt's supposed sins.

'You'd rather have him a thief than a coward, eh?' he observed.

'I'd rather have him neither. But yes, if you like.'

There was no arguing with that, and shortly afterwards the two of them parted, agreeing to meet for breakfast the next day and begin their search.

## Chapter Four

The Villa des Fleurs was tucked away in the hills above Villefranche, where the air was cooler. It was a fine-looking house, surrounded by sloping gardens thick with lush vegetation, through which the sea could be glimpsed far below, and which afforded the villa a good deal of privacy from other nearby houses. Freddy and Nugs took a taxi from the hotel, for even in the early evening it was still very warm, and an uphill toil did not appeal. Nugs had fortified himself for the coming ordeal with a couple of whiskies before they left the hotel, which made him garrulous and inclined to talk nonsense. He was fascinated by Angela Marchmont.

'Delightful woman,' he said enthusiastically. 'Are you sure she didn't blow her husband's head off?'

'Quite sure,' replied Freddy.

'I must say she didn't seem the type, although one can never tell. But even if she did do it, I dare say he died happy. Who wouldn't like to meet his end gazing upon the face of a pretty woman—even one who's irked enough to put a bullet in you?' He seemed to think he could pay a lady no higher compliment. 'Rather she than your Great-Aunt Ernestine, for example. Can you imagine spending your last moments on earth gawping at that bulldog's jaw? Odd, because she wasn't bad-looking when she was younger, if you like the stern, commanding type. Your Great-Uncle Algy did, but then he'd been in the army.'

He then embarked upon a long, rambling reminiscence about an illegal bare-knuckle prize fight between two women which he had witnessed in his youth. Freddy had heard the story many times before, and it had long since ceased to hold his interest.

'Have you decided what you're going to say to Baba?' he interrupted.

'Bah! What is there to say? Besides, you don't suppose I'll be able to get a word in edgeways, do you? I'll listen and nod, and if we're in luck we might get a drink out of them. Then we can go back to the hotel and enjoy a few days' peace and quiet.'

'But you'll have to say something—come to terms, at least, to keep things civil and stop the press crawling all over it when it gets to court.'

Nugs huffed.

'I don't see why any of this is necessary. The woman's been bouncing from one poor fathead to another for the past forty years or more. Why she's suddenly decided to be respectable at her age is beyond me.'

'Well, you can ask her now,' replied Freddy, as the taxi drew up at the villa and they alighted.

The door was answered by a stiff manservant who looked very British and out of place. After a minor skirmish in which he affected not to recognize the visitors, despite having known them both for many years, he admitted Freddy and Nugs to the house.

'Who is that, Henry?' came a loud voice. 'Is it my great-nephew?'

The voice was followed by its owner, who emerged from a door to the left.

'Hallo, Aunt E,' replied Freddy. 'Here we are, as promised—or threatened, if you like.'

Ernestine, Dowager Duchess of Purbeck, was a short, well-built woman with a firm jaw and an impressive bosom rather like the prow of a ship. She was over-dressed for the weather, wearing clothes more suited to a British autumn, for she held to the firm belief that since September is not summer in Britain, it is not summer in France either, and therefore one must wrap up warmly. Despite having lived in Villefranche for ten years now, she only ever allowed herself to shed her outer layers between the months of June and August, and since she never seemed to suffer the heat, Freddy had always set it down as an example of the triumph of mind over matter, although she herself would have ascribed it to a proper approach to dress.

She greeted them with the distant civility which was the nearest she ever got to affection, and led them into a grand drawing-room. It had once been the dining-room, but had been converted for the Duchess's use when it became clear that she and Baba were never going to get along, and would have to live in separate parts of the house. Fortunately, the villa lent itself naturally to being divided into two, and while Great-Aunt Ernestine might have balked at being relegated to the lesser apartments, she could at least console herself with the fact that the windows in her half of the house had an uninterrupted view all the way to the sea, which had ceased to be the case for Baba's drawing-room after someone had built a house nearby that partially blocked it out.

Freddy wandered over to gaze at the ocean as his aunt and Nugs exchanged preliminaries with wary and exaggerated politeness. The Duchess had been married to Nugs's eldest brother, the seventh Duke, and had always strongly disapproved of her brother-in-law, but it appeared that under the circumstances she had decided that old enmities must be put aside for the greater good. From her manner, it was evident she thought that Nugs saw things as she did, although had she known Nugs's real feelings on the subject the atmosphere would undoubtedly have been much frostier.

'We cannot have this sort of thing happening,' she said. 'Why, it's a disgrace! I have tolerated her foolishness for many years, but this cannot be countenanced, especially at her age. Lucian, you must speak to Cecily and tell her she is making a fool of herself.'

'But you know she won't listen to me,' replied Nugs, who had no intention of even trying.

'You must catch her the right way. Naturally she will not listen if you pin her in a corner and lecture her. You must think of some other way to convince her.'

'Where is Baba, by the way?' asked Freddy.

'Gone out with this man to play tennis, of all things. It must be a deliberate snub, since I told her you were coming, but I imagine she will be back soon.' Great-Aunt Ernestine closed her eyes briefly. 'I simply cannot tell you how trying she is being about this. One could turn a blind eye to the other ones, who were all rather to be pitied than not, and at least had the decency not to intrude themselves here. But this count has turned her head completely. Divorce, indeed! Why, whoever heard of such a thing? I have tried to make her see that she must let the man go for the good of the family, but since she is not a Wareham by birth and merely married in, she does not seem to understand the importance of preserving our good name. Divorce simply cannot be allowed.'

Great-Aunt Ernestine had some time ago taken upon herself the rôle of preserver of the Wareham family name, and nobody could have played the part with more devotion than she. It would therefore have been plain bad manners to point out, first, that she, too, had married into the family, and had once been plain Ernestine Hepple, a vicar's daughter; and second, that none of the other Warehams—with the possible exception of Cynthia—cared nearly as much as she did about what others thought of them. Freddy reflected that it was a good thing his aunt was unaware of the conduct engaged in over the years by some of the more disreputable branches of the family, since it would have ruined the appearance of unsullied respectability over which she had laboured with such dedication.

Servants came in and began bustling about, setting out glasses, plates and other appurtenances that indicated company. It was too much to hope for that the reception was for Freddy and Nugs, since Great-Aunt Ernestine was frugal with the provisions where relatives were concerned.

'Are you expecting guests, Aunt?' Freddy asked.

'Just a small gathering,' she replied. 'You may stay if you like, but you must be on your best behaviour. We have the Weekses coming. It's too bad that Cecily couldn't have made the effort to be here when they arrive.'

'The Weekses? Not Jessie Weeks?' asked Freddy in surprise.

'Yes, do you know them? I knew Jessie's mother as a girl, but she moved to America when she married that mining magnate with the dreadful foreign name. He was rich, and Ethel came from the poor part of the family and hadn't two pennies to rub together so had little choice, but still, one can't help feeling she lowered herself. I don't know Jessie well, but Mr. Roche has assured me she is perfectly unexceptionable and that her daughter, Garnet, is quite the beauty. Mr. Roche himself is coming too. He is always most considerate, even if he is French. He moves in the highest circles, and I have been given to understand that he is somewhat influential.'

Mr. Roche, whoever he was, was clearly approved of.

'Now,' she went on. 'I must just go and see that the napkins have been folded properly.'

Nugs, who had been eyeing the glasses longingly as she talked, took the opportunity afforded by her absence from the room to pour himself a drink, which he swallowed in one gulp.

'Whew!' he exclaimed. 'Can't we go now? Baba isn't here, and I don't want to waste the evening waiting for her. Why don't we go to the casino? As a matter of fact, I shouldn't be surprised if we found her there now. There's nothing she likes better than throwing my money away at the tables, and at least we might have a little fun while we talk to her.'

Freddy was half-tempted by the idea himself, since there was no saying when his grandmother would return, and a night at the casino appealed to him greatly, but his interest had been aroused by the news that Jessie Weeks was expected. Rather than impose upon Mrs. Weeks at the hotel and perhaps be rebuffed, here was an easy way to effect an introduction to her and perhaps drop a hint or two that she might be wise to keep a close eye on her jewellery—useful advice even where there was no suspicion that a crime was intended. That done, he could spend a day or two inquiring at hotels in the area to please Angela, and if no sign of Edgar Valencourt were found, he could consider his job complete and return to London—although even then there was no need to do so immediately, since nobody would be expecting him back at the *Clarion* until his fictitious German measles had cleared up. Freddy liked the prospect before him, and began to look forward to a few days' unexpected holiday.

# Chapter Five

Jessie Weeks's appearance spoke of a life of ease and comfort. She was sleek and well-nourished, with a face that bore no sign of the cares which tend to line the faces of less fortunate mortals, while her clothes were of the latest fashion and would not be worn more than a few times before being discarded for new ones. She was frequently the centre of attention but was good-mannered enough to affect an air of surprise on such occasions, for her wealth had not spoilt her. She had brought with her not only her daughter, Garnet, but also a young Frenchman who was introduced as Jacques Fournier, the son of the French Prime Minister. Young Fournier had for some years been a staple of the French gossip columns for his wild and ungovernable habits and tendency to fall into bad company, and after one too many scandals it was said that his father had begun to despair of him. However, the young man had lately shown signs of settling down a little, and in an attempt to encourage him to continue the good work and instil a sense of responsibility in him, the Prime Minister had charged him with the pleasant task of escorting Mrs. and Miss Weeks from The Hague to the Riviera, since the reparations talks were dragging on longer than expected, and the ladies had been longing for some warmth and sea air.

One could hardly blame the young man for jumping at the chance to spend some time by the sea—especially in the company of Garnet Weeks, who was nothing less than a beauty, with large, expressive brown eyes, dimpled cheeks and a beautifully shaped mouth that turned up slightly at the corners and looked permanently about to break into a smile. Indeed, it seemed that M. Fournier *père* had hit upon a happier solution than he knew, for although they were doing their best to hide it, it was perfectly obvious that Jacques Fournier and Garnet Weeks were quite smitten with one another. He in particular could not keep his eyes off her, and although with her looks she must have been accustomed to attention from men, she flushed a very becoming shade of pink whenever he spoke to her. She seemed disposed to scatter her happiness over everyone in the company, and declared she was exceedingly charmed with the Riviera.

'I've never seen anywhere like it!' she exclaimed to Freddy. 'It rained for a week straight in The Hague and I thought I should never dry out until I came here. But the Riviera is so beautiful! Who could resist it?'

She shook her dark curls at him and opened her eyes wide, and Freddy had no choice but to agree—in fact, would have agreed had she told him that the sea was yellow and that cows had wings. He noticed she was wearing a pretty ring set with a red stone. He commented on it, and she held it up so he could see it better, and said:

'Do you like it? Daddy gave me it for my birthday. He's always so kind.'

'And I suppose it's a garnet, not a ruby.'

She laughed.

'Yes. I never seem to be able to get away from them—understandable, given my name! I have more garnets than I can count.' She lowered her voice. 'Truth to tell, red isn't my favourite colour, but I guess people will be giving me garnets until the day I die!'

'Do you like jewels, then?'

'I don't mind them, if they're pretty. Mother loves them, though. She doesn't go anywhere without her jewellery-box.'

Freddy looked across at Mrs. Weeks, who was preening under the flattery of Nugs. It was too early in the evening for the most showy finery, but Freddy saw a delicate cluster of sapphires and diamonds glittering at her throat, while something else sparkled in her ears, and now and again she put her left hand over her right, as though comforting herself with the feeling of the large diamond ring that she wore there. Freddy seemed to recall having read that the Mariensee diamond was set in a brooch, but Mrs. Weeks was not wearing a brooch. Still, whether she had brought the famous jewel with her or not, it was clear she would be rich pickings for a thief. He saw no harm in giving Garnet a hint.

'Ah, yes, I believe I read something about it in the newspapers,' he said. 'Rather dangerous to be travelling about with it all, what?'

'Oh, Mother is always very careful,' replied Garnet. 'Everything stays safely locked up unless she's wearing it.'

Jacques Fournier had gone across to the window and was staring out morosely, his formerly cheerful expression nowhere to be seen. Freddy wondered for a second whether he were upset that Garnet was talking to another man, but the thought was immediately dispelled when Fournier turned away from the window with a despairing, almost tormented look on his face that clearly had nothing to do with Freddy. Garnet did not see it, but Freddy could not help wondering what it meant.

They were interrupted by the arrival of Benjamin Roche, a distinguished-looking Frenchman of about fifty who, it seemed, was a permanent fixture of the Riviera, and the star around which its high society orbited. He was remarkably tall and thin, but despite his unusual height he stood up very straight, perhaps to throw into deliberately sharp relief his fine head of greying hair. Such an aspect might have been a forbidding one had it not been for his dark eyes, which twinkled benevolently upon everyone, and his manner, which was never less than kind and cordial. He was the proprietor of an old and venerable French newspaper, *Le Moniteur*, and was delighted to discover that Freddy worked for the *Clarion*, for he declared he was a great friend of its owner, Sir Aldridge Featherstone. Roche was immensely rich, owned a magnificently palatial villa on the Cap de Nice, and was fond of throwing his home open to company. In conversation he spoke of the Dowager Duchess and Lady Lucian Wareham with familiarity, and talked of many other important people of his acquaintance, and from the pleasure he evidently gained from doing it, Freddy deduced that he was something of a snob. He was a connoisseur of fine things, and had filled his house with many works of art and valuable antiques. His particular pride and joy was his collection of historic jewellery, much of which had belonged to women of the royal and most noble houses of Europe, and he liked nothing better than to show it off to guests whenever they came to visit.

Freddy was alarmed. Everywhere he went he seemed to hear of valuable jewellery. He glanced around involuntarily, almost as though he expected to see Edgar Valencourt peering in at the window, then shook himself, exasperated. Angela had got herself worked up about nothing, he was sure of it.

Mr. Roche was very pleased to add the Duchess's great-nephew to his collection of fine things, and confided that he was overjoyed to have been introduced to Mrs. Weeks.

'I understand she is also a lover of beautiful jewels, and indeed she has promised to show me the pinnacle of her collection, the Mariensee diamond. I myself keep my jewels in a glass case, but they are much better off in a live setting, so to speak. I shall be delighted to see Mrs. Weeks at my little party on Thursday. You will come too, of course, Mr. Pilkington-

Soames? I know you won't say no—indeed I won't hear a refusal.'

Freddy, always happy to attend any social event, accepted the invitation with alacrity. Mr. Roche went to speak to Jacques Fournier, with whom he was obviously well acquainted, and Nugs came over, a peevish expression on his face.

'Ernestine has been lecturing me for the past fifteen minutes so I couldn't get at the drinks, and it looks as though Baba isn't going to turn up, so why don't we go?' he demanded.

Freddy was about to reply when Nugs spotted something and stiffened. Before Freddy could turn around to see what it was, a woman's voice cried out:

'Freddy, darling, is it really you? My, how you've grown!'

It was Baba. Freddy found himself enveloped in an affectionate embrace, then his grandmother turned to Nugs.

'And Lucian.' She plucked a stray thread from his jacket. Nugs shied and shuffled.

'Hallo, Baba, you're looking well,' he said formally.

Cecily Wareham bore a startling resemblance to her daughter Cynthia, and indeed, looked very little older. She had been only sixteen when Nugs, captivated by her beauty, had married her (possibly with some urgency, according to uncharitable rumours) and taken her home to his family. The marriage had proved a turbulent one from the start, punctuated by several periods of separation, and their estrangement had been more or less permanent since an episode in 1918, during which Baba had returned to her husband with the declared intention of nursing him through an attack of pneumonia which threatened to carry him off. The experiment was not a successful one, and after concerned friends hinted that her presence was possibly causing him more harm than good, she departed for the last time, and had been sunning herself on the Riviera ever since. As Nugs had said, she was looking very well—radiant, even—which might have had something to do with the man who was standing respectfully a short distance away, watching the little scene.

'This is Yves,' said Baba, blushing slightly. 'The Comte de Langlois. Yves, this is Lucian, and this is my—this is Freddy.'

She spoke the last words in some confusion, and Freddy raised his eyebrows as the Comte and Nugs bowed stiffly to one another and murmured acknowledgment of the introduction.

The Comte de Langlois could not have been more than forty-five or so, and was the very picture of sun-tanned health. One could imagine him swinging a racquet professionally, or driving a racing car, or dancing the tango with great style and panache. He was at least six feet tall and beautifully built, with a full, thick head of hair and features that were so regular they might have been chiselled out of marble. Freddy noticed that Nugs had straightened up to his full height, which was not considerable, and appeared to have sucked in his breath.

'I'm so pleased you've come!' exclaimed Baba gaily. 'I'm sorry we were late, but we got so caught up that we quite forgot the time.' She lowered her voice. 'We can't speak now, of course. How long are you staying?'

'A few days,' replied Freddy, seeing that if Nugs spoke he would be forced to let out his breath, causing him to lose several inches in height and gain several more in girth.

'Splendid. Then you and I shall have a cosy little chat tomorrow, Lucian. Now, Ernestine is looking rather cross, so I must just go and make myself amenable.'

Baba took the Comte's arm and fluttered off. Nugs let out his breath and sagged.

'That might have gone worse,' said Freddy, but Nugs was in a state of outrage.

'What's the woman thinking, bringing the fellow into the house?' he demanded.

'Why? Do you think she ought to have left him tied outside with a bowl of water?'

'She oughtn't to have brought him anywhere near the place. I don't know how the young people behave nowadays, but in my day one kept one's paramour at a tasteful distance from one's lawful wedded.'

'You know Baba has never been one to follow convention.'

'She might have made an effort for once. A man likes to feel master in his own house.'

'This isn't your house,' Freddy pointed out.

'It's more mine than it is his. If Cedric and his lot were carried off by bubonic plague tomorrow I'd come in for the whole boiling, including this place.'

'You'd have to fight Aunt E. and Baba for it first. But since pestilence is not threatened and we dwell in the merely hypothetical, I suggest you forget about it for now and go and get a drink.'

Nugs needed no further encouragement. He took himself off and Freddy observed the Comte de Langlois discreetly from a distance. He was certainly a handsome fellow, with perfect English and just enough of a French accent to make him charming but not incomprehensible. Baba hung upon his every word, and the other women of the company—with the exception of Great-Aunt Ernestine—also seemed to find him fascinating.

The sun had now almost set and the guests showed signs of preparing to leave. Nugs seized at the opportunity with alacrity, tossed back one final glass of whisky and made a bee-line for the door. Baba followed Freddy and whispered to him:

'Listen darling, I don't suppose you've noticed it particularly, but Yves is a *little* younger than I am. Not that that sort of thing matters, but one doesn't wish to stand out, so I may have taken just a *few* years off my age. Of course I'd never tell Yves an untruth as such—at least, nothing that makes any difference—but I'd be awfully grateful if you wouldn't draw too much attention to the fact you're my grandson.'

Freddy looked at Baba in surprise.

'Why the devil not?'

'Because I haven't told him I have one. I'm not old enough for one, you see.'

As far as Freddy was aware, Baba's real age must be about sixty-three or four. He did some quick calculations in his head and felt a dawning suspicion.

'Just how many years did you knock off?' he asked.

'Only twenty. I didn't mean to!' she went on hurriedly, as she saw his eyes widen. 'I meant to stop at ten, but it just slipped out, and then I realized what I'd said, but by that time it was too late to correct myself, and I thought, well there's no harm in it, is there? After all, everyone tells me how well I'm ageing.'

'No harm in it? Don't you think he'll find out sooner or later? Aunt E. will tell him even if you don't.'

'No she won't. She can barely bring herself to speak to him let alone tell him anything about me.'

'But I thought you wanted to marry him. Surely you've told him all about yourself?' He saw her face, which was mutinous, and suspicion began to dawn. 'Look here, Baba, what exactly does he know about you?'

'Only what I choose to tell him,' she replied haughtily. 'A woman ought to be a mysterious creature if she wants to hold a man's interest.'

'A woman ought to be a *what*?'

'Shh! Keep your voice down!' The Weekses were now within earshot and the bustle of departure had begun, and she went on, 'Now, go, and tell Nugs I'll see him tomorrow.'

Freddy began to protest, but he saw it was no use, for she was now bidding a loud and affectionate goodbye to Jessie Weeks, so he had no choice but to leave the house.

Mr. Roche had put his car at the service of the ladies and

their escort, but regretted that there was no room for the other two gentlemen. Darkness had fallen now, and it was much cooler and more pleasant, with the scents of evening flowers all around them, so Freddy and Nugs were sincere in their assurances that it did not matter and they were quite happy to walk back to the hotel, which was not more than a mile or so away. They waved the car off, and Freddy was just wondering whether to tell Nugs what had passed between him and Baba when his grandfather burst out:

'Why did she call me Lucian? She never calls me Lucian, except when she's telling me off.'

'Perhaps she was being polite.'

'Polite? So that's the way she wants it, is it? We'll see about that!'

'What?'

'If Baba thinks I'm giving her a divorce to marry that mountebank she's very much mistaken.'

'You've changed your tune,' said Freddy, regarding his grandfather in astonishment.

'Didn't you see him? Why, the fellow practically oozes brilliantine! Never trust a man who thinks more of his own looks than anything else. I saw him glancing at his reflection at least three times. Oh, yes—his face might fool the women, but I saw through him immediately. I've met the type before. He's after nothing but her money—my money, in fact. I could almost see him eyeing up the silverware and calculating how much it would fetch. What the devil has got into Baba? The woman's a damned fool, and he'll take her for every penny she has if we don't do something.'

'What do you mean if *we* don't do something? Who is we?'

'You and I, of course.'

'But what have I to do with it? This is between you and Baba. If you've changed your mind and don't want to let her have the divorce then tell her so, but I'll thank you to leave me out of it.'

'Have you *no* family feeling?' said Nugs in a tone of deep hurt. 'No thought of the disgrace that divorce will bring upon the Warehams?'

'It didn't seem to bother you this morning. As I recall, two hours ago you were more than happy to let her go—couldn't wait to get rid of her, in fact.'

'I've changed my mind.'

'But what am I supposed to do about it?'

'Why, help me find out what he's up to, of course. The man's nothing but a parasite, and we must find proof and tell Baba.'

'You don't think it will make any difference, do you? When did she ever listen to a word you said?'

'Well I shall *make* her listen. I've already told Ernestine I'll move into the villa tomorrow, to keep an eye on Baba, and she quite approves. She says you must come too.'

Freddy saw the pleasant prospects he had been entertaining of a peaceful few days' holiday evaporating before his eyes. The last thing he wanted was to stay at the villa under the watchful and disapproving eye of Great-Aunt Ernestine, who would force him to pour tea for elderly ladies every afternoon and ration the whisky ruthlessly every evening.

'I can't move to the villa,' he replied. 'I've promised Angela I'll give her a hand with something tomorrow.'

'Oh, I see. You choose this woman over family.'

'I'm not choosing anyone over anyone, but I told her I'd help, and I can't very well—'

He broke off and froze.

'What is it?' asked Nugs.

'Shh!' Freddy listened for a moment. 'Hi! You there!'

Nugs turned to look, but Freddy had already shot off and disappeared into the bushes. There was the sound of rustling and cracking, as of someone ploughing through undergrowth, then Freddy re-emerged a little way down the street.

'Too late—he's gone,' he said.

'Who's gone?' demanded Nugs.

'Didn't you see him? There was a man. He must have been lurking in the Great-Aunt's garden. He crept out in front of us and disappeared into the bushes just ahead.'

'But who was it?'

'I don't know. I didn't get a proper look at him, but he had no business being there.'

'Perhaps he was lost,' suggested Nugs.

'Hardly. There's no path through this way. If he was in the garden, then it was deliberate.'

'Well, he's gone now, so I shouldn't worry about it.'

But Freddy was not so sure. The man had taken some pains not to be seen, and it was only quite by accident that Freddy had caught sight of him. Who could it have been, and what had he been doing in the garden of the Villa des Fleurs? He walked back to the hotel, deep in thought.

## Chapter Six

THE NEXT MORNING Freddy came in to breakfast a little late, having been occupied in assisting Nugs with his departure for the Villa des Fleurs, and in resisting all attempts to persuade him to follow suit. When he went into the dining-room, he found that Angela was just finishing breakfast. He sat down at her table and spent some little time considering the menu.

'Now, to business,' said Angela once he had ordered and the waiter had gone. 'If we split up, then we ought to be able to get much more done. Villefranche is a small place, but there's Beaulieu further along, and Cap Ferrat, and there must be a few hotels on the Cap de Nice too. I'll start at the harbour and work back in the direction of Nice, and you can work your way through Villefranche itself and towards Cap Ferrat, and we'll meet back here at one o'clock. How does that sound?'

'Do you really think he's here?'

'If he is, we'll find him. If not—I don't know. At any rate, I shall have to try and get in with Mrs. Weeks somehow, just so I can say I've done everything I could.'

'Nothing easier,' said Freddy, who had just seen the

Weekses come into the dining-room. 'I met them last night at the Great-Aunt's. We're quite old friends already.'

'Oh!' said Angela, following his gaze. 'Well, then, you'd better introduce me when you've finished your breakfast.'

The introductions were duly made. Mrs. Weeks made pleasantries about the weather, while Garnet dimpled and shook her curls. Jacques Fournier was nowhere to be seen.

'Pretty girl,' remarked Angela with a sly glance at Freddy as they came away.

'Don't look at me—she has eyes only for another. Besides, I am a model of decorum these days.'

'Ah, yes, Gertie.'

'Don't you approve?'

'Gertie is a splendid girl,' she replied. 'I like her very much.'

This was not precisely an answer, but Freddy let it pass. It was already ten o'clock and the sun was warm, so they lost no more time in beginning their search. Freddy spent the morning wandering up and down the steep, narrow streets of Villefranche until he was hot and weary, but gained nothing to show for it: there was no sign of the man he was searching for. At one o'clock he trudged back to the Hotel Bellevue and found Angela already there. One look at her face told him she had been no more successful than he.

'Not a thing,' she said in answer to his inquiry. 'Perhaps I've made a mistake. Perhaps he's not here at all.'

They had lunch, dispirited.

'You realize even if he is here he's probably using a false name,' said Freddy.

'I know.'

She prodded at a slice of tomato with her fork and looked unhappy. Freddy felt a pang of sympathy.

'Cheer up! Never say die! There are still a few more hotels at the other end of the bay. We'll do those this afternoon. But let's search together this time—things are much more fun in company.'

'I suppose so,' she replied without enthusiasm.

The sun was directly overhead now and it was far too hot to tramp the streets, so they agreed to begin again later that afternoon. At four o'clock, therefore, they reunited and walked out and down the hill, into the centre of the town and onto the promenade. They had been intending to start their search here, but it was a pleasant afternoon, and people were sitting at tables with cool drinks, watching the fishing-boats chug to and fro. It was a tempting scene, and without much thought they decided to sit down and have a drink instead. They spent some time absorbing the sunshine and idly watching people go by, then at last they remembered they had a job to do, and began to think about resuming their search. As Freddy was gesturing to the waiter he happened to spot a woman sitting at a table in the next café. She was small and handsome, and finely dressed in a rose-pink frock of the latest Parisian fashion, with golden hair shingled neatly against her head under a wide-brimmed hat. She was sitting sideways on and Freddy could not get a full view of her face because there were other people in the way, but he was certain he recognized her from somewhere. He frowned, trying to recall. Just then the woman turned her head and the memory came back.

'Good Lord, it's Mrs. Dragusha!' he exclaimed.

'Who?'

Freddy turned away.

'Don't look now, but the woman in pink sitting at the table to your left over there is a thief. We had some trouble with her at Belsingham earlier this year when she tried to relieve us of a valuable family heirloom, but she skipped before the police could get hold of her. I wonder what she's doing here.'

After a discreet interval Angela turned her head to look, then immediately went white in the face and gave a gasp.

'It's La Duchessa! Freddy, it's La Duchessa, I'm sure of it!'

'Who?'

'I came across her in Italy a few years ago. She was dark-haired then, and much dressier, but I'm certain it's the same woman. What did you call her? Mrs. Dragusha? In Italy she was calling herself La Duchessa di Alassio. She shot Edgar.'

'She shot him? What for?'

'I don't know, exactly. He was rather cagey about it, and told me something I'm fairly sure was a cock-and-bull story about a dispute over a stolen necklace.'

'But didn't the Boehler gang shoot him last year, too? Is it something he makes a habit of?'

'You'd almost think so, wouldn't you? Luckily she didn't do him any serious harm, but I shouldn't like to get in her way when she's in a bad mood.'

'I quite agree with you. As it happens, she waved a gun at me, too, a few months ago, and gave me no doubt she meant business. If she's the armed and impetuous type I suggest we maintain a judicious distance.'

'No! We can't let her disappear just like that. It can't be a coincidence—Edgar's here, I know it!'

They both covertly eyed Mrs. Dragusha, who did not seem to have seen them. As they did so, a heavily built and rough-looking man wearing an eye-patch approached her table. He said something rapidly and she glanced around then shooed him away.

'A man with one eye,' said Freddy, watching him as he sauntered off. 'Didn't you say Valencourt left Perpignan with someone of that description?'

'I certainly did,' replied Angela. 'Quick! Let's pay the bill and be ready to follow her when she goes.'

A few minutes later they were following the pink dress at a discreet distance. Mrs. Dragusha had made it easier for them by raising a parasol, which acted as a useful sign-post and enabled them to keep her in sight without having to get too close. She led them all the way along the water-front almost as far as Beaulieu, and then turned into a large, grand hotel close to the beach, with palm trees flanking the entrance. It was evidently a popular establishment, and many people were wandering in and out.

'A big hotel makes it easier to disappear among the crowds, I suppose,' said Angela.

They waited a moment before following Mrs. Dragusha in, and were just in time to see her disappear into the lift. Angela and Freddy went up to the hotel reception desk.

'I'm looking for an Edgar Merivale,' said Angela to the man standing behind it.

He consulted the register.

'We have no-one of that name here,' he replied.

'What about Edgar Valencourt?'

'I am afraid not.'

'Edgar de Lisle?' suggested Freddy.

The clerk replied in the negative. Angela tried again.

'Perhaps Edgar Smart?'

'Do you not know his name?' asked the man, amused.

'She has several cousins, all called Edgar. Extraordinary, isn't it?' replied Freddy. 'She hasn't seen any of them in years, but they're all staying in the area at present, only they forgot to tell us at which hotel.'

'Ah, I see. Well, you are fortunate, because we do have a Mr. Edgar Smart. He is staying here with his wife.'

There was a short silence.

'I beg your pardon, his wife?' inquired Angela.

'Yes, she is that blonde lady in the pink dress who came in just before you. Mr. Smart is out at present but I dare say he will be back soon.'

Another silence descended. Freddy glanced at Angela fearfully, but he need not have worried about any public unpleasantness. She drew herself up very straight and regarded the clerk down her nose.

'Thank you,' she said with dignified politeness. 'We'll wait for him. Come, Freddy.'

They followed the man's directions and went out onto the hotel terrace. Angela placed herself at a table and drummed her fingers. It was impossible to tell what she was thinking. At last she spoke.

'Fetch me a martini, Freddy. And you'd better make it a large one.'

'Ought we to be here? What if he comes?'

'I want him to come,' she replied ominously.

They did not have long to wait, for they had barely started their drinks when a good-looking man in a light, beautifully pressed suit strolled onto the terrace, seeming wholly relaxed and at ease with the world. His eyes rested on Angela and Freddy for the merest second and slid away smoothly without so much as a spark of recognition, then he glanced at his watch, turned on his heel as though he had just remembered an appointment, and walked straight out again. Freddy rather admired how coolly he did it. He stole a nervous look at Angela, who glared at him.

'Don't squint at me like that! You don't suppose I intend to hare down the street after him, brandishing a rolling-pin and screeching like a fishwife, do you?'

She sat and brooded for a few minutes, and smoked several of Freddy's cigarettes.

'We must find out what he's up to,' she announced at last.

'It seems pretty clear what he's up to,' said Freddy, half under his breath.

'Not to me, it isn't.'

'But the chap at reception said—'

'Never mind what the chap at reception said. There's something going on. He's in some sort of trouble, I know it.' She glanced at him. 'You're still squinting.'

'Sorry,' said Freddy.

Angela finished her drink in one gulp.

'Well, there's no use in waiting any longer. It's obvious he won't come near the place again as long as we're here. Let's go back and think about what to do next.'

She bristled with indignation all the way back to the hotel.

'Wife, indeed!' she muttered. 'That woman? I can't believe it!'

Freddy saw that any remark from him would be useless, and, indeed, would most likely only serve to increase her irritation, so he said nothing, but he was thinking. Mrs. Dragusha was the last person he had expected to see, but he supposed it was not such an extraordinary coincidence that she should be acquainted—in one way or another—with Edgar Valencourt, given her history and the fact that criminals tended to band together. He could not say whether or not Valencourt were trifling with Angela's affections, but Mrs. Dragusha's presence here certainly increased the likelihood that something illegal was afoot, if nothing else—and it was no stretch of the imagination to surmise that it would involve the Mariensee diamond. In that, at least, he agreed with Angela's deductions.

It was past six o'clock by the time they arrived back at the Hotel Bellevue, and they went up to change, then met again in the reception hall, where Angela was informed that a note had arrived for her. She read it, then handed it to Freddy. It looked as though it had been scribbled in a hurry. It read:

*Come to the casino this evening. Don't let on you know me or you'll be in danger. E.*

Freddy frowned over the note.

'Danger?' he said. 'I don't much like the sound of that.'

But Angela seemed oddly relieved.

'He must have followed us back here. At least he hasn't run off again—I suppose that's something. Perhaps he's even thought of a convincing story. I look forward to hearing it.'

'How are you supposed to pretend you don't know him, though? If Mrs. Dragusha is there this evening, surely she'll recognize you?'

'There's no reason she should,' replied Angela, considering. 'I don't think I exchanged so much as a word with her at the time, and would she be likely to recognize someone who happened to stay at the same hotel as she did a couple of years ago? I was there when she shot Edgar, but it was dark, and I doubt very much she was paying any attention to me.'

'Perhaps not, but don't forget she knows *me* very well, or she ought to. If she sees me with you something might jog her memory.'

'I suppose you're right. We'd better keep apart as much as possible, then.'

'Don't you think it might be wiser if I didn't come at all?' asked Freddy.

Angela pondered the matter.

'No, I don't,' she replied. 'As a matter of fact, since you know who she is, and she knows you know, your presence might even be enough to frighten her off whatever she's planning.'

'I've had plenty of practice at frightening women, but I doubt Mrs. Dragusha will be put off. She's a brazen one all right.'

'We'll see,' said Angela.

The casino at Beaulieu was busy that evening, and as soon as they arrived Angela and Freddy separated as agreed. Freddy wandered around the place, looking out for Mrs. Dragusha or Edgar Valencourt, but could not see either of them, although they would be difficult to spot among the crowds. He did, however, see his grandmother, who was at a table with the Comte de Langlois, watching adoringly as he played with great concentration. Freddy surveyed the room, certain that Nugs would be somewhere in the vicinity, but could not see him. Since everybody else seemed to be enjoying themselves Freddy saw no reason why he should not do the same, and settled himself to a game or two.

'Any sign of them?' came Angela's voice next to him after a few minutes.

'No, and aren't you meant to be keeping away from me?'

'I've come for a rest from your grandfather.'

'Oh, so he is here, is he? I thought he must be. He hasn't been bothering you, I hope.'

'He is perhaps just a *little* freer with his hands than I like,' replied Angela delicately.

'Ah. He must have been at the whisky again. I'll have a word with him.'

'No need, thank you. I extricated myself gracefully. So, then, am I to look to him as a model of what you'll be like in about 1980?'

'Certainly not!' exclaimed Freddy, outraged.

Angela looked around.

'He seems to have gone now. I think I shall go and play some roulette. Would you care to join me? We can pretend we don't know each other.'

Freddy had no objection, so they bought some chips and prepared to play. Just then Edgar Valencourt appeared at the opposite side of the table. They had not seen him come in. Next to him, Freddy felt Angela start slightly.

'*Faites vos jeux*,' said the croupier. 'Place your bets, please.'

Angela and Valencourt both pushed their chips towards red at the same time.

'After you,' said Valencourt politely. Angela opened her mouth then shut it again. Freddy placed his bet on the last twelve numbers, and they all watched as the wheel spun round and the ball landed firmly in the zero. The croupier collected their chips, then Valencourt shrugged, excused himself and headed for the door. They watched as he paused for a second then left the casino without looking behind him.

'Off you go, then,' murmured Freddy to Angela.

'Watch out for La Duchessa,' she returned quietly, and went out likewise.

The street outside was quiet, but there had not been time for Valencourt to have gone far. Angela crossed the road to the little harbour and looked about her. There was no sound but that of the rippling water, and nothing to see in the darkness but the gleaming white of the boats that bobbed up and down in the gentle swell. The place seemed quite deserted, and she hesitated, wondering whether he had come here at all. To her left was a boat hut, and she walked towards it.

'Well, this is a merry dance you've led me,' she said, as he stepped out of the shadows.

# Chapter Seven

A SHORT WHILE LATER—BUT not too soon—Angela said, 'Enough of this nonsense. I'm too old to be kissing disreputable men behind boat huts. Besides, what *will* your wife say?'

'Hmph!' replied Valencourt. 'I guessed you must have inquired at the hotel. Blast the woman! I imagine it was her notion of a joke.'

'Please tell me you're not actually married to her.'

'Of course I'm not—what do you take me for?'

'Many things. I didn't really think you could be, but one never knows. You've sprung an unexpected wife on me before.'

'Not this time, I promise. I don't collect them. Besides, I'm keeping that position in reserve for you.'

'If you want to get married then running away from your intended without telling her where you've gone is not the best way to go about it,' said Angela severely.

'None of this was my idea, I assure you, but I didn't have much choice other than to go along with it. As I expect you're about to ask, however, I draw the line at sharing a room.'

She was about to reply tartly but he forestalled her by kissing her again. She pulled away, glancing about.

'No, really, what if we're seen?'

'I suppose you're right. They'll be looking for me any minute. I'm sorry about all the hole-and-corner stuff, but these people are capable of anything, and I'd much rather you kept out of it.'

'This isn't a game, is it?' she said, observing his brows, which were knit closely together.

'No.'

'Then sit on this bench, and I shall sit at the other end, and if anybody comes you can dive behind the hut again, and I'll send them off in the other direction. Now, tell me.'

'I was hoping to avoid all this, but the cat's out of the bag now so I suppose it can't be helped.' He sighed. 'Very well, then. It started in Saratoga a couple of months ago, when a fellow called Gino came to me looking for a job. He was the cousin of one of my stable-hands, just arrived from Italy, and I didn't take to him much—he was a bit shifty-looking for my taste—but he knew horses, so I took him on. That was a mistake on my part, because a day or two afterwards he came to me, told me he knew who I was and tried to extort money in return for his silence. I'd thought when I met him that he seemed oddly familiar, and at any other time I'd have been on my guard, but things were frantically busy just then because two of the horses were lame and we had several cases of ring-worm, so my mind was elsewhere.'

'He was going to report you to the police?' demanded Angela, aghast. This was the thing she had feared above all else, for whatever little peace of mind she had gained in the past year would be lost if the world knew Valencourt was still alive.

'Not the police. This Gino was a hanger-on of the Boehler gang, whom you might remember I had an unpleasant encounter with last year. He knew they believed they'd killed me, and he saw what he thought was a nice opportunity to fleece me. Of course I wasn't having that, so I gave him an earful and sent him packing.'

'Oh dear.'

'Well, I was hardly going to pay him. I thought he might do some petty damage by way of revenge, and told the men to keep a sharp eye on the horses just in case, but I've seen the type many times before and didn't really expect him to squeal. I thought no more about it, and a couple of weeks later came over to France. I'd obviously underestimated him, though. It seems he went to his cousin, found out where I'd gone and wired Fritz Boehler—he's the one who shot me last year, by the way, so you might say he has a personal interest in my being dead. As far as I understand it, Fritz was all set to turn up in Perpignan and have another try at finishing me off, but the gang happened to be working with Bettina at the time, and she persuaded them not to. I owe her that, at least.'

'Bettina? Is that what you call her? Freddy knows her, by the way.'

'Does he? That's unfortunate. You'd better make sure she doesn't see him, always assuming she hasn't already. Anyway, it turns out there's a big job planned, and Bettina thought I would be much more useful to them alive than dead, given my particular expertise. Naturally they needed to exert a little persuasion, so they put Gino to work back in Saratoga. The first I knew about the whole thing was when I got a telegram from old Dan at the stables saying that Nightshade had been kidnapped, and that they'd received a note warning them not to let the police know or we'd never see the horse alive again.'

Angela put her hands to her face.

'Oh, Edgar, poor Nightshade!'

'Yes. It came as an awful shock, and when I got the wire I was all set to take the first boat out from Bordeaux back to the States. Then Fritz and Rolf Boehler turned up and told me they had a proposition for me, and said that I'd better not try and make a run for it, because if I did then Nightshade would be dead before I'd got as far as the station. I didn't see I had much choice just then, so we came here, and they explained what they were planning and gave Bettina the job of chaperoning me—just to be on the safe side, I imagine. I didn't like the sound of the job at all, but I couldn't see any way to get out of it without ending up with a dead horse on my hands, so I went along with it for the first few days, to give myself some time to come up with a plan. But the longer things went on the clearer it became that Nightshade was most likely doomed whatever I did. As a matter of fact, I began to suspect they'd killed him as soon as they got hold of him.'

'Oh, no, surely not! Who could do that to such a beautiful horse?'

He set his jaw grimly.

'They're a ruthless lot, as I have reason to know, and they bear grudges. I've crossed them twice—once by taking something of theirs and once by failing to die as instructed, and they won't forget it in a hurry. Now it seems they've decided I must do this job whether I want to or not.'

'But what is the job? No, don't tell me, I know already—the Mariensee diamond.'

Valencourt looked surprised.

'You have done your homework. Does the whole Riviera know about it?'

'Not as far as I'm aware. I saw something in the paper and suspected I shouldn't find you far away. What is it? Are you to seduce Jessie Weeks into handing it over?'

'I shouldn't put it like that, exactly. Originally it was Bettina who was meant to do it. She has a talent for dressmaking, and she's very good at worming her way into the confidences of women who have more money than sense. She tried it in The Hague with the Weekses, but on this occasion she failed to scrape an acquaintance with them. But the gang were determined to get their hands on the diamond, so they followed the Weekses down here and they're now preparing to try again, only with yours truly doing the dirty work. It ought to be easy enough—nothing more than the usual routine: I put on my best manners, talk to the lady and admire her jewels, then somehow she goes home with a paste imitation while I do a vanishing act with the real thing—I'm sorry, darling, I know you don't like it—'

'Was I wincing? Don't mind me. Go on.'

'—but I don't know, Angela. There's something distinctly fishy about the whole business.'

'How can there possibly be anything fishy about a plot to steal an enormous diamond? I beg your pardon, facetious of me. I'll try again. Do you mean you think they have something else planned in addition to that?'

'I shouldn't put it past them for a second. I can't put my finger on it, but I've had enough experience over the years to sense when something's not quite right. I don't like it, Angela. There's something they're not telling me. At the very least I'm sure they don't intend to keep their side of the bargain.'

'Then you don't think they'll let you go once the job is done?'

'Oh, I haven't the slightest doubt they mean to put a bullet in my head and dump me over the side of a boat as soon as they've made use of me.'

'Rude of them.'

'Not the sort of manners one learns at finishing-school, certainly,' he agreed. 'So here we are. I'm in a tight spot, all told. They've got the horse, and they've got me, and I can't see a way out of it that will save us both.'

'But if you can't save Nightshade you can at least save yourself. Couldn't you have made a bolt for it?'

'I could have, yes. And that's exactly what I'd been planning to do until you turned up this afternoon,' he replied dryly.

'Oh. I see,' said Angela, taken aback.

'Quite. And you also see why they mustn't find out who

you are. A horse three thousand miles away is an uncertain means of persuasion, but you, here, are another matter altogether. If they see us together and discover your connection to me, then the situation becomes even more impossible. To be perfectly frank, I wish you hadn't come at all, because I have quite enough on my plate at present.'

'What was I supposed to do when I found out you'd disappeared into thin air?' demanded Angela indignantly. 'Sit at home, knitting? I've been worried sick about you.'

'Have you?'

'Don't sound so surprised, of course I have. I've been imagining all sorts of horrors—none of which, I might add, come close to the reality. But what are we going to do?'

'*You* will do nothing at all,' he replied firmly. 'You'll pack your things and leave Villefranche first thing tomorrow—or tonight, preferably. And tell Freddy to do the same, before he gets caught up in it too. What is he doing here, by the way?'

'I brought him along for moral support. And you can forget any nonsense you might be entertaining about my keeping out of the thing. Do you really think I'm going to leave you to face this all alone? I'm here now and I intend to help.'

Valencourt made an exasperated noise.

'God preserve me from interfering women! Don't you realize how dangerous this is? They'll put a bullet in you just as soon as they will in me. Your presence here isn't helping anyone—least of all me. I'd have been halfway to Bordeaux by now if you hadn't turned up.'

'Yes, and with a dead horse waiting for you when you got back to the States! And possibly the police, too. If you give the Boehlers the slip then what's to stop them turning you over to the law? Besides, what sort of coward should I be if I ran away while all this is going on?'

'It's not a question of courage—' he began.

'No, it's not. It's a question of principle. I won't stand by and see them drag you back into all this when you'd been trying so hard. No,' she went on, 'there must be something we can do. For a start, I don't believe whoever has Nightshade will kill him—or not yet, at any rate. He's worth far too much money, and with things the way they are at present it's bound to be a temptation. They're much more likely to try and sell him before they do anything else. Are your men searching for him?'

'I hope so, but there's only so much they can do without me there.'

'Then we'll send William to help them. If anybody can find Nightshade he can. I'll wire him as soon as I get back to the hotel and we'll leave it all to him. But we'll have to give him a few days, which means you can't leave as you were planning to, or the gang will certainly give the order to kill the horse. In the meantime, we must decide what to do about this diamond business. When is the theft to take place?'

'There's to be a big do on Thursday night at a house on the Cap de Nice. Chap by the name of Benjamin Roche, who owns a newspaper and likes to surround himself with a fashionable crowd. The Weekses will be there, along with about three hundred other people, so it ought to be easy enough to slip away unnoticed once the thing's done. Of course, there are all sorts of things that might go wrong—and frequently do in this kind of job. There's only so much I can do to create the right opportunity, and even then the exchange has to be made in a matter of seconds. If it got to the point where I had to do it, my original plan was to fumble it and then make a discreet exit under cover of the crowd before the Boehlers realized what was going on. Not ideal, because they'd come after me, but I couldn't see any other way out of it without actually pinching the thing. I don't suppose you have any better ideas?'

'No,' replied Angela after a moment. 'Not while there's a slim chance we can save Nightshade. If you can convince the Boehlers they have you in their power until the night of the party, then that will give William two vital days. I don't expect there's much chance of his succeeding, but nobody will be able to say we haven't given it a jolly good try.'

'I wish you'd stop saying "we". This isn't your problem.'

'Yes it is, and you may as well save your breath. I'm here now and I'm not leaving without you. We'll get you out of this somehow. I don't know exactly how, but there must be a way.'

There came the sound of footsteps on the road behind them and Valencourt retreated swiftly behind the boat hut. Whoever it was passed by, and he emerged, glancing around uneasily.

'Bettina will be after me any moment. She's been breathing down my neck for days and I've hardly had a second to myself. She only lets me out of her sight if Fritz or someone else is watching me.'

'Is Fritz the man with the eye-patch?'

'Yes. I don't know how he lost his eye, but the experience didn't improve his temper at all. Now, listen, if I had time I'd talk you out of this ridiculous idea of your staying here, but we don't have much longer. Just promise me you'll keep out of sight of Bettina. She's the only person here who might conceivably recognize you, and I don't want to give them any more ammunition against me.'

'Very well, I'll do my best. There's one thing I don't understand, though: why did Bettina persuade the Boehlers not to kill you? There must be any number of ways to get at the diamond without bringing you into it, and since she's taken a gun to you before I should have thought she'd be only too glad to see you dead. Why did she want to save you?'

'I don't know, exactly. She can't still be angry with me after all this time, so I can only suppose she retains some sentimental regard for me.'

There was a heavy pause, and a certain frost percolated into the atmosphere.

'You beastly Frenchman,' said Angela. 'I knew you were fibbing about her in Italy.'

'Was I? What did I say?'

'You said there'd never been anything between you, and then gave me some trumped-up tale about a mysterious collector who wanted the Poldarrow necklace.'

'Oh. Well, the part about the necklace was true, at any rate. And if my memories of that evening are correct, it wasn't exactly the most appropriate moment to bring up anything more personal.'

'Perhaps not, but if you will insist on telling me lies, you might at least pay me the compliment of giving me the same story each time.'

'I didn't think it was important. It was a long time ago and there's certainly nothing between us now. Attempted murder tends to sour relations irrevocably, I find.'

Angela was feeling increasingly nettled by the whole conversation.

'Look here,' she said suddenly. 'Would you ever have told me about all this if I hadn't come after you?'

'Would you have felt any better for knowing?'

She sighed and shook her head. There was still a long way to go with him.

'What am I to do with you, Edgar?' she said.

'Just as you always do, of course—forgive me and tell me you love me.'

'It's not funny. How can we continue like this? I thought we were safe. We *were* safe as long as everybody believed you were dead, but this is the worst thing that could possibly have happened. Now the Boehlers know you're alive you'll be in danger again. They know where you live and they'll never let you go. We can't even report them to the police because they'll certainly talk, and then you'll be in danger of arrest.'

'Oh, well, I've been in worse fixes.'

The remark was accompanied by a careless shrug which only served to irritate Angela further.

'And so have I, but after all the horrid things that have happened in the past couple of years I've had enough of danger, and of being frightened all the time. I was hoping life would be pleasantly dull from now on.' She stood up. 'I'd better get back to the casino. I'll telegraph William this evening and send him up to Saratoga. And I'll see if I can get myself invited to this party. An extra pair of eyes can't do any harm. In the meantime, don't worry, I'll keep as far away from you as I can. I think it's unlikely this Bettina—La Duchessa—Mrs. Dragusha—whatever her name is—will recognize me, but there's no sense in taking any chances. Besides, I'd hate to intrude upon your married bliss,' she added pointedly.

'If you're going to be all womanish about things—' he began, but Angela had already stalked off. She knew she was being a little unreasonable, but Edgar's story—and the discovery that he had lied to her about his past history with La Duchessa—had disturbed her more than she cared to say, and she was in no mood to continue the conversation. She left the little harbour area and crossed the road to the casino. As she went in she almost bumped into the man with one eye she now knew to be Fritz Boehler. Valencourt had now also emerged onto the promenade and was standing under a street-lamp, engaged in lighting a cigarette, the very picture of innocence. Fritz Boehler saw him and went over to join him. Angela pressed her lips together and slipped back into the casino.

# Chapter Eight

It was very shortly after Angela followed Valencourt out of the casino that Freddy spotted Mrs. Dragusha. She was wearing an evening-dress of shimmering gold that must surely have been one of her own creations, and the lights of the casino glinted off the precious stones at her throat and in her ears. She seemed a proud, exotic creature, her attire far removed from the elegantly understated look she had adopted as dressmaker to his family earlier that year, and her demeanour that of a woman fully at home in her surroundings. She was prowling around the casino like a restless lion, watching the people at play. She paused by a card table, and Freddy saw the man with one eye playing. He and Mrs. Dragusha did not acknowledge one another. Not far away was another man, much fairer than the one-eyed man, but bearing an unmistakably close resemblance to him. The second man came across and muttered something to Mrs. Dragusha, but she favoured him with a glare and moved away without replying. Freddy wondered what to do. Sooner or later she would see him, and he could not decide whether it would be wiser to approach her first in order to have the advantage, or to keep out of sight as much as possible. He decided upon the latter, and watched her closely for a while. After a few minutes she glanced around, frowning, as though looking for someone. The one-eyed man was watching her, and she seemed to give him a signal, for he rose from his table and went outside. Shortly afterwards Angela reappeared at Freddy's elbow.

'Don't let her see you!' she hissed.

'What?'

'She mustn't see you. I'll explain later, but we'd better go before she spots us. Quick!'

'Oh,' said Freddy, surprised. 'Very well, then.'

He cast a regretful eye at all the chips he had surrendered to the croupier that evening and prepared to depart. But they had reckoned without Nugs, who just then arrived at the roulette table looking highly agitated.

'You won't believe who I've just seen,' he said urgently. 'That Dragusha woman! Do you remember? Of course you do. She nearly got away with the Belsingham pearls that weekend when old Coddington got bashed on the noggin. She's wandering around here dressed up to the nines, as cool as you please. We must fetch the police!'

'No!' exclaimed Angela involuntarily.

'Why not? She's not a friend of yours, is she? I hope not, because the woman's a thief—I'm sorry to put it so bluntly, my dear, but there's no other word for it.' Nugs cast his eyes about. 'Now, where is the telephone?'

'Please don't call the police,' pleaded Angela. 'You'll ruin everything!'

'What do you mean?'

'Why—' Angela broke off and glanced appealingly at Freddy, who saw his assistance was needed and came to her rescue.

'Because they already know about her,' he replied. He lowered his voice. 'Listen, you mustn't say a word, but Angela is working under cover for the French Sûreté. They've been watching Mrs. Dragusha secretly for some time now, while they gather enough evidence to arrest her. They're still waiting for a vital piece of proof, but if Mrs. Dragusha finds out she's being spied on she'll make a run for it and all their efforts will have been wasted.'

Nugs seemed impressed.

'By Jove! Is that so?' he said.

Angela nodded vigorously.

'Yes. So it's very important we keep the police out of it, at least for now. Don't worry, we know who she is, but many lives depend on your silence. I know I can rely on you to keep it under your hat, Lord Lucian.'

'Oh, very well, then,' said Nugs. 'I shall do as you ask. But I'd hide my pearls away if I were you.' He eyed Angela with interest. 'Are you really working for the Sûreté? Young ladies didn't do that sort of thing in my day. I'm not sure I like it.'

He muttered to himself a little, then departed.

'French Sûreté, indeed!' murmured Angela to Freddy.

'It was the first thing that came into my head. But look here, what's all this about?'

'Let's go and I'll tell you later. We must get out before she sees us.'

Unfortunately for them, Mrs. Dragusha chose that very moment to present herself at their table. She threw the merest glance at Angela and seemed to dismiss her, then gave Freddy a nod of recognition.

'Good evening, Mrs. D,' said Freddy, as Angela took the opportunity to withdraw discreetly.

Mrs. Dragusha inclined her head.

'Mr. Pilkington-Soames. I thought it was you—I saw your grandfather a moment ago.'

'Place your bets,' said the croupier.

Freddy could hardly walk away now, so he bought some more chips and allocated them at random. Mrs. Dragusha placed some chips on black. She appeared quite at ease.

'Having a holiday?' asked Freddy idiotically as the croupier spun the wheel.

'In a manner of speaking,' she replied. 'I am here with my husband.'

'Mr. Dragusha?'

She threw him an amused look.

'Do not be absurd. Of course that is not my name.'

'Then what is your real name? Sangiacomo? Like Valentina?'

'Ah, she told you who she was, did she? Foolish girl. She would have done better to keep her mouth shut.'

Freddy glanced behind him, half-expecting to see Valentina Sangiacomo loitering somewhere nearby.

'She's not here, is she?' he asked.

'No. She is in England as far as I know. Better for her, as I have a—what do you call it? A bone to pick with her.'

'I don't see why. She did you a good turn when she stopped you from taking the pearls. We'd have had the police after you in a trice if you'd got them.'

A complacent smile spread across her face.

'No doubt you would. And they would have found nothing. Your English police, they are no match for me.'

As if to prove her point, the ball landed on black. Mrs. Dragusha scooped up her winnings.

'I dare say we shall see one another again,' she said coolly, and walked away, leaving Freddy to wonder whether a constitution formed largely of brass was a common feature of all jewel-thieves. He went in search of Angela and found her sitting unobtrusively in a quiet corner.

'What did La Duchessa say?' asked Angela as soon as they were outside.

'Not much. She merely told me how clever she was, and said she was on holiday with her husband,' replied Freddy.

'Hmph. Well *that's* not true, at any rate. But I suppose she was hardly likely to tell you what she's really up to. Let's find a taxi.'

They sat in silence as the cab wound through the hills back to the Hotel Bellevue, where they found a quiet corner of the lounge, and Angela recounted what Valencourt had told her. Freddy whistled.

'Then you were right about the Mariensee diamond. I say, well deduced on your part! It certainly sounds like a bold scheme. And it's the Boehler gang, is it? My word, I don't wonder Valencourt is nervous about being mixed up with them after what they did to him last year.' He hesitated, then said tentatively, 'But are you sure he was telling the truth?'

'I can never be sure he's telling the truth, but I've no reason to doubt him in this instance. He knows that if he's lying then I'll find out as soon as William arrives in Saratoga. And speaking of William, I must just send him a wire.'

She went off and returned a few minutes later.

'There! If he gets it immediately he should be able to make it to Saratoga by midnight American time, and then that will give him two days or so to find the horse. I hope it's enough, but I fear it won't be. Poor Edgar—he'll be devastated if anything happens to Nightshade. I do believe he loves that horse more than he loves me. The poor animal was a champion once, but when Edgar found him late last year he was neglected and sick, and had to be nursed back to health. Now he's worth a lot of money, but Edgar will never sell him, as he's far too fond of him and wants to run him in races. I only hope the men who took him are treating him well.'

'I should imagine they are, if he's as valuable as all that,' said Freddy. 'So, then, assuming everything is as your chap says it is, William will spend the next two days looking for a missing horse, but in the meantime what are we going to do?'

'I want to go to this Benjamin Roche's party. You see, the idea is that Edgar will only pretend to exchange the jewels then make himself scarce, but I'd like to be there, just to be on the safe side. If he says he smells a rat, then something is almost certainly going to happen, and if it all goes wrong then I might be able to help in some way. But I don't know how to get myself an invitation.'

'I can get you an invitation—or an introduction, at least. Roche invited me to the party himself last night.'

'Did he, indeed?' said Angela in surprise. 'Goodness me, you only arrived yesterday. That was fast work. Do you know everyone on the Riviera?'

'It was quite a coincidence, I assure you. Roche is a distinguished old French aristocratic type with a love of fine possessions and fine people—not that I class myself as the latter, but I have the advantage of family, and I was at my great-aunt's yesterday when he turned up and included me in the general hospitableness. But I'm sure he'd be happy to invite you, too. I'll speak to him tomorrow and tell him you're the sister of Sir Humphrey Cardew. He won't be able to resist an English title.'

'Splendid! I always hoped Humphrey would come in useful sooner or later, although he'd be horrified if he knew what I was getting up to these days. Very well, you shall get me an invitation to Roche's party, and we'll go and keep a lookout for squalls. If all goes to plan the job will go wrong and Edgar will get safely away, and if fortune is truly on our side William will have found and rescued Nightshade by then.'

'But Valencourt will still be in danger from the Boehlers.'

'We'll cross that bridge when we come to it. I only wish we could report them to the police, but they'll talk if they're arrested, and then Edgar will be in danger from the law, too.'

'He'll always be in danger from the law, old girl,' said Freddy.

She sighed.

'Yes, I'm beginning to realize that. Why couldn't I have found myself a nice, respectable farmer or banker, as my family always meant me to? I could be living happily in

Banford Green now, baking cakes and fussing about chicken-pox instead of chasing gangsters around the South of France.'

'Sounds rather dull to me.'

'I dare say it would be after a while, but the idea is quite appealing at present. Now, as to practicalities: until Thursday night I think it will be better if we're not seen together, because I don't want La Duchessa looking at me too closely. I'm sure she didn't recognize me this evening, but if she gets the slightest inkling that there's any connection between Edgar and me they'll have another threat to hold over his head. Not that these people frighten me for a second, but Edgar would be tiresome about it, and I'd have to leave Villefranche, or at least go into hiding, and then what use would I be? No, we'll lie low until Thursday evening, then go to the party, make sure Edgar gets away from the Boehler gang *without* absent-mindedly stealing a large diamond from force of habit, and take our own departure at our leisure.'

'You make it sound very easy. Almost too easy, in fact.'

'Oh, something is bound to go wrong, but one might as well start out from a position of optimism, don't you think?' said Angela.

So it was agreed, and shortly afterwards they parted and went up to their respective rooms, Freddy shaking his head. He was by no means convinced that Edgar Valencourt's story was true, for it would be an easy enough lie for him to tell. Angela's faith in Valencourt's promise to give up his old life was touching, but Freddy had encountered enough criminals in his time at the *Clarion* to know that old dogs were reluctant to learn new tricks as a rule. However, even if Valencourt were participating in the theft willingly, surely the fact that Freddy and Angela now knew the Boehler gang had the Mariensee diamond in their sights would be enough to cause him to warn his associates off the job? Whatever the case, it was clear that *something* was going to happen at Benjamin Roche's party, and Freddy had no intention of missing it. With that resolution, he went to bed and fell quickly asleep.

If Freddy was to be left in peace with his own thoughts, the same could not be said of everyone. In another part of the hotel, long after midnight when all was quiet, a casual observer might have seen the shadowy figure of Edgar Valencourt slipping unobtrusively along the corridor and knocking softly at the door of Angela's room. After a few moments the door was opened, and voices could be heard conferring in low tones—but what he said to her, and whether she let him in, it is not the purpose of this work to inquire.

## Chapter Nine

La Falaise was a magnificent house set back against the cliff-side of the Cap de Nice promontory. It had been built for a foreign prince some fifty years earlier, and was one of the most well-known villas on the Riviera. Its original owner had spared no expense in creating the finest residence money could buy: large and imposing, the house's exterior was elaborately decorated with cornices and curlicues and other ornamental features—so much so that in the approach from the sea it looked from a distance rather like a lavishly iced cake. Access to the house from the land side was via a long drive which wound down from the scenic headland road to the main entrance. Set close to the cliff as it was, this side of the building was dark, and guests arriving were quickly ushered through the entrance-hall and into the grand, palatial rooms used for entertaining, all of which were on the sea-facing side of the house. The gardens were necessarily limited in size, given the short supply of level land on the Cap de Nice, and were set out in the form of a large, formal terrace laid to lawn and paths, and planted with cypresses. Surrounding the terrace was a balustrade beyond which was an almost sheer drop to the sea. The views in the daytime were usually spectacular, but the weather had turned cloudy, causing darkness to fall earlier than usual, and there was an unseasonable chill in the air produced by a strengthening breeze which fore-warned of an approaching storm, and so the festivities were confined to indoors. When Freddy and Angela arrived they were greeted warmly by Benjamin Roche.

'Delighted to see you, Mrs. Marchmont!' he exclaimed. 'You look quite radiant—that shade of green suits you very well. And Mr. Pilkington-Soames. The Duchess and Lord and Lady Lucian are already here, in the ballroom. You'll find quite a mixture of people here this evening.' He snapped his fingers at a nearby waiter, who approached obligingly with a tray of drinks. The man looked ill at ease in his smart waiter's jacket, and Freddy was startled to see a familiar eye-patch. He helped Angela and himself to drinks and they went into the crowded ballroom, with its high ceilings, tall windows and glittering chandelier. A smart band was playing at one end of the room, and the noise was very loud.

'Did you see him?' hissed Angela. 'Fritz Boehler!'

'I'll say,' replied Freddy. 'What the devil is old Roche doing hiring crooks as waiters?'

'He can't possibly know who he's taken on. So something is happening, then—I'd almost begun to wonder.'

'There's been no sign of Nightshade, I take it?'

Angela shook her head.

'No—at least, I don't think so. William has been most remiss in communicating with me. Either he's hot on the scent and hasn't had time to wire me, or he's had no luck and is still searching. But the Boehlers are determined that the theft must take place this evening, so I'm afraid it looks as though we've run out of time—whether Nightshade has been found or not we must make sure Edgar gets away safely.' She looked around. 'I can't see him, but I suppose he must be here. I'm going to circulate. Keep your eyes peeled.'

She went off, and Freddy shortly afterwards spotted Mrs.

Dragusha, looking magnificent in deep amber satin and chiffon, talking to a group of people. At least two of the gang were here already, then. He glanced around, but could see no sign of Valencourt. Thinking that he might as well throw himself into the fray, he danced with several pleasant girls, then stopped for a drink and to observe proceedings from the side of the room. Angela was in conversation with Mr. Roche, while the Comte de Langlois was dancing with Baba. Freddy went to exchange a few words with his Great-Aunt Ernestine, who was watching the couple disapprovingly.

'Hallo, Aunt, splendid do, what?' he said.

She saw him and gave a cluck.

'Your grandfather seems to think there is something dishonest about this count. He has been muttering darkly about information he has received about the man's character. Do you know anything about this?'

'Not a thing. Did Nugs say what it was?'

'No, but if it is true, then it is doubly important that we get Cecily away from him.'

'I take it Nugs hasn't had much luck with that so far.'

'Cecily won't listen to him. I fear she is lost to this man forever, and the family will never get over the scandal.'

'Cheer up, Aunt, I'm sure we've weathered worse,' he said bracingly. 'I say, come and dance.'

She seemed flustered at his invitation.

'Goodness me! I don't believe I've danced since Algernon was alive. I don't know—'

'Then all the more reason to do it now,' said Freddy firmly.

He conducted her to the floor and they danced in great state. She was quite flushed and bright-eyed by the time they had finished, although she claimed it was due to the unaccustomed exertion rather than any enjoyment she might have derived from such frivolous activity. He left her to the compliments of Mr. Roche and went to take a turn around the room, mindful that he was meant to be paying attention to the crowd. He soon spotted Garnet Weeks with Jacques Fournier. The young man had a distracted air about him, and as Freddy watched he saw Garnet upbraid him laughingly for it. Fournier's brow cleared and he smiled at her. Freddy passed on. Fritz Boehler had come into the room holding a tray of drinks, and Freddy eyed him covertly for a minute or two, then turned to find Edgar Valencourt standing by his side, apparently also engaged in watching the crowd.

'You'll keep an eye on Angela, won't you?' said Valencourt without looking at him.

'She's rather good at keeping an eye on herself. But yes, of course I will. What's the plan? Are you leaving now?'

Valencourt was still scanning the room.

'No—they're watching me like hawks and they'll be after me in a second if I do that. They must see me with the thing in my hands, so they can be sure I've done the deed. Then they'll be off their guard—for a little while, at least.'

'But you're going to give Mrs. Weeks the original back rather than the paste one you have in your pocket, I trust,' said Freddy.

'Naturally.'

'Then what?'

'Then I return the fake one to Fritz and make myself scarce. The chap who made the replica isn't here this evening, and it's difficult to tell one from the other in this light, so they oughtn't to realize they've been had until I'm well away.'

Freddy glanced at him, but his face was unreadable.

'And where will you go after that?'

'I dare say I'll think of somewhere,' replied Valencourt vaguely, and then he was gone. A few minutes later, Freddy saw him dancing with Jessie Weeks, talking and smiling at her as though she were the most fascinating woman in the world. The change in his manner was almost palpable, and Freddy blinked. For her part, Jessie Weeks seemed mesmerized, and was hanging on his every word. Freddy studied her more closely, looking out for the thing that interested him most. There it was: the Mariensee diamond. She had worn it as promised—or, at least, Freddy assumed the ornament she wore on her breast must be the famous jewel, for surely no inferior diamond could sparkle quite as brightly at him from across the room? Even from several yards away he could see it was magnificent. He began to calculate idly the cost of insuring such a gem.

'Tell me I don't look like that when he talks to me,' said Angela at his side.

'I beg your pardon?'

She nodded towards Mrs. Weeks.

'The poor woman has a face like a stunned sheep. It's quite unsettling to watch. I don't know how he turns it on and off like that.'

'I should never call you a stunned sheep, but he is rather good at it, isn't he? How are you enjoying the do? Seen anything suspicious?'

'Not as far as I can tell, but I don't exactly know what it is we're meant to be looking out for. I mean to say, we know what Edgar is supposed to be doing, but he seems to think the Boehlers are planning something else, too. But what? I wish there were something we could do. I'm feeling useless as it is.'

'Well, presumably he knows his job, so there's nothing we *can* do until he's pretended to make the exchange—and even then I don't know how you think we can help.'

'Nor do I,' replied Angela. 'I just can't help thinking we might be needed, somehow. Let's be ready, just in case. Oh, goodness, there's La Duchessa. I'd better go.'

'Does it matter if she sees you now?'

'I don't expect so, but better to be safe than sorry.'

Angela slipped away and Freddy resumed his observation of the crowd. The one-eyed waiter was clearing a table nearby, and did not so much as look up as La Duchessa swept past. Everyone was enjoying themselves hugely, and had it not been for the presence of several known criminals, it would have been difficult to imagine that anything untoward was about to happen.

The song came to an end and Valencourt escorted Mrs. Weeks to a table at the side of the room at which several other people were already sitting. She was flushed and laughing, and seemed to be complaining of the heat. Valencourt went to fetch her a drink, and had just returned when all the lights went out without warning. Immediately the room was full of shrieking and giggling, and a cheer went up among some of the rowdier members of the party. The band gamely continued for a bar or two but then gave it up, and the party came to a temporary standstill.

For a moment Freddy did not understand what was happening, and was as inclined as anybody to cheer the mishap, until it struck him that this was not an accident at all, and that something was afoot. He had just reached this conclusion when a woman screamed loudly. Suddenly all was confusion, as everybody began to blunder about and bump into one another. Freddy was sure the scream had come from the part of the room where Mrs. Weeks had been sitting, and he began to move towards it—or where he thought it was, at least—but his way was blocked by crowds of people. He fumbled his way along the window side of the room, into which a little light was entering from outside, then pushed into the throng, raising protests as he went.

'Excuse me, do you mind?'

'What do you think you're doing?'

'*Pardon*.' (This as somebody blundered into him and trod on his foot.)

'Is that you, Wilfred?'

Freddy wormed his way through the crush of people, dispensing apologies freely, and emerged just as the lights came back on to find himself by the table at which Jessie

Weeks had been sitting when darkness fell. An odd little tableau was before him: Mrs. Weeks had jumped to her feet and was clutching her breast, a look of horror on her face, as Edgar Valencourt stood next to her, a drink in his hand, his expression closed, wary. Several people were staring at Mrs. Weeks, including her daughter, who looked surprised and disconcerted. Baba stood just behind them, glancing around frantically, while Angela stood nearby, very still, her eyes on Valencourt.

'My brooch!' cried Mrs. Weeks wildly. 'Somebody's stolen my brooch! Quick! Catch him!'

Instantly there was an uproar as everybody began talking at once. Mr. Roche was by Mrs. Weeks's side in a moment.

'What happened?' he demanded.

'He tore it off me! Look!'

They all looked as instructed, and saw a tear in the blue fabric of Jessie Weeks's dress where the thief had wrenched the diamond away.

'It must have been somebody standing next to me. But who—' she cast about, her eyes falling first on one person, then on another. One man, a burly American, grasped the situation quickly.

'It must be someone here,' he said. 'Mr. Roche, sir, I suggest you don't let anybody leave the house. We'll search all the guests if necessary—turn out their pockets.'

He turned out his own to demonstrate. Benjamin Roche looked taken aback.

'Oh—er—I don't quite—' he began.

Freddy glanced sideways and saw Angela and Valencourt staring at one another in silent communication, Angela's expression one of inquiry. Valencourt shook his head almost imperceptibly, and at that moment Freddy remembered the paste jewel Valencourt was carrying in his pocket. He had been standing nearest to Mrs. Weeks when the lights went off, and would be first to be searched. If that happened he would be caught and the game would be up. Something must be done. Freddy racked his brains quickly, but Angela had got there before him.

'Oh!' she exclaimed loudly. She put a hand to her head and swayed as everybody's eyes turned in her direction. 'I think I'm going to faint.'

And she did.

# Chapter Ten

WHILE IT MIGHT BE SUPPOSED that any true gentleman would have rushed to the aid of an unconscious woman, Freddy did nothing of the sort. Instead, he took advantage of the confusion caused by Angela's fainting act to retreat into the crowd —as he assumed Valencourt had also done. With any luck the few seconds' distraction would give Valencourt time to get away, but Freddy was not thinking of him, for he was more interested in what had happened while the lights were off. A man had pushed past him and trodden on his foot as he did so. This in itself was not odd, but what was odd was the fact that the unknown person had been heading quite purposefully away from the screaming Jessie Weeks, and towards one of the grand French windows which led out onto the terrace. The doors had been closed and the curtains drawn across them all evening to keep out the draught, but Freddy was almost sure he had felt a gust of cold air blow in from the terrace shortly after the man had passed. Why had he chosen that particular moment to go outside?

The party-goers were all enjoying the excitement of the stolen jewel and the spectacle of the fainting lady far too much to pay any attention to Freddy as he slipped out onto the terrace into the chill night air and glanced about. The light blazed out through the windows, and if anybody had remained close to this part of the house he would have seen them easily, but he saw no-one. Freddy moved cautiously away from the building, winding his way among the cypress trees, listening as he went. The wind was stronger now, and he could hear nothing but that, together with the faint, distant sound of waves dashing against the cliff below the balustrade that surrounded the terrace perhaps thirty yards away. The place seemed quite deserted, but Freddy was almost certain someone had come out here. The darkness grew thicker the farther away from the house he got, and after a few minutes of fruitless stumbling about he began to think that he must have been mistaken. It was damp and uncomfortably cold, and all the excitement was surely happening indoors. If someone had come outside then perhaps he had gone straight back in again—and even if he had not, it would be nearly impossible to find him in the pitch dark, so what was the use in remaining outside?

Freddy had just made up his mind to return to the house when a hand reached out suddenly and clutched at his arm. He started violently and very nearly let out a yell.

'Where is it?' rasped a hoarse voice in French.

'What?'

At his reply, the questioner seemed to realize that Freddy was not the person he was seeking.

'*Pardon,*' he said, and would have retreated, but Freddy had by now gathered his wits. The man was wearing a rough jacket and cloth cap, and was clearly not a party guest, so what was he doing in the garden?

'Not so fast,' said Freddy, and grabbed at the man in turn, with some idea of restraining him and taking him up to the house. Too late he became aware that the man was much bigger and brawnier than he was, and had no intention of being restrained. There was a scuffle, then a punch was thrown which caught Freddy awkwardly on the jaw. It was merely a glancing blow and not in itself powerful enough to fell him, but it knocked him sideways, and then somehow he got his feet tangled up in the other man's legs and hit the ground heavily. The fall exasperated him more than the punch had, and he scrambled to his feet, ready for a fight despite his disadvantage in size. Before he could throw himself back into the fracas, however, the man grabbed him by his jacket and jammed something hard and metallic into his ribs.

'Now look here,' began Freddy.

'Shut up!' hissed the other, in English this time.

There was the tell-tale sound of a revolver being cocked, and Freddy froze, but he had no time for anything more than the briefest of prayers before his assailant paused and turned his head, as though listening. Before Freddy knew what was happening, the man raised his arm and landed him a sharp sideways clip to the head with the butt of his gun, knocking him to the ground again, then departed quickly.

The blow had not been hard enough to knock Freddy out, but it was enough to make him see stars. He lay for a few moments, waiting for the pain to recede; then, when it failed to do so, he eased himself up gently into a sitting position, since the ground was cold and hard and added little to his overall comfort. He felt his head gingerly and let out a quiet whimper, then rose carefully to his feet and walked unsteadily back towards the lights of the house, just in time to see Angela emerge onto the terrace in a hurry.

'I thought I saw you come out,' she began, then saw immediately that something was wrong. 'Goodness! What's happened?'

'Nothing much. Just one unsatisfactory brawl and a mild concussion,' replied Freddy with a wince, then, as she exclaimed, went on, 'I don't know what's going on in there, but out *here* there's a man with a gun, and I rather think he's expecting someone to hand him the diamond.'

'Good heavens! Where is he?'

'He was heading back this way a few moments ago, as far as I could tell from a horizontal position.'

'Oh dear,' said Angela. 'Do you think we ought to go after him?'

'You might ask whether I'm all right,' said Freddy, with an injured expression.

Angela glanced at him impatiently.

'Freddy, you are quite the most indestructible person I've ever met. I doubt whether anything less than Armageddon could finish you off. If you're on your feet then you'll forgive me for assuming there's nothing much wrong with you. Besides, I've seen you in worse condition—at least this fellow didn't bite your ear off.'

There was clearly no use in expecting any womanly sympathy from her, so he asked:

'Did Valencourt get away?'

'I think so. At least, I hope so. If he didn't then I've ruined my frock and given myself a fine crop of bruises for nothing.'

'What happened? This wasn't the plan, was it?'

'No,' replied Angela. 'Something's gone very wrong. Edgar was right when he said there was more to this than meets the eye. The whole place is in an uproar at present, but it won't take long until they spot he's missing and pin the blame for the whole thing on him.'

She turned and looked along to the darker end of the terrace.

'Is there a way out along there?' she asked, and walked off in the direction in which Freddy's attacker had disappeared.

'I say, be careful,' said Freddy, catching up with her. 'I came within a whisker of being shot just now. Don't let him see you.'

'Shh!' said Angela suddenly. 'What's that?'

Ahead of them they could hear the sound of a man's voice, rough and impatient. Then came a cry of surprise, followed by the unmistakable report of a gun. No good could come of such a sound. They jumped and stared at one another, then Freddy put his finger to his lips and pulled Angela against the side of the house into deeper shadow. They crept along the terrace, following the walls of the building, then turned right onto a section that fronted one of the side wings of the house. Here there was little light, but it was enough to see the scene before them, and they stopped. Before them, lying on the ground, was the man who had attacked Freddy, his gun clasped loosely in his hand, a pool of blood seeping out from under him. He was obviously quite dead. Standing over the body was Edgar Valencourt. He glanced up at them as Freddy and Angela took in the scene in silence.

'Why are you still here?' asked Angela at last, since it was as good a question as any.

'I couldn't get out through the front entrance, and they've got people searching the house,' replied Valencourt, regarding the dead man dispassionately. 'That American was quicker off the mark than most, so I had to hide and look for my chance. But at this rate I'll be here all night.'

Freddy stared at the body and recognized it for the first time as the man he had seen the other night at the casino talking to La Duchessa.

'Who's this? Rolf Boehler, I take it?'

'Yes. I can't say I'll miss him.'

'You didn't kill him, did you?' asked Freddy.

'No, of course I didn't,' replied Valencourt tetchily. 'I was trying to make a discreet exit through this door and down the cliff path when somebody decided to throw a spanner into the machinery and leave a dead body lying around for me to trip over. I got here a second before you did.'

'Then who did kill him? Did you see who it was?'

'No. I heard the shot from inside, but whoever it was must have disappeared pretty quickly.'

'None of this was meant to happen, was it?' said Angela. 'The lights, and the theft in the dark. It was a trap, wasn't it?'

'Yes, I rather think so,' answered Valencourt.

'You didn't take the diamond?'

'No.'

'Then where is it?'

'I don't know.'

'Look, what the devil is all this?' demanded Freddy.

'I've no idea, but I think it's fair to say this job is not going well,' replied Valencourt dryly.

'I admire your facility for understatement,' said Angela, 'but perhaps this will be better discussed later. They'll be out looking for you in a moment.'

'You'd better make yourself scarce, old chap,' agreed Freddy.

'And don't run off again,' Angela called after Valencourt as he melted away into the darkness.

# Chapter Eleven

'THIS IS TURNING out to be quite the oddest evening,' remarked Angela.

Freddy's head was still turned in the direction in which Valencourt had disappeared. He went off and returned a moment or two later.

'There's a cliff path leading from the terrace,' he said. 'It's too dark to see where it goes, but it looks like a handy means of escape. I wonder how Valencourt knew it was there.'

'I should think the worse of him if he hadn't had the sense to come here beforehand and "case the joint," as I believe they call it. If I really must cast in my lot with a jewel-thief, then better a competent one than not.' Angela gazed down at the prone figure of Rolf Boehler. 'I suppose one ought to be sorry a man is dead, but from what I've heard of him we needn't mourn his passing. If the newspaper reports are correct he's murdered two innocent people at least, and most likely more. So you think he was waiting here to take delivery of the diamond, do you? Then where is it now?'

Freddy crouched down and made a brief but efficient search of the dead man's pockets.

'Rolf doesn't have it, at any rate,' he said.

'Then whoever shot him must have it. But who? Was it someone from inside or did they come up the cliff path?'

'I don't know. It might have been either.'

It had begun to rain. Angela shivered.

'I don't know about you, but I don't much relish the thought of staying out here in the cold and dark with a possible murderer on the loose. Besides, I expect the police will be here soon, and no doubt Mr. Roche would like to know about the dead body cluttering up his terrace. Let's go indoors.'

Freddy made no objection to the proposal, since the bump on his head had begun to throb painfully, making it difficult to think. In spite of the fuzziness clouding his brain, however, two things were very clear: a man was dead and the Mariensee diamond had vanished. There was nothing they could do for Rolf, so there was no sense in remaining outside. This was a job for the police now.

Once inside they found that the band, in the absence of any instructions to the contrary, was still playing, and a number of hardy couples were dancing, while most of the other guests sat at tables, chattering excitedly. The police had not yet arrived, and servants had been stationed at all the doors of the ballroom in order to prevent anyone from leaving. Freddy looked around, but saw no sign of La Duchessa or Fritz Boehler. He spent several minutes searching fruitlessly for Benjamin Roche, who was also nowhere to be seen. He found his great-aunt sitting down, and asked her whether she had heard any news. She was horrified at the events of the evening.

'What is to be done?' she quavered. 'Is anything or anyone safe, when such wickedness walks among us?' She put a hand protectively over her diamond necklace, which Freddy's Great-Uncle Algy had bestowed upon her some fifty years earlier. 'We are all lucky not to have been murdered!'

'I say, Aunt, I shouldn't go that far. And I shouldn't worry

—why, they'll have the brooch back in a jiffy and lock up the fellow who did it.'

'Oh, I do hope so. It is too early to say who was the culprit, of course, but it seems a man has disappeared most suspiciously. He was standing next to Mrs. Weeks when the lights went off, but when Mrs. Marchmont fainted he vanished in all the confusion. There you are, my dear,' she went on, seeing Angela. 'We were all terribly worried about you. Are you sure you ought to be still here? Perhaps a taxi might be brought.'

'That's very kind of you, Duchess, but I'm quite all right now, thank you,' replied Angela unblushingly.

'Any sign of Roche?' asked Freddy.

'There he is,' said Angela, and Freddy turned to see their host just coming into the room, leaning on the arm of one of the men who had been searching the house. He was helped to a chair and sat down unsteadily.

'I have been attacked!' he exclaimed as they approached.

'Goodness me!' said Angela. 'Are you all right? Perhaps we ought to call a doctor.'

'Thank you, there is no need, my dear. I believe I shall be quite well in a moment. It is only the shock.'

He brushed dazedly at some dust on his sleeve, then brought out a handkerchief and wiped his face. A manservant had come in and was hovering anxiously around him.

'Thank you, Werner, I am quite all right. Is everything cleared away?'

'Yes, *monsieur*. Everything is done.'

'Then go and see to the waiters.'

The manservant departed, and Roche burst out indignantly:

'The miscreants were hiding in my salon. They threw me to the ground as though I were an old rag and made off with a necklace of great historical value. They smashed a case to get it, and left broken glass all over the room—ah, but I forgot to tell Werner to clear it up.'

'Better leave it for the police, sir,' said Freddy.

'Of course, of course. You are right. But great heavens—first the Mariensee diamond and now this! It is all dreadful, quite dreadful!'

'I'm afraid it gets worse, sir,' said Freddy, and gave a brief account of what had happened on the terrace, without mentioning Edgar Valencourt. Roche looked as though he could not believe his ears, and all but wrung his hands at the news that his party had been ruined not only by the theft of several thousand pounds' worth of valuable jewellery, but also by the appearance of a corpse in his garden.

'Oh dear, oh dear!' he lamented. 'What is to be done?'

He was saved from having to answer his own question by the arrival of several efficient-looking policemen, who spread out and took charge of proceedings. Their leader was a man in plain clothes, who introduced himself as Chief Inspector Guichard and reacted phlegmatically to the news that the theft had now turned into a murder investigation. He barked instructions to his men to see to matters indoors, and requested to see the body.

'It was at the West end of the terrace, you say?' asked Roche of Freddy. He rose to his feet, brushing off all attempts to support him. 'Thank you, I am perfectly well now. Just a momentary shock, that is all. Now, perhaps it will be better not to go through the ballroom. Please come this way.'

He led them through several grand rooms to a small library which had a door leading out into the garden. Freddy saw that it was the same door through which Valencourt had come out. They stepped outside to find that the rain was now little short of a downpour and the wind was threatening to rise to a gale. They all huddled together in the shelter of the doorway.

'Where is it?' asked the chief inspector patiently.

Freddy and Angela were staring at the ground before them. The body of Rolf Boehler was not there.

'How odd,' said Angela. 'It was here a moment ago. Are we sure this is the right place?' she asked of Freddy.

'Unless somebody lifted the building and set it down somewhere else while we were inside, yes,' he replied, looking about him in puzzlement.

'Are you quite certain of what you saw?' said Roche.

'Of course I am.' Freddy gazed at the spot where Rolf Boehler had breathed his last, as though he could will the corpse back into visibility. 'I tell you he was here. He bashed me on the head with his gun and ran off, then somebody shot him. We heard it.'

'It's true, inspector,' agreed Angela.

Guichard regarded them both doubtfully.

'He was lying here, you say?'

He shone a torch on the ground. There ought to have been bloodstains, but even had they been visible in the dark it was clear that the rain would soon wash the last remaining trace of them away, if it had not done so already. The chief inspector turned back to them, his face the very picture of polite incomprehension.

'Somebody must have moved him,' said Angela.

The chief inspector pulled his coat tightly around him then ducked out into the rain. He ran quickly the length of the terrace and back.

'Nothing,' he said as he returned.

Roche, looking at Angela, was struck by a sudden thought.

'Mrs. Marchmont, you have already fainted this evening, and you really ought not to be out here. It's too cold and wet. You must come indoors.'

'You are not well?' inquired the chief inspector of Angela. Those were his words, but his expression said clearly, 'You have drunk a little too much champagne?' His gaze slid from Angela to Freddy, whose dinner-suit had derived little benefit from its close encounter with the ground, and he appeared to draw his own conclusions.

'There is nothing to see here at present,' he said at last. 'We shall inspect the terrace properly tomorrow, and I dare say all will be explained, but in the meantime we had better do as M. Roche says and get out of the rain.' He ushered them inside and shut the door firmly. 'Now then, M. Roche, I should like to speak to this Mme. Weeks. She has lost a brooch, they tell me. And you also have been burgled?'

'Oh, yes. I needn't tell you that this is no ordinary theft. It is no exaggeration to say that Mrs. Weeks's husband is a man who quite possibly holds the future of France in his hands, and my own loss, although most distressing, is wholly unimportant by comparison with the loss of the Mariensee diamond. R. G. Weeks is a busy and important man who has agreed to help broker a vital agreement between France and Germany. To allow his wife to be robbed in this fashion is quite unconscionable, and does nothing to foster good feeling among nations. And to think it happened in my house! I feel responsible for this terrible event.'

They went off, Roche talking incessantly as they went, leaving Freddy and Angela to stare at one another in consternation.

'What on earth is going on?' demanded Angela.

'I don't know, but I don't like it,' replied Freddy grimly.

# Chapter Twelve

THE STORM BLEW itself out overnight, and the next day dawned warm and sunny. Freddy slept later than he had intended, and woke up to find the sun streaming in through a gap in the curtains. He sat up carefully and felt his head, thinking of what had happened the night before. After the police had carried out a fruitless search for the Mariensee diamond and Benjamin Roche's missing necklace, all the party guests had finally been allowed to leave. Angela and Freddy had protested, but Chief Inspector Guichard had been firm. There was nothing they could do to help at present, but he would be obliged if *madame* and *monsieur* would leave their addresses with the sergeant at the door, so that the police might find them again if necessary. It was clear that Guichard considered them *de trop*, and quite possibly drunk, and so they had had no choice but to depart along with the rest of the guests. On their return to the hotel Freddy would have kept Angela up all night talking, but by that time she had got a good look at the state of him and firmly instructed him to go to bed—which, he had to admit, had probably been the wisest course of action, since, having had a decent night's sleep, he felt little the worse from the scuffle with Rolf apart from a sore spot just above his left ear and a slight headache.

He was anxious to talk over the previous evening's events with Angela, so he dressed quickly and went downstairs, where he found Angela speaking to the man at the desk. She turned away, a discontented expression on her face.

'Nothing from William,' she said. 'I thought we might have had news of Nightshade by now, one way or the other. How is your head?'

'Harder than I supposed. Join me for breakfast?'

'I've already eaten, thank you, but I'll come and sit with you and we can talk about last night. Inside or out?'

Freddy opted for inside on the grounds that the terrace was crowded and less conducive to private conversation. They sat in a quiet corner of the dining-room and Freddy gave his order.

'Now, tell me again exactly what happened when you went outside last night,' said Angela, once the waiter had furnished them with coffee.

Freddy recounted his tale and she listened attentively.

'Do you think the person who trod on your foot was the one who tore the brooch from Mrs. Weeks's dress?' she asked.

'It might not have been, of course, but it seems rather too much of a coincidence that when I followed him into the garden I encountered old Rolf, to the great detriment of my cranium. We do know for certain that the Boehlers were planning to steal the diamond, so I don't think it's too much of a stretch to assume that the foot-treader had come outside to deliver it to Rolf.'

'Then "where is it" presumably referred to the Mariensee diamond. But who was the man? Fritz Boehler?'

'That was my first thought, but it couldn't have been Fritz,' replied Freddy. 'I saw him with a tray of drinks by the door at the opposite end of the room when the lights came back on. He couldn't possibly have had time to go outside and come back in again.'

'Another member of the gang, then?'

'Presumably, but who?'

'Are you sure it was a man?'

'Well it wasn't La Duchessa, if that's what you mean. His voice was far too deep. It might have been my Great-Aunt Ernestine, I suppose, but I think it's unlikely she's begun dabbling in thievery as a side-line.'

Angela stirred her coffee thoughtfully.

'Very well, let's get things straight. When the lights go off our thief—let's call him X—tears the brooch from Jessie Weeks's dress and creeps outside to deliver it to Rolf, but fails to find him in the dark. In the meantime, Rolf, who's waiting for X, grabs you, realizes his mistake and is about to shoot you when he hears a noise and decides to hit you over the head instead. He runs off, then I come outside and find you just staggering to your feet. Then what?'

'Then what? That's the question, isn't it?' said Freddy. 'We're assuming Rolf heard X and went to get the diamond from him, but why did X then shoot him?'

'Perhaps he'd decided not to hand it over, but to keep it for himself.'

'But then why come outside at all? Why not simply pocket the thing and make a run for it? There was no need to kill anybody.'

'No, there wasn't, was there?' agreed Angela.

Freddy's food arrived and they were silent for some minutes as he attended to that important business, then Angela said:

'I wonder why they decided to rob Mr. Roche as well. You'd think they might have concentrated their attention on one thing at a time.'

'Perhaps they couldn't resist it.'

'I dare say. But it seems an awful risk to take when they'd made such careful plans. And where did Rolf's body disappear to? Chief Inspector Guichard obviously thought we were a pair of idiots, but we did see him, didn't we? I mean, we weren't imagining things?'

'No, he was there all right. I saw him just as clearly as you did.'

'Might we have been mistaken, though? Perhaps he wasn't dead after all, but merely injured, and took himself off when we went inside.'

'You don't believe that any more than I do,' said Freddy. 'We've both seen enough dead bodies in our time to know when someone's beyond help, and it was perfectly obvious that Rolf was no longer at home to visitors.'

'Then someone else must have moved him. But who? And where to?'

'Let's go back to La Falaise and find out,' said Freddy.

Angela looked doubtful.

'Will they let us in, do you think?'

'We can but try. The police are unlikely to speak to us but Roche or one of his servants might be prepared to spill the beans. A wandering corpse isn't the kind of thing one can keep secret for long.'

'It's possible nobody even knows about it, since the police didn't believe us.'

'Then all the more reason for us to go and search the place ourselves. More coffee?'

'Edgar was right, at any rate,' said Angela, as the waiter filled her cup.

'What do you mean?'

'Why, that the Boehlers tried to double-cross him. They led him to believe that it was his job to steal the diamond from Jessie Weeks, but it's clear now that they had quite a different plan, and merely arranged things so that he'd get the blame when the lights went back on. They had a grudge against him and I suppose that was their idea of revenge.'

'That seems a reasonable conclusion,' agreed Freddy. 'While Valencourt was working up to taking it by charm, someone else barged in and ripped the thing off her frock. Terribly vulgar.'

'I wonder whether it was La Duchessa's idea to pin the blame on him. It seems a lot of effort to go to just to do someone a bad turn.'

'It does, doesn't it? But from my long and glorious experience at the *Clarion*, I've learned that criminals don't think the same as the rest of us.' He glanced at Angela. 'I really ought to tell the police about her, you know, since it's more or less public knowledge that I know her. We certainly can't rely on Nugs to keep his mouth shut forever.'

She sighed.

'I dare say you're right. It would be nice if you could keep Edgar out of it, though.'

Freddy hesitated, and she saw it.

'Look, if you're thinking he shot Rolf then you can stop thinking it. I know exactly what he is and has been, and I have just as many doubts as you do about the theft. But one thing I do know is that Edgar isn't a murderer, and if you're going to start thinking he is then I'm afraid we can't be friends. Besides, the body disappeared, remember? You don't think he came back, slung it gaily over his shoulder and scampered off with it down the cliff path, do you?'

'When you put it like that—' admitted Freddy.

'No,' she went on. 'Whoever killed Rolf must also have been responsible for the removal of his body, so you'll have to take it on trust that Edgar really did stumble over him just as we did.'

'Oh, very well. But you can hardly blame me for being cynical. Where is Valencourt now, by the way?'

'I couldn't tell you. I promise, I have no idea,' she insisted, on seeing his disbelieving expression. 'But if I were in his position I'd go and find myself a big, anonymous hotel in Nice, where nobody could possibly recognize me. I expect we'll hear from him soon.' A fleeting look of uncertainty crossed her face. 'At least, I hope we will.'

## Chapter Thirteen

ON ARRIVAL at La Falaise they were informed that Chief Inspector Guichard had left the house and was pursuing his investigations elsewhere. A sergeant who had remained on duty regarded them askance, and seemed inclined to turn them away, but Freddy had had the foresight to telephone his Great-Aunt Ernestine before they set off, the results of which could be seen when Mr. Roche came bustling to the door before the policeman could send them about their business.

'My dear boy, I had no idea you were a detective! The Duchess informs me that you were responsible for recovering some priceless pearls that were stolen from your family last spring. How very fortuitous. Come in, come in! And Mrs. Marchmont. I hope you are none the worse for your adventure of yesterday evening—no, I can see you are well—so glad, so glad. Yes, I am quite well, too, thank you—none the worse for my little contretemps, unexpected as it was. I am much stronger than I look, and fortunately the thieves were more anxious to make their escape than to do me any serious harm. Just one or two little cuts and scrapes from the floor. Now, I am afraid I have just a little business to attend to with my lawyer, who is here—very troublesome, but unavoidable—

but I do hope you will wait and give us the benefit of your expertise. I shall have Werner bring you tea.'

'No need, thank you,' replied Freddy. 'As a matter of fact, that's exactly why we came. We were hoping to scout around and see if there was anything we could do to help.'

'Naturally, I shall be more than grateful for any assistance you can provide that might lead to the recovery of the Mariensee diamond and my necklace—although of course my own loss is paltry by comparison with Mrs. Weeks's.'

'We'll do anything we can, sir. Might we go into the garden?'

Roche hesitated.

'Ah, yes, the dead body.'

'I don't suppose the police found any sign of it?'

'No. Some of Guichard's men made a search of the terrace this morning, but found nothing.'

'Hardly surprising, given the rain last night,' said Angela.

'Perhaps. I confess the whole thing appears most odd.' Mr. Roche coughed. 'In truth, I rather wonder whether you might not have been mistaken as to what you saw.' The suggestion hung delicately in the air. 'Might it have been that—is it possible that the man you saw was not dead at all, but had—let us say—lain down for a rest? It was very hot in the ball-room, and some people do react badly to the combination of that and too much champagne. And it was very dark outside, so it would be entirely understandable if, upon finding a man who had taken a little too much to drink lying prostrate on the ground, you came to an erroneous conclusion. Yes,' he went on, warming to his theory. 'I should not be at all surprised if this man, whoever he was, woke up while you were looking for me, and went back indoors to rejoin the party.'

It was evident that he was as unconvinced about their story as Chief Inspector Guichard had been, and there was little use in insisting upon the point, since there was no body to prove them right, and no evidence apart from that of their own ears that a gun had been fired at all. Freddy therefore agreed that it had been very dark, and that he was perfectly prepared to accept they might have been mistaken, but they should like to take one last look if it were not too much trouble. Mr. Roche had no objection to make and went off to speak to his lawyer, declaring that he would be only too grateful if Mr. Pilkington-Soames and Mrs. Marchmont succeeded in finding any clues as to who had committed the dreadful crimes which had taken place under his own roof.

'You seem to have quite the reputation as a detective among your family,' remarked Angela as they walked along the terrace towards the West wing of the house.

'I must say I had no idea Aunt E. would be so fulsome in her praise,' replied Freddy. 'It makes a change from her usual air of pained disappointment. It feels a little odd but I think I rather like it.'

'Let's hope we can live up to the billing, then.' She stopped at the place where Rolf's body had lain the evening before. 'Well, there's certainly no corpse here. Leaving aside the absurd idea of anyone's having had so much to drink that the cold, wet ground looked a suitable place to sleep it off, where did Rolf go after we went indoors, and who took him?'

Freddy stood, absorbing his surroundings. The rain had washed the terrace clean, taking with it any traces that indicated a man had died on that spot. The sea was calm and deep blue beyond the balustrade, and the events of the night before seemed almost unbelievable in the light of day.

'Where were you when he grabbed you?' asked Angela.

'Just over there.'

They walked across to the spot he had indicated. Freddy spied something on the ground and picked it up. It was a button from a dinner-jacket.

'So that's where my top button went. I noticed it had gone when I went to bed. It must have come off in the struggle. This is certainly the place, then.'

They turned and contemplated the house, and Freddy frowned.

'What is it?' asked Angela.

'I'm just thinking of what we were talking about at breakfast. Why did X come outside at all if he had no intention of giving the diamond to Rolf? There seems no sense in it.'

'Did he come out for the purpose of handing it over and then change his mind for some reason? Was there a dispute over it?'

'It's possible,' replied Freddy. 'But I don't think there was enough time. I was only on the ground for a minute or two, then I walked towards the house and met you, and that's when it started.'

'Was it Rolf we heard speaking?'

'It sounded like his voice, yes. But I couldn't hear what he was saying, could you?'

Angela shook her head.

'From the tone it sounded as though he were telling X to go away or asking what he wanted, or something of the kind.'

'Yes, it did, didn't it?' agreed Freddy. 'And I think that exclamation we heard was Rolf realizing he was just about to meet his Maker, because a second after that came the gunshot. It didn't sound like much of a row to me—rather that someone caught Rolf by surprise and then shot him before he knew what was happening.'

'I've just thought of something,' said Angela. 'When I found you last night and you said the man who attacked you had headed back towards the house, my first thought was that he must have gone inside, and I've just remembered why.'

'Oh? Go on.'

'After I fainted, they picked me up and sat me on a chair on that raised area at the side of the room, and that's when I saw you going outside. I said I needed some air and got away as soon as they'd let me, but as I was making my way through the crowd to follow you into the garden I saw the French window open again and someone come in, and I thought it was you. After a second I realized it wasn't, so I went outside and found you, as you know. But someone certainly did come in—only I don't know who it was, because there was an awful scrum of people between me and the door and I couldn't see over their heads. But what if it was X—the person who took the diamond to Rolf? If that's the case, then X didn't shoot Rolf at all. He gave Rolf the diamond and then came back in, and it was someone else altogether who shot him.'

'By Jove, that's a thought!' exclaimed Freddy. 'It would certainly explain our difficulty: X handed over the diamond exactly as he was meant to, then returned to the ballroom and disappeared among the crowd. Then Rolf headed along to this part of the terrace, intending to make his escape down the cliff path, but was forestalled by someone else who came out, shot him in cold blood and relieved him of the diamond.'

'That must be what happened,' said Angela. 'It must. It's the only thing that makes sense. Although of course it doesn't answer the question of who X is.'

'No, it doesn't. And it complicates matters by giving us a second person to look for: the murderer of Rolf, who is also now the proud possessor of Jessie Weeks's favourite sparkler.'

'Oh dear, this whole thing is turning into rather a muddle. It seems as though half the people at the party were running around shooting each another and stealing each other's trinkets. Or might the killer have been someone who wasn't a guest at all? A servant, perhaps, or someone from outside who came up the cliff path.'

'If it was someone from outside how would they know exactly when to turn up?' said Freddy.

'The lights went off, didn't they? I assume that was Fritz's doing. He could easily have arranged it to happen at a certain moment.'

'But that implies Fritz had something to do with Rolf's death.'

'Don't you think it's possible? Criminals fall out all the time, and I'm sure it's the same even when they're brothers.'

'Perhaps,' answered Freddy doubtfully. 'But then who disposed of Rolf's body? Fritz was in the ballroom when we came in to report the murder. I saw him wandering up and down collecting glasses, and he was still there when we came back after talking to Guichard. He might have shot Rolf but he couldn't possibly have had time to take him away.'

'Well then, other members of the gang who were waiting outside.'

'If that's the case then there must have been a lot of people milling about in the garden while I was out there. I wonder I didn't bump into more of them.'

'It does seem unlikely,' agreed Angela. She walked slowly back towards the place where Rolf had been. 'Let's think this through. Our murderer—let's call him Y—knows that Rolf will be here to collect the diamond from X. He lies in wait, shoots Rolf, takes the diamond and leaves immediately. Then Edgar turns up, followed shortly by us.'

Freddy hesitated, but kept his thoughts to himself. Angela went on:

'Edgar escapes down the cliff path, and we go inside to tell Mr. Roche what happened. In the meantime Y, who assumes nobody knows about the shooting, returns and removes the body. How long were we away from the terrace? It couldn't have been more than ten or fifteen minutes.'

'That's plenty of time to take him away,' said Freddy.

'Do you think so? Have you any idea how heavy a dead body is? I don't suppose you've ever moved one, have you?'

Freddy coughed.

'As a matter of fact, I have.'

'Really?' Angela regarded him for a moment, her head on one side. 'I ought to be surprised, but somehow I'm not.'

'I'll admit it wasn't one of my finer moments, and I shall tell you about it another time. However, I can assure you I know exactly how heavy a dead body is, and that it's tricky—not to say nearly impossible—to move one without either assistance or transport, but as long as you have at least one of those then ten or fifteen minutes ought to be enough. I don't suppose they keep a wheelbarrow around here?'

They looked about them, but there was no shed or store where a wheelbarrow might be kept.

'In that case our mysterious Y must have had an accomplice,' said Freddy. 'Let's call him Z and hope we don't run out of letters. Unless Z is X, in which case why didn't X merely hand the diamond to Y and leave Rolf out of it?'

'The whole thing is most perplexing. Let's leave that matter aside for a moment and stick to the problem of Rolf. Where could the body have gone? Down the cliff path? Or even into the house?'

'It's a big house, but surely somebody would have noticed two men lugging a corpse from room to room,' replied Freddy. 'And which door would they have taken him in by? Not the French windows—there are two sets of those, but they both lead into the ballroom. Then there was the door from the library that Valencourt came through and we came through ourselves with Guichard.'

'There are doors at the other end of the house. Several of them, in fact.'

'Yes, but to take Rolf into the house that way they'd have to have carried him along the whole length of the building, and someone might have come out through the French windows at any time and caught them.' Freddy rubbed his chin. 'It would be helpful if we knew where the murderer came from—I mean to say, whether he came from outside or inside the house. If he came up the cliff path he might have had an accomplice waiting, ready to dispose of the body. If it was someone from inside, then that brings us back to the question of who? And who helped him?'

'Not only that, but if it was someone inside the house then

which door did he use?' said Angela. 'He couldn't have come through the library door, because that's the way Edgar came a minute later, and Edgar would have seen him.'

'Ye-es,' replied Freddy.

Angela threw him an exasperated look and walked off and around the side of the building. Freddy heard an exclamation.

'There's a door here,' she called.

He followed and found her standing by a glass-paned door, on the other side of which was a short passage with a red-tiled floor. The door was unlocked, so they went in and discovered the passage led past the kitchen, around a corner and thence to the main part of the house.

'The murderer *might* have come out through this door,' said Angela. 'But I doubt very much they brought Rolf this way. They would have been seen. Is there any other way they might have gone?'

'Only upwards,' replied Freddy, gazing up a flight of steps which led up the side of the building, presumably to a roof terrace. But the steps were barred by an iron gate which was firmly fastened with a padlock. They examined the lock, but it was encrusted with dirt and salt, and clearly had not been unlocked recently. Rolf had certainly not come this way. Angela gazed at the gate, considering.

'Well, then, if he didn't go into the house or onto the roof he must have gone down the cliff path. It can't have been much fun carrying him all that way in a storm, though.'

'There is another possibility,' said Freddy. 'Although it's not a pleasant one.'

He went across to the stone balustrade and peered over it. A hundred feet below the sea dashed against the rocks at the foot of the cliff. Angela joined him and stared down at the roiling water.

'Oh, I see.' She grimaced. 'Yes, of course. They threw him over the balustrade. How horrid.'

'It would be much the easiest way, don't you think? And one man could do it himself.'

They walked the outer length of the terrace, gazing over the edge.

'It's unlikely they carried him far,' said Freddy. 'If they did chuck him in then it was probably at the point nearest to where he was shot. Somewhere around here.' He examined the section of balustrade in question, then gave it up. 'The rain will have washed any traces away.'

'Very likely,' agreed Angela. She looked a little sick. 'I know he was a bad man, but I hope he went straight in and didn't hit anything on the way down.'

It was an unpleasant thought, and they stood in silence for a few moments, then Angela said:

'But why did they dispose of him at all? Surely the most important thing was for them to get away with the goods rather than waste time hiding a dead body?'

'I dare say they wanted to conceal the fact of there having been a murder at all, in case they were caught. Better a gaol sentence than the guillotine.' He pointed. 'Look, there's a cove down there, and a boat. Is that how Rolf was planning to spirit the Mariensee diamond away, do you think?'

'If he was, then he was taking an awful risk in that storm.'

'Perhaps he had another plan just in case the escape by boat wasn't possible. At any rate I'd like to take a closer look.'

They set off down the path, which had been cut into the rock and ran steeply backwards and forwards along the side of the cliff. Here and there, where the route became too steep for a path, steps had been cut. A short way down it split into two. One branch continued down towards the cove, while the other led back upwards, ending at a locked iron gate through which they could see another house.

'Edgar must have climbed over this gate and escaped that way,' said Angela. 'And I expect Rolf would have done the same in the end, since the sea was too rough to leave by boat.'

They returned to the downward path and arrived at the cove, which was natural on two sides and shaped by human hand on the third. Here a boat with a furled red sail bobbed merrily on the water. It bore the name *Neptune*. Freddy approached it.

'Hallo! Anyone aboard?' he called.

There was no reply. He jumped onto the boat and put his head into the cabin, which contained nothing but a few coils of rope and a tiny berth covered with an untidy heap of blankets. There was nothing to say whom the boat belonged to, or whether the Boehler gang had ever been there.

'Any clues?' asked Angela, as he emerged onto the deck and sprang across to land.

'Not that I can see,' he replied. 'There's nothing in the way of personal possessions that might indicate whose it is.'

'Perhaps it was hired.'

'I imagine it was, if this was how Rolf was planning to leave.' He glanced at his watch then turned to contemplate the upward toil that lay ahead of them. 'I suppose old Roche has finished with his lawyer now, so we'd better go back. I must say, the way up doesn't look nearly so much fun as—hallo, who's that?'

Angela followed his gaze.

'I can't see anyone.'

'There was a man there, just where the path forks, looking down at us.'

'Why wouldn't he look at us? We're the only people here,' said Angela reasonably.

'A fair point, except that he ducked down behind a rock as soon as he realized I'd seen him.'

'Oh. How odd. But I expect there's some simple explanation. Perhaps we'll see him again on the way up.'

'I have the feeling we won't,' said Freddy.

## Chapter Fourteen

THEY TRUDGED up the path back to La Falaise, but met no-one on the way—as Freddy had expected, for the man he had seen had had a furtive air about him, and had altogether given the impression that he wished to remain out of sight. They reached the house to find that the lawyer had left and Mr. Roche was looking for them.

'I am sorry to have kept you waiting for so long,' he said. 'Might I ask whether you have found anything interesting? No dead bodies tucked behind the cypresses?'

His eye twinkled as he said it, and there was evidently little use in telling him of the conclusions they had reached, since they still had no proof that a man had died at all.

'Not a dead body to be seen,' replied Angela pleasantly. 'It's quite a mystery.'

'We've been down to the little cove to look at a boat there,' said Freddy. 'Do you know it? Does it belong to the house?'

'No, it is not mine.'

'What about the house next door, perhaps?'

'The house next door? Ah, you mean the little villa at the top of the other fork in the path? That house is empty at the moment as far as I know.'

'We thought perhaps the boat might have been moored there to allow the thief or thieves to make a quick getaway, although of course they didn't use it in the end as the sea was too rough.'

'Perhaps you are right. I imagine Guichard will have seen it, since the police were outside this morning, but I will mention it to the sergeant here in case they missed it.'

'Any sign of the Mariensee diamond?' asked Freddy.

Roche's face fell.

'Alas, no. I am very much afraid that if they cannot get it back soon then it will be too late. The police have put a watch on the ports and the border crossings, but it would be only too easy to smuggle such a small thing out of the country, especially since we do not know whom we are looking for. This will cause a dreadful scandal at a most inopportune time. The talks in The Hague have reached a critical point, and it is not too much to say that the fate of the reparations agreement hangs in the balance. The last thing France needs is for Mr. Weeks to be distracted by a calamity of this kind. They are doing their best to keep the story out of the papers, but it is difficult as everyone who was here last night knows what happened, and some of the foreign newspapers are unlikely to co-operate, especially the German ones. I shall not publish, naturally, but if the story gets out before the diamond is recovered then I cannot bear to think of what will happen. I am quite beside myself. The Prime Minister will be very angry with me, and rightly so, for it was in my house that all this happened.'

'What was taken of yours?'

'I will show you.'

Roche led them to a grand, high-ceilinged room off the entrance-hall which he evidently used as a kind of museum, for the furniture was all antique, while a proliferation of china vases and figurines stood on display around the room. Against the panelled walls were several glass cases, one of which had been smashed open and its contents taken.

'It was a necklace,' said Mr. Roche, as they all gazed at it. 'It belonged to one of the ladies-in-waiting of the Empress Joséphine. Quite an ugly thing, and not even especially valuable, but interesting nonetheless for its historical significance. As a matter of fact I was thinking of selling it.' He gestured to another case. 'Now, this ring here belonged to the Empress herself, and is worth much more money. I wonder they did not steal this instead.'

'What exactly happened?' Angela asked.

'It is difficult to recall, since it was all very quick. I had gone to speak to Werner for a moment about the incident with the lights, while some of the male guests searched the house for the diamond. When I came back I saw the door to this room was ajar, and wondered if the thief was perhaps hiding in here. I came and found the light was off, so naturally I went to try the switch to see whether all was working. As soon as the light came on they sprang and knocked me to the ground. Two of them, there were—at least, I did not see any more. There was a little scuffle—which I fear was my own fault, since I am sure they were far more concerned with escaping than with fighting—and they ran off. Once I had gathered my thoughts I got to my feet and found the case as you see it.'

'Did you get a look at them? I mean to say, would you recognize them again?'

Roche grimaced regretfully.

'I fear not. I was caught so much by surprise that I did not see their faces properly.'

Freddy turned to look at the room.

'The broken case is nearest the door,' he said. 'Perhaps it was an opportunistic theft, since they'd obviously come for the Mariensee diamond. I expect they thought there was no harm in filching something else before they left the house, but didn't have time to take anything more than the necklace.'

'It is as you say,' agreed Mr. Roche.

'I wonder—might we speak to the chap who was in charge of the waiters?'

'Certainly,' replied Mr. Roche.

The man was duly summoned, and stood before them. He was solid, bland and impassive, and looked as though it would take much more than a mere robbery to shake his self-possession.

'Werner, be so good as to answer Mr. Pilkington-Soames's questions,' said Mr. Roche.

'Very good, sir,' replied Werner, and turned with polite attention to Freddy, who asked:

'Do you know who turned off the lights? How did they do it?'

'I do not know who was responsible,' the man replied, 'but the fuse-box is located just outside the kitchen, and has a switch to the mains, so anyone might have done it as they were passing. We have had trouble with wiring in the past, and we have had people in to fix it, so when this happened I sighed as I thought the problem must have started again. But when I went to the box I saw that somebody had merely turned off the main switch, so I turned it back on.'

'And nobody saw who did it?'

'No. We brought in several hired waiters for the evening, and it might have been any of them, although they all denied having done it. It is most distressing to think that I might have inadvertently employed such people,' he added.

'Now, now, I do not suppose for a second that you did it deliberately,' Mr. Roche reassured him. 'At any rate, the police are looking into that.'

'You turned the lights back on, then what?' asked Freddy.

'I went about my business for some minutes—there was a great degree of confusion when it all happened, you understand, and I had to give firm instructions to the waiters, who were inclined to shirk their duties and talk about what a great joke it had been. Then M. Roche came to find out what had occurred, and told me that a valuable jewel belonging to one of the guests had been taken. He went away to help in the search of the house, and perhaps ten or fifteen minutes later someone came to tell me that he had been attacked, so I went into the ballroom to assist him if I could. Soon after that the police arrived.'

There was nothing else he could tell them, and he was dismissed.

'I say, sir, you'd better be careful,' said Freddy to Roche. 'It's obvious there are some dangerous thieves in the area at present, and this house must be a temptation to them. They've already got a couple of things, but I shouldn't be a bit surprised if they were to come back soon and try again for the rest.'

'I am quite of your opinion,' replied Roche gravely. 'And I promise you I mean to be careful. I am only sorry I was not more vigilant before the party, because then Mrs. Weeks might still be in possession of her brooch.' He shook his head in distress. 'This is a terrible thing which has happened, and very much my responsibility. If you discover any clue as to where these criminals have gone, then I wish you will tell me.'

They promised to let him know if they found out any further information and took their leave.

'Well, I don't think much of Werner,' said Angela as they left La Falaise. 'Far too good to be true.'

'You thought that too, did you? Yes, he did rather look as though butter wouldn't melt in his mouth.'

She wrinkled her nose in dissatisfaction.

'This business is becoming more and more confusing. Why the necklace? Were the Boehlers behind that, too? Or was it an inside job?'

'What, all the servants tangled up in the matter in addition to the Boehlers, Valencourt and La Duchessa?'

'It does seem a little excessive,' she admitted. 'In fact, the whole thing is nonsensical.'

'Perhaps Valencourt will be able to tell us what happened. I'll bet he knows more than he's letting on.'

'Of that we can be quite certain,' replied Angela dryly.

'With any luck he'll have sent you a note by now to tell you where he's staying, and we can go and ask him ourselves.'

Freddy was engaged to have lunch at the Villa des Fleurs, so they parted, Freddy promising to find out whether any of his relations had noticed anything untoward at the party. When he arrived he found that Jessie Weeks was there, as well as Chief Inspector Guichard, who was pursuing his investigations. Mrs. Weeks was pink-eyed and inclined to burst into tears at intervals, and Guichard was doing his best to be patient with her.

'Randall is so terribly angry with me,' wailed Mrs. Weeks, wringing her hands. 'But what could I have done? It all happened in a matter of seconds. He's threatening to pull out of the talks, and if he does then Germany will invade France, or France will invade Germany, and it will be all my fault!'

'Now, my dear, you must not think such dreadful thoughts,' said Great-Aunt Ernestine. 'You have nothing to reproach yourself with. You could not have expected this. Besides, you need not worry—Freddy has vowed never to rest until your brooch is recovered and the thieves have been brought to justice.'

Chief Inspector Guichard stared hard at Freddy, who shuffled uncomfortably.

'I didn't—' he began, but Mrs. Weeks had begun weeping again.

'Please do not distress yourself,' said Guichard. 'We, the *police*—' here he glanced pointedly at Freddy again, '—are doing everything we can to find the Mariensee diamond. From a description we have received of one of the waiters, we believe the theft was organized by a well-known gang. They have vanished, but it cannot be long until we track them down. But if there is any information you can give me, then please do so.'

Baba, who was hovering nearby, exclaimed:

'A gang? Then it wasn't the man who disappeared?'

Guichard looked at his notes.

'Which man? I did not know about this.'

'Oh yes,' said Great-Aunt Ernestine. 'They were just about to search everybody when a lady most unfortunately fainted, and he vanished while everyone's attention was elsewhere.' She turned to Mrs. Weeks. 'You were dancing with him, my dear. Who was he?'

'Why, I don't know,' replied Mrs. Weeks. 'I first saw him at the casino the other night. I dropped my purse and it burst open and he very charmingly helped me pick everything up. Then he was at the party last night and we danced.'

'What was his name?' asked the chief inspector.

She thought.

'How odd!' she replied. 'I didn't think to ask. I was sure he must have told me, but now you come to mention it I have no idea.'

'What did he look like?'

There was some confusion as they all tried to describe him at once, but since it was clear that none of them had noticed more than the fact that he had blue eyes and was rather handsome, Guichard gave it up.

'I dare say he was part of the gang,' he said. 'Please, if you see him again, then be sure to let me know.'

Henry, Great-Aunt Ernestine's manservant, just then appeared to announce that luncheon was served, and the chief inspector prepared to take his departure. Freddy sidled up to him.

'I say,' he murmured. 'I expect you don't think I'm much use, but I know the gang you're talking about.'

'Ah, *oui*?' said Guichard.

'Yes. It's the Boehlers, isn't it?'

Guichard stiffened and regarded Freddy suspiciously.

'And what exactly do you know about them?'

'We're not old school pals, if that's what you're thinking. As a matter of fact I'm a newspaper reporter of sorts, and I remember the gang from a couple of years ago when they were rampaging around England, smashing windows and coshing people rudely over the head. I've seen police photos of Fritz Boehler and I know he was at the party last night—he's hard to miss, really, what with having just the one eye—but I didn't remember who he was until this morning.'

'I see,' replied Guichard non-committally.

'But I think someone else was involved, too. A woman.'

'Oh? Who?'

'I don't know her real name, since she seems to change it according to the weather. I first knew her as Mrs. Dragusha, but I gather she also uses the name La Duchessa di Alassio on occasion. She was working the stately homes of England earlier this year, sweeping up unattended tiaras as she passed, but she's here now, and was at the party last night.'

'And what does this woman look like?'

'Shortish, stands up very straight, blonde at the moment but I don't suppose that's natural. Has the look of a panther about to spring. I shouldn't like to cross her.'

'Ah!' said Guichard with satisfaction. 'Yes, we know this woman. A few years ago she was well known to the police as the wife of a—what do you call it?—a fence called Philip Laurentius, but he went to prison for a while, after which she began to operate upon her own account.'

'Laurentius?' exclaimed Freddy. 'Good Lord, I've met him, too. Stiff little man who exudes respectability from every pore. He was her accomplice in England, but he was posing as her brother, not her husband. Is he here in Villefranche?'

'As far as I am aware he is at present back in prison, serving a six-month sentence for receiving stolen goods.'

'Perhaps that's why she's here, then—she must be at a loose end. At any rate, I believe she and the Boehlers are in league with one another.'

'Yes, this seems possible,' replied the detective thoughtfully. 'And what about this man the ladies have mentioned? The one who danced with Mrs. Weeks shortly before the theft of the Mariensee diamond. Do you know anything about him?'

'Not a thing,' lied Freddy.

Chief Inspector Guichard took out his notebook and scribbled a note or two.

'Very well, I shall look into this connection between the Boehlers and the woman who calls herself La Duchessa. In the meantime, please tell me if you see her again, or any of the gang. We are particularly interested in apprehending Fritz Boehler, who is a most dangerous man.'

'So I've heard.' Since Guichard by now appeared slightly less inclined to consider him a confounded nuisance, he went on, 'By the way, Angela and I really did see a dead body, you know. I think it was one of the thieves—possibly Rolf Boehler.'

He explained to Guichard their theory that someone had handed the diamond to Rolf, who had then been shot for it. He did not mention Valencourt. Guichard listened intently.

'It is possible, what you say,' he said at last. 'To dispose of the body over the balustrade would take a matter of seconds, and would explain why it had gone by the time we arrived. And you did not see who fired the shot?'

'No.' That was true, at least, although Freddy felt a twinge of guilt as he said it. 'I hope you find the diamond,' he said as Guichard prepared to leave.

The detective turned an ironic eye upon him.

'So do I. I have been told this morning that the Prime Minster and M. Weeks intend to come down to Villefranche this evening or tomorrow, and I imagine things will be somewhat unpleasant for me if I cannot report any progress. If you have any information you have not told me, I should be obliged if you will let me know.'

Freddy experienced another pang of guilt. How far did his loyalty to Angela stretch? He was keeping Valencourt's presence a secret, but what if it turned out he had been part of the plot all along? By now Freddy was as anxious as Angela to see Valencourt and satisfy himself that he really knew nothing of all this, but for now he had promised to say nothing, so he merely assured Guichard he had told all he knew, and the chief inspector departed.

# Chapter Fifteen

Luncheon was an uncomfortable affair, since everybody appeared out of sorts—apart from Great-Aunt Ernestine, who was impervious to atmosphere as a rule, and who talked loudly and continuously of the previous night's events. Jessie Weeks was still upset, and dabbed a handkerchief to her eyes throughout the meal. Garnet Weeks seemed very little better: she sat silent and subdued, not looking at anybody, while Jacques Fournier, who was still in attendance, pushed his food around his plate, his face like stone. Freddy noticed that the Comte de Langlois was not present.

'Where's your intended?' asked Freddy of his grandmother, who was sitting next to him. She flushed.

'Why, he's—I—he had business to attend to,' she replied in some confusion. 'Besides, Ernestine had a word with me about not inviting him when we have company. She appears to think it's in bad taste to have him at the house now that Nugs is here, although I don't see why.'

'Well, I mean to say, it's hardly the done thing to expect one's present and future husbands to exchange polite nothings over the *salade niçoise*, is it? The more faint-hearted of the company won't know where to look.'

'Now, don't you start! One might expect that sort of attitude from someone like Ernestine—at her age she could hardly be expected to think differently, but for the young-spirited among us who like to move with the times, it's simply too old-fashioned.' She lowered her voice. 'Although, as a matter of fact, darling, Yves seems to feel the same way. He doesn't like it at all that Nugs is here. I've told him there's nothing to be jealous of, but he's insisted on staying away for the time being.' She pouted. 'It's too bad. Why can't people be civilized about things?'

Freddy noticed just then that Nugs was trying to catch his eye across the table, and deduced that his grandfather wished to speak to him about something. Sure enough, once lunch was finished Nugs followed him into the garden.

'What was she saying to you?' he demanded. 'Where's the lounge lizard today? Why didn't he come to lunch?'

'She says the Great-Aunt has told her not to parade him in front of everybody,' replied Freddy.

Nugs snorted.

'Poppycock! Ernestine's been telling her that for weeks, but she's carried on doing it out of pure defiance. But since I arrived she's seen less of him, and I'm rather hoping I've scared him off. The silly woman's easy enough prey when she's on her own, but he won't find it so easy to get past *me*. Sooner or later I'll have to go home, however, so before I leave I must find a way of convincing Baba that the man's up to no good—otherwise he'll be after her again the second I'm gone. Now, listen, I've been doing a little investigating on my own account, and I've found out some disturbing information.'

'Oh yes?' inquired Freddy.

'Yes. I've been speaking to one of Ernestine's maids—a comely little minx, and not at all a prude like some of these English girls—'

He paused to give full rein to this thought. Freddy dug him in the ribs.

'You were saying?'

'Ah, yes,' said Nugs, coming to himself. 'Now, this girl is from Paris originally, and has worked in some of the grand houses. She tells me the Comte de Langlois is well-known all over town for mixing with the lower sort of company—including a number of famous criminals. He was rumoured to have had dealings with Théodore Archambault just before the banking scandal blew up.'

'Hardly surprising. As I recall half of Paris was forced to deny ever having known the man, including the Prime Minister himself.'

'Is that so? At any rate, Archambault isn't the only crook the Comte has been mixing with—Paulette says he has friends in all sorts of low places, although he takes care to maintain his position at the higher end of society too. He has a taste for the finer things, and keeps an apartment in Paris full of valuable antiques and paintings and wine and the like. In the past his name has been associated with various film actresses, and he showers them with furs and jewels, although nobody seems to know where his money comes from.'

'Do you think his wealth has something to do with his criminal connections?' asked Freddy.

'It wouldn't surprise me. According to Paulette, there was an incident a few years ago in which a priceless painting was stolen and eventually found in the Comte's apartment. He claimed he'd agreed to look after it for a friend, and no action was ever taken, but there were rumours that all was not as it seemed, and suspicion has followed him around ever since. I can't let Baba marry a man like that. Why, it wouldn't be right!'

Freddy looked sceptical.

'Have you told Baba any of this?'

'Not yet.'

'And is there proof, or is it all talk?'

'Does it matter? The man's clearly a scoundrel.'

'Of course it matters! Don't you know anything about women? There's nothing more likely to make them cling to a man like a limpet than the discovery that he's a rotter.'

'Don't be ridiculous,' said Nugs. 'Baba might be a nit-wit, but I'm sure she has more sense than that.'

'She married you,' Freddy pointed out.

Nugs glared.

'Of all the damned impudence—'

'Don't think I haven't heard the stories.'

'None of them were true. Which stories?'

'Never mind,' said Freddy. 'But think on what I said.'

'Perhaps you're right,' Nugs conceded grudgingly after a minute. 'But then what are we to do?'

'We? She's *your* wife.'

'And she's your grandmother. Besides, there's something else I'd forgotten—this diamond business.'

'What of it?' asked Freddy, suddenly alert. 'Don't tell me you think the Comte had something to do with the theft.'

'I can't say for certain, but I have my suspicions. I saw him dancing with Mrs. Dragusha last night. They seemed on very friendly terms, and I shouldn't be a bit surprised if they cooked the thing up between them. By the way,' he went on, 'wasn't this Marchmont filly supposed to be in charge of things? I thought you said the French Sûreté knew all about Mrs. Dragusha and were just waiting for the right moment to pounce.'

'Oh, they are, they are,' replied Freddy airily.

'But surely she must have had something to do with the theft? I wanted to mention it to that French inspector this morning, but since I'd promised to keep my mouth shut I didn't. When may I speak?'

'Don't worry—there's no need. I've already mentioned her to Guichard and told him about the affair at Belsingham.'

'And they haven't arrested her yet? Upon my word, the

Sûreté don't appear to be very efficient. That's what happens when you let women do men's work.'

He went off, grumbling, leaving Freddy to think about what he had just heard. Nugs's suspicions of the Comte seemed to be founded upon very little except his dislike of the man, but the rumours of his association with criminals, and the fact that he had danced with La Duchessa were suggestive. Freddy tried to remember where the Comte had been when the lights had come back on, but had no success. He could not quite see the Comte tearing a valuable jewel from a woman's dress, but it might be worth while to look more closely into his background.

The party broke up soon afterwards, and Freddy decided to walk back to the hotel for the benefit of his digestion. He set off down the hill, but was struck by a thought, and instead turned and bent his steps towards the hotel in which La Duchessa and Valencourt had been staying, with some idea of questioning La Duchessa. But when he inquired at the reception desk he was informed by an affronted clerk that Mr. and Mrs. Smart had slipped out some time in the night without paying their bill, and did *monsieur* know anything of where they had gone?

Freddy could tell the man nothing, and came away, thinking. Valencourt had of course made his escape the evening before, but when had La Duchessa disappeared? He cast his mind back to the party at La Falaise, but could not remember having seen her after the lights had gone out. He was feeling increasingly uncomfortable about the whole thing. They had only Valencourt's word for it that he had been forced to do the job, and that he was an innocent victim of dangerous criminals. What if he had been lying all along? What if he and La Duchessa had arranged the theft between them, using the Boehler gang as dupes, and then gone off together with the diamond? Freddy was not sure exactly where Rolf came into the thing, but it was easy enough to surmise that he must have got in the way somehow. True, when he and Angela had found Valencourt standing over Rolf's body he had had no gun in his hand, but that was not to say he had not shot him. Valencourt had been tried and found guilty of murder in the past, and although he had eventually been pardoned of that particular crime, the suspicion would forever hang around him. Might Valencourt have shot Rolf with his own revolver and then hurriedly put the gun back in Rolf's hand when he heard Angela and Freddy coming? They would never know for certain now that the body and the gun had vanished.

To Freddy's eye it looked as though Valencourt and La Duchessa were in league together, and he feared Angela was in for a grave disappointment. Valencourt had saved Angela's life once and she had stood by him loyally ever since, but Freddy suspected that he was the sort to tire easily of a woman once he had won her over, and that his interest already lay elsewhere. Freddy was saddened by the idea, and quite disconsolate for half the walk back to the hotel, but the day was such a beautiful one that it was impossible to remain downcast for long. The sun was still shining, the sky was the colour of cornflowers, and boats bobbed merrily on the ocean, and as Freddy absorbed the warmth his mood began to lift. Angela was one of the most capable women he knew, and he was sure that if anybody could triumph in such a situation it was she. With such thoughts he consoled himself, and by the time he arrived back at the hotel he was restored to all his customary cheerfulness.

# Chapter Sixteen

On his return Freddy sought out Angela and related what Nugs had told him of his suspicions about the Comte de Langlois.

'It's a good story, but rather thin on evidence,' she said doubtfully.

'That's what I thought, but remember we still don't know who X is—that is, the person who tore the diamond from Jessie Weeks's dress and took it outside to Rolf. I don't suppose you remember where the Comte was when the lights went off, do you?'

She thought.

'He was with your grandmother, and they were both standing not far from the table where Jessie Weeks was sitting.'

'I wonder,' said Freddy thoughtfully. 'Stay here. I'm going to make a telephone-call.'

He was put through to the Villa des Fleurs and ran the gauntlet of both Henry and Great-Aunt Ernestine before he eventually succeeded in speaking to Baba.

'Oh, he was there with me all the time, darling,' she said. 'At least, until the lights went out. I was terrified—I've been frightened of the dark ever since I was a child, and even now I do rather prefer to sleep with the lights on than not, so you can imagine how I felt last night, and it was so odd, the way the orchestra tailed off in that horrid discordant way. It quite gave me the shivers.'

'About the Comte,' prompted Freddy.

'Oh, yes, when the lights went out I reached for his arm, but he wasn't there. I was cross with him, but of course there wasn't *really* anything to be frightened of, because everyone was squealing and laughing, and eventually I saw the funny side myself, but then Mrs. Weeks screamed and the lights came back on and she said her diamond had been stolen, and then Mrs. Marchmont fainted, and a minute later Yves came back with a drink for me. It turned out he'd gone off as soon as the lights went out to fetch it from one of the waiters because he knew I'd need it to calm my nerves. So kind and thoughtful of him, don't you think?'

'Did he stay with you after that?'

'Yes—well, he went off to find Mr. Roche a little while later, to see if he could help search for the diamond.'

'How long was he away?'

'Why, I've no idea. Not long. Five minutes? Ten? You know I never have any idea of the time, darling, especially not when I'm enjoying myself. I was speaking to Mr. Lenoir, who was most complimentary about my new dress, although I hadn't been altogether sure of it since it's not a colour I'd usually wear, but he assured me it suited my complexion beautifully, and said that nobody was likely to steal my ruby earrings, since the thieves were most likely miles away already, and that set my mind *quite* at ease, although one can never be sure of anything, can one?'

Freddy eventually managed to extricate himself from the conversation and returned to Angela.

'So the Comte might have been either the thief *or* the murderer,' she said, after he had related the telephone conversation to her. 'He wasn't with your grandmother when the lights went off or at the time when the murder took place.'

'I hope for Baba's sake he's neither, but one has to think of all possibilities. I must say, though, even if I can perfectly well imagine him consorting with undesirables I can't quite see him in the part of an active criminal. No,' he went on, considering, 'I find myself unconvinced by the theory.'

'I wonder where Edgar has got to,' said Angela. 'I still haven't heard from him, but I should have thought he'd have managed to get a message to me by now. I do hope he hasn't made a bolt for it again. By the way, I forgot to tell you I've finally heard from William. He says he's had no luck in searching for Nightshade so far, but he's had a lead and is going to follow it, and he'll let me know more about it as soon as he can. Pity—I was so hoping he would have found the horse by now. I only hope Gino and his accomplices are treating him well, although I fear they're not. And if Fritz Boehler didn't get his hands on the Mariensee diamond I dread to think what he'll do in revenge.'

'That sort of thinking won't do you any good. Look on the bright side—perhaps no news is good news.'

'Perhaps. But I can't help worrying about this whole thing. I wish I knew where Edgar was.'

'I'm sure your chap can look after himself.'

'Of course he can. But what are we going to do once this is all over, now that half the criminals in France know he's still alive and where he lives? Fritz has already tried to murder him once, and from what I hear of him he's not the sort to give up until he gets what he wants.'

This was indeed a difficulty, Freddy had to admit, but he had no time to say so because just then a note arrived for Angela.

'At last!' She tore it open eagerly and read it. 'He's in Nice, as I thought. I'm going to see him. You'll come, won't you? I'm sure between us we can get the truth out of him if he does know more than he's telling. Besides, we need a plan, and three heads are better than two.'

Freddy was as keen as Angela to question Valencourt, and so they set off immediately. The address Valencourt had given turned out to be a small, dingy hotel down a dark side street in the old quarter of Nice. There was nobody at the reception desk when they went in, so they made their own way up to the third floor, which had a sticky carpet and a musty smell. Angela made a face.

'Goodness, couldn't he have picked somewhere nicer?'

'I expect it was all he could find in a hurry at one o'clock in the morning,' Freddy replied reasonably.

'Still, though, I'd have thought he might have tried one of the big hotels on the Promenade des Anglais first,' she said.

The room was close to the stairs—most likely for ease of escape should it prove necessary, Freddy guessed. Angela knocked at the door. Valencourt opened it quickly, but before she had a chance to speak his eyes darted to something behind his visitors.

'Bruno!' he snapped.

They turned just in time to see a man disappearing through the door to the stairs. Quick as lightning, Valencourt was after him, followed closely by Freddy. The man barrelled down the stairs but they caught up with him on the second landing down. He saw he was cornered and reached a hand towards his pocket, but Valencourt grabbed him and shoved him face first against the wall before he could bring out the gun, pinning his arms behind his back with a grip of iron.

'Get the gun off him,' he commanded.

Freddy dug in the man's pockets and brought out his revolver as instructed, and between them they hauled the protesting Bruno back up the stairs, bundled him into the room and sat him in a chair.

'Oh dear, did we inadvertently bring an unwanted guest?' said Angela.

'Couldn't you have been more careful?' demanded Valencourt.

'How was I supposed to know he was following us?' she replied crossly.

'This is the fellow who was watching us when we were down at the cove this morning,' said Freddy. He looked more closely at the man, who was small and sullen, with a rodent-like face and the reddened, mottled cheeks of a man who drinks to excess. 'And you were hiding in the bushes outside my great-aunt's house the other day too, weren't you?'

The man swore at length in French, then spat on the floor.

'I don't think much of your friends, dearest,' remarked Angela to Valencourt. 'Let's not have them to dinner again.'

'Now listen here, Bruno,' said Valencourt, regarding him with distaste. 'You'd better talk, and quickly. What are you doing here? I suppose Fritz sent you, did he?'

Bruno smirked but said nothing.

'All right, if that's how you want to play it.' Valencourt took the gun from Freddy, pointed it directly at the man's head and cocked it.

'Edgar!' exclaimed Angela.

He ignored her, his face hard. Freddy was surprised at how dangerous he looked. He had never thought of Valencourt as anything more than an opportunistic confidence-man, but at that moment he saw a streak of ruthlessness laid bare which indicated it would be wise not to underestimate him.

'Now,' Valencourt said. 'What were you doing, following these two? Who put you on to them?'

Bruno regarded the gun warily, then indicated Angela.

'Fritz saw you giving her the signal to create a distraction last night when the lights went back on. He told me to stick to her like glue today because he was sure she'd come and find you sooner or later. Then when she did I was to come back and tell him where you were.'

He darted Angela an insolent look and said something in

French which caused Freddy to raise his eyebrows, although Angela affected not to have understood it. Valencourt cuffed Bruno neatly over the side of the head with the gun and he yelped.

'You'll refer to the lady politely if you know what's good for you. Why does Fritz want to know where I am? I did what I promised—or would have if he hadn't tried to put one over on me. But surely he got the goods and doesn't need me any more?'

Bruno rubbed his head, glowering.

'He didn't get the diamond. He wants to know who double-crossed him and where Rolf is.'

'Where Rolf is? Doesn't he know?' asked Freddy.

'No. Rolf was meant to wait outside until someone passed it to him, but he never came back to the boat. Fritz says people were talking about a stiff on the terrace and he wants to know whether it was Rolf. Did you kill him?' he asked Valencourt with interest.

'No. And I'm asking the questions, so you'll speak when you're spoken to. Now tell me: what was supposed to happen last night? I know the idea was to frame me, but why? Why did the plans change?'

'I don't know much, only that it was because of Bettina,' replied Bruno. 'It all happened before you joined us. Fritz was all for getting the diamond away immediately and having it broken up for sale, but Bettina said she had a better buyer, although she wouldn't say who. Anyway, she was throwing her weight about as if she knew something we didn't. Then you came, and Fritz could see which way the wind was blowing with all this *Mr. and Mrs.* business she insisted on, and taking you to a fancy hotel, and he guessed you were cooking something up between you. He was sure you'd both double-cross us in the end and run off with the diamond, so he decided to double-cross you first. He switched off the lights and had someone else take the jewel while you were standing there with a copy of it in your pocket, primed and ready for them to find it and nab you. What a way to kill three birds with one stone, eh? We get the jewel, Bettina gets nothing, and having you sent down was the icing on the cake!'

He let out a wheezing chortle.

'You should have heard Fritz laugh at the idea of it! He said it would be worth letting you live just to see the look on your face when you realized what had happened. You have to admit it was a pretty idea. Fritz doesn't forgive easily, so you should have expected something of the kind.'

'But you didn't get the jewel, it seems,' said Freddy. 'Who tore it from Jessie Weeks's dress? It wasn't Fritz, was it?'

Bruno shrugged.

'I don't know. Not Fritz. He said he'd found someone who would never be suspected. Whoever it was did it all right, but I don't know what happened after that. Gaston and I were to wait in the boat until Rolf arrived with the diamond and then set sail for Marseilles, and Fritz would join us later. But Rolf didn't come back and the weather took a turn for the worse. By three o'clock we were tired of waiting and worried something had gone wrong, but we couldn't get away by boat because of the storm, so we went up the cliff path and got out over the gate.'

'At the empty villa?'

'Yes, you don't think we went through the big house, do you? With all those *flics* crawling around the place?'

He spat again.

'Must you?' said Angela, a pained look on her face.

Bruno went on:

'Then Fritz turned up, raging because the job hadn't gone as planned and Rolf and the diamond were missing. He gave Gaston and me a hard time of it, wanting to know why we hadn't gone to help Rolf.' He cringed at the memory. 'Well, how were we to know what was happening? Our orders were to stay out of sight and help get the boat away quickly. Is Rolf really dead?'

Nobody answered.

'Who took Roche's necklace?' Freddy asked. 'Was it Fritz?'

Bruno looked blank.

'I don't know about that. As far as I know we were only in it for the diamond. But it looks like the joke's on us. I guess you got it back off Rolf, did you?' he said.

'If I had the diamond do you really think I'd be hanging around in this flea-infested hole?' replied Valencourt. 'What about Bettina? Where is she?'

'I thought she was with you.' Bruno eyed Angela. 'But perhaps not. Did you frighten her off?' he said to her with a leer.

'I doubt it,' Angela replied.

'No, it will take more than the likes of you,' he agreed, then turned to Valencourt. 'I'd watch out if I were you. When Bettina gets her claws into a fellow she never lets go.'

He made another crude remark in French and guffawed.

'Yes, well, this is all quite delightful,' said Angela briskly, 'but if Bruno has nothing more of interest to tell us, I have several other things I'd rather be doing at present. Can we let him go now?'

'Hardly,' replied Valencourt. 'He'll run straight to Fritz and squeal.'

He weighed the gun in his hand thoughtfully, and Bruno quailed.

'Edgar!' exclaimed Angela again.

'Suppose we tie him up and leave him here,' suggested Freddy. 'Someone will come in and rescue him eventually, and in the meantime we can find you somewhere better to stay.'

'Oh, yes,' said Angela, jumping at the idea. She cast her eye around the room. 'What can we use?'

There was nothing resembling rope in the room, so they were forced to tear up one of the none-too-clean sheets from the bed. Then Bruno's hands and feet were bound firmly together and a gag placed in his mouth. Freddy and Valencourt would have shut him up in the wardrobe, but Angela protested at the unnecessary discomfort, and in the end they put him on the bed, ignoring the murderous looks he was directing at them.

'Someone will find him sooner or later,' said Valencourt as they went out. 'Although possibly later, given how infrequently they seem to clean the rooms.'

# Chapter Seventeen

There was still nobody at the reception desk when they came out. Valencourt and Freddy walked past it and prepared to step out into the street, but Angela stopped.

'You must pay the bill,' she said.

Valencourt stared at her incredulously, then put his hand into his pocket and threw one or two notes onto the desk.

'I'm making a deduction for the fleas,' he said.

Angela did not move.

'But they'll have to clear up Bruno. You ought to leave a tip.'

He sighed and threw another note down.

'Is that better?'

'A *little* better,' she replied. 'Oh, well, if that's the best you can do then I suppose we'd better go and find you another place to stay.'

After taking suitable steps to ensure that nobody else was following them, they went in search of another hotel, and eventually found one that met with Angela's approval, in a slightly more salubrious quarter of Nice, but at a discreet distance from the Promenade des Anglais. Then they went to sit in a café as they debated what to do next. They chose a dark corner at the back, well out of the sight of prying eyes.

'Well, so much for keeping my presence a secret from the Boehlers,' said Angela. 'I'm rather put out that Fritz spotted my fainting fit wasn't real. I thought I'd been perfectly convincing. I certainly *ought* to have been convincing, to judge by the bruises I woke up with this morning. They seem to have sprung up in all sorts of unlikely places.'

'Fritz is a sharp one, all right,' said Freddy to Valencourt. 'He must have been watching you like a hawk, even with just the one eye.'

'Oh, I should never make the mistake of underestimating him,' replied Valencourt. 'It's interesting they don't know about Rolf, though. I'd half-thought Fritz must have shot him, given that they hate each other most of the time and fight like cat and dog. But it's clear Fritz doesn't know what happened to him either—or what happened to the diamond.'

'Were you and La Duchessa planning to double-cross the Boehlers, as Bruno said?' asked Freddy curiously.

'I can't speak for Bettina, but I certainly wasn't.'

'Are you sure?' said Angela before she could stop herself.

'It's rather tiresome, trying one's best and not being believed,' he remarked evenly. 'Yes, I'm sure. Everything happened just as I told you. As far as I knew, I was to exchange the real diamond for a paste one, but someone else got in first. In fact, until we talked to Bruno just now I assumed Bettina had been in on the plan to frame me, but it seems they'd decided to cut her out too.'

'I shouldn't be a bit surprised if she got one up on all of you and took the diamond for herself,' said Freddy.

'Nor should I.'

'I wonder where she is now,' said Angela. 'I don't suppose she's still at the hotel.'

'I passed the place and asked earlier, and the man at the

desk told me Mr. and Mrs. Smart had skipped without paying,' replied Freddy unthinkingly.

Angela glared at Valencourt, who glared at Freddy in turn.

'What did you expect?' he demanded. 'I was hardly going to return and pack my things, with half the Cap de Nice hot on my heels, was I?'

This was unarguable, and Angela was forced to concede the point.

'Who was Bettina's buyer?' she asked instead. 'Did she tell you?'

'No, but I expect she planned to pass it on to her husband to sell—he's a crooked jeweller who's well-known as a fence in criminal circles.'

'Philip Laurentius?' said Freddy.

Valencourt looked at him in surprise.

'What do you know of him?'

'I've met him.'

Freddy related the incident of the Belsingham pearls, and how Mrs. Dragusha, as she had then been known, had escaped the police but had failed to obtain the pearls thanks to quick thinking on the part of Valentina Sangiacomo.

'But Laurentius is in gaol at present, according to Guichard, so I doubt Bettina was intending to pass the diamond on to him,' he finished.

'It must be someone else, then,' said Valencourt. 'At any rate, she must be slipping if she let those pearls out of her grasp. She'd never have been foiled so easily at one time. And by her own daughter, too! I shouldn't like to be in Val's shoes if Bettina catches her.'

'I can't imagine Bettina with a daughter, somehow,' said Angela.

'She must be quite grown up by now. She was about thirteen or fourteen when I knew her. The little brute lifted my watch,' he said darkly. 'It was rather a good one, too.'

Angela seemed highly entertained at this.

'I'd like to meet this girl,' she said.

'She's an interesting study,' replied Freddy. 'One can never tell what she's going to do next. But she's certainly carrying on the family trade—in a small way, at least. Like father and mother, like daughter.'

'She's not his daughter,' said Valencourt. 'Laurentius must be Bettina's second or third husband—if they're married at all, which I doubt. She had the girl in tow long before she met him.'

'So, then, what are we to do now?' said Angela. 'The Mariensee diamond is missing, Rolf is dead, La Duchessa has disappeared, and now Fritz Boehler is out for your blood. And goodness knows where Nightshade and William have got to,' she added as an afterthought. 'We're in rather a fix, but there must be something we can do.'

'That's what you said the other night at the casino,' replied Valencourt. 'And we only had the horse to worry about then. *Doing* things doesn't appear to be helping us at all, so I say we cut our losses and leave before any more disasters occur.'

'Oh, but we can't leave now, not with things the way they are. Besides, do you really think Fritz will let you go just like that? He'll follow you to America and make life difficult for you one way or another.'

'That's a given,' he agreed. 'But I'd prefer to be back there, looking after things in person than relying on others. The men at the stables have the horses to attend to, and I can't expect them to know how to deal with this sort of situation. Besides, I don't want any more horses going missing or perhaps being hurt—and I want to find out what's happened to Nightshade, since William doesn't appear to have had any luck. No, it will be wisest all round if we leave as soon as possible.'

His tone was firm. Angela chewed her lip.

'Bother. I do hate leaving a job unfinished.'

'I thought you'd given up detecting,' said Freddy.

'So did I, but it seems to have got into my blood, somehow. I'd feel much happier if we could find the diamond before we went, at least.'

'The diamond is none of our business, and we're only getting in the way, so the best thing we can do is stay out of it and leave the police to do their work,' said Valencourt.

'But—'

'But nothing. I'll go to Cook's and get the tickets this evening, and we'll leave first thing tomorrow.'

It was clear he had made up his mind. Angela opened her mouth to argue, but seemed to think better of it.

'There'll be the devil of a diplomatic row if this brooch doesn't turn up soon,' said Freddy. 'R. G. Weeks is already threatening to pull out of the reparations talks, and one can hardly blame him. I mean, it's a bit thick, offering one's assistance to a nation in need, only to have said nation run off with one's wife's favourite toy. They've made a lot of progress thanks to Weeks's work, but if he withdraws the talks will most likely collapse.'

Angela did not reply, but her face assumed an expression of noble suffering. She appeared to be directing it at Valencourt, who ignored it resolutely.

Freddy went on:

'If only we knew where La Duchessa had got to. She's a slippery one, but if she's fallen out with the Boehlers then she might be in enough of a rage to tell us what happened. For my money, she found out what they were planning and decided to forestall them.'

'That's certainly possible,' agreed Valencourt.

'In which case she either has the diamond or knows where it is.'

'I wonder why she didn't let you know about the change of plan,' said Angela. 'After all, you nearly got caught, and she can't keep her hooks in you if you're in gaol.'

'What do you mean by that?' demanded Valencourt. 'She hasn't got her hooks in me.'

'Hasn't she?' replied Angela distantly. 'Bruno seems to think she has, and since she's been going around calling herself your wife, I don't think it's too much to speculate that she has designs on you, at the very least. I don't see why she'd be saying it otherwise—unless you gave her the wrong idea, somehow.'

The look of noble suffering shifted subtly, to be replaced by one of tragic betrayal with just a hint of reproach.

'If you think I'm a party to any of this—' began Valencourt.

'Of course I don't. I trust you implicitly,' she said, avoiding his eyes and gazing bravely at a spot just above his head.

'Well, then.'

'But if she really doesn't want you back—'

'Of course she doesn't want me back—she tried to kill me, don't you remember?'

'I've been tempted to do the same myself on occasion,' said Angela sweetly. 'And yet here I am.'

'Besides, if she did take the diamond she'll be miles away by now if she has any sense.'

'Not if she's planning on taking you with her,' put in Freddy unhelpfully. 'She doesn't know anything about Angela, so as far as she's concerned the way is clear. She seems to have a pretty high opinion of herself too, so I don't suppose she's given much thought to your own inclinations.'

'I haven't the slightest interest in what the woman's thinking or doing,' replied Valencourt testily. 'She can run off with all the diamonds on the Riviera for all I care. We're leaving tomorrow.'

Angela examined her fingers.

'Of course you're right. Quite aside from what Bettina has in mind, I can't blame you for wanting to leave before Fritz

Boehler gets hold of you again. I'd be frightened too if I were in your position.'

'Who said I was frightened? I'm not—' He stopped and regarded her narrowly. 'Look here, don't think I don't know what you're doing.'

'I'm not doing anything.'

'Yes you are. You're trying to goad me into staying.'

'We-ell,' she said. 'Don't you want to know what really happened?'

'It's obvious you do.' He looked at her for a moment then sighed. 'Am I to take it you'll be giving me the quivering lip and tearful eye all the way back to the States if you don't get your own way?'

'Yes,' replied Angela.

'Oh, very well, then,' he said resignedly. 'We'll stay a little longer if you like.'

Angela beamed and clapped her hands together.

'Oh, thank you, darling! Just one more day, I promise.'

'That's all. Then we're going, even if we haven't found the diamond, d'you hear?'

'Yes, Edgar,' she said meekly.

'I don't see what you think we can do, though.'

'Do you still have the paste imitation?' asked Freddy suddenly.

Valencourt felt in his inside pocket and brought something out. Freddy examined it closely, then passed it to Angela, who did the same.

'I don't know what I expected to see,' she observed. 'It looks real, but I shouldn't know a real one from a fake.'

'Nor should I,' said Freddy. 'Are we sure it isn't the real one?'

They both looked at Valencourt speculatively.

'It's certainly a fake, but a good one,' he replied. 'If Bettina's original plan had worked, Jessie Weeks most likely wouldn't have found out for months or possibly years that her diamond had been stolen, and probably couldn't have said *when* it happened, either, so nobody would have been able to trace the theft back to any of us.'

Freddy took the brooch back from Angela and regarded it, thinking.

'I wonder if we mightn't use this to draw her out,' he said.

'How do you mean?' asked Angela.

'Why, suppose we go back, spread it around publicly that we've recovered the diamond—we'd have to think of a good story about how we found it—and hand it in to the police. They'll pronounce it a fake, of course, but by that time word will have got about and La Duchessa will show herself out of either curiosity, doubt as to whether she stole the right jewel, or because she'll assume Valencourt must be somewhere close by.'

'Then what?' inquired Valencourt. 'Do you expect her to stand there and let you hand her over to the police?'

'Hardly, but she might give away some clue as to what happened to the real diamond—and that's the most important thing, after all.'

'That's not a bad idea,' said Angela.

'Then let's try it.'

'There's no mystery about it if you ask me,' said Valencourt. 'Bettina pinched the thing and is probably halfway to Antwerp with it by now.'

'If she is, then Freddy's plan won't work,' replied Angela simply.

They all returned together to Valencourt's hotel room, then Angela and Freddy prepared to depart. Valencourt was grumbling at the necessity of kicking his heels in Nice like a coward.

'Nobody's accusing you of being a coward,' said Angela. 'But everyone at Mr. Roche's party saw you putting the 'fluence on Mrs. Weeks, and the police are looking for someone of your description, so it would be foolish in the extreme to go parading around the streets of Villefranche just at present. If you get arrested it will defeat the whole purpose of the thing.'

'Hmph. Well, then, if you're allowed to go parading around the streets of Villefranche and I'm not, you'd better take this, just in case Fritz turns up.'

Valencourt brought Bruno's gun out of his pocket as he spoke.

'Not I—I've sworn off guns,' said Angela firmly. 'And I should say you need it far more than I do.'

'But they know who you are now, and they'll have you in their sights.'

'Never mind that—I'm not afraid.'

'Will you listen to reason, damn you?'

Freddy saw a row brewing and departed discreetly. He went out into the street and smoked a cigarette, and after a few minutes Angela joined him.

'Which of you has the gun?' asked Freddy curiously.

'Why, Edgar, of course,' answered Angela, as though surprised at the question. 'Now, have you got the fake jewel?'

He showed it to her by way of reply.

'Good. Then let's hope your plan works. I'd like to hear what La Duchessa has to say for herself.'

'Do you really think Valencourt has been dallying with her behind your back?' he could not help asking.

'Certainly not,' replied Angela. 'It can't do any harm to let him think I do, but I have no doubts at all on that head. Which reminds me—we'd better hurry, because there's something I want to do before dinner.'

---

AT THE HOTEL de la Plage, the afternoon rush had died down, and the reception hall was quiet. Gustave, the clerk on duty, was contemplating the possibility of stepping away from the desk for a few moments, when a woman came in.

'I've come to pay the bill for my cousin and his wife,' she said. 'They were called away urgently in the night and most unfortunately didn't have time to settle up. The name is Smart.'

Gustave was all attention.

'Certainly, *madame*. Yes, Mr. and Mrs. Smart did not return last night and we discovered this morning that they had gone. I am glad you have told me, for one does not like to deal with unpleasant incidents of this kind, but if it is as you say, and the bill is to be paid—'

He made an expressive gesture.

'Yes, yes, I'll pay it. They've asked me to pass on their deepest apologies for the inconvenience, and I'm to collect their things, too. I assume you still have them?'

'Some of them, I believe. It seems Mrs. Smart took her luggage with her, but Mr. Smart did not.'

'How odd. He must have been really flustered to have left everything behind like that. Ordinarily he'd never dream of doing such a thing, let alone leaving without paying. I do hope it won't be necessary to bring the police into it, since it was entirely unintentional on his part.'

Gustave assured her that he had no interest in bringing the law into the matter if *madame* really intended to pay the sum owed, and began adding up the total.

'Room 23 was their room, wasn't it?' she said carelessly as he scribbled the figures down.

'No, *madame*. They had two rooms. Mrs. Smart was in room 54, but there were no other rooms free on that floor so we were forced to put her husband in room 47, on the floor below.'

The news appeared to afford the lady more gratification than one might have supposed it warranted, for she closed her eyes briefly and said something under her breath that sounded like, 'Oh, thank heaven!'

Gustave looked at her in surprise and she coughed, and added:

'I mean to say, I'm pleased they were so high up—the views must be glorious from the fourth and fifth floors.'

'That is so,' he agreed.

Angela paid the bill and left instructions for Mr. Smart's luggage to be sent on to the Hotel Bellevue. Then she bestowed a brilliant smile upon the clerk and departed with a light step.

# Chapter Eighteen

FREDDY HAD BEEN WONDERING how best to hand over the fake diamond to the police in order to achieve the maximum éclat, but as it turned out Chief Inspector Guichard did his job for him, by turning up at the Hotel Bellevue just before dinner with the declared intention of questioning all those guests who had been present at Benjamin Roche's party the night before. First of all, Guichard said, he had a few words he wished to say to Mrs. and Miss Weeks, if he might request the honour of their presence in the lounge. Mrs. and Miss Weeks had no objection to make, and the eyes of all the guests were on them as they went in and sat down. There could not have been a more perfect opportunity for Freddy to carry out his plan. He strolled across to where they were sitting.

'I say, I don't mean to be a bother, but I was hoping to speak to you, chief inspector,' he said, taking care not to lower his voice.

Guichard regarded him with impatience.

'I am afraid it will have to wait. As you can see, I am speaking to Mrs. Weeks.'

'Oh, but I rather think this is something Mrs. Weeks will want to hear.'

He produced the fake diamond from his pocket and handed it over with great ceremony. The cry of surprise and delight from Jessie Weeks was everything he could have hoped for.

'My diamond!' she exclaimed.

Freddy glanced around and saw with satisfaction that every head in the lounge was turned towards them. Jacques Fournier, who was sitting nearby, was staring as though he could not believe his eyes.

'Where did you find it?' demanded Mrs. Weeks.

'I should also like to know where you found it, M. Pilkington-Soames,' said Chief Inspector Guichard, regarding him with not a little suspicion.

'Well, it all happened quite by chance,' replied Freddy, who was beginning to enjoy himself. 'I was taking a stroll in Nice this afternoon, when I happened to find myself in a part of the city with which I was unfamiliar. Mother always warned me it was dangerous to stray far from the Promenade des Anglais, you know, and said that as long as I remained within sight of La Jetée I couldn't go far wrong. However, I'm afraid on this occasion I must have been thinking of something else, because at a certain point it came to my attention that the scent of the sea had been replaced by something altogether less fragrant, and that the people slinking through the streets around me were not exactly of the *haut monde*—in fact, I can only describe them as positively objectionable in appearance. I come here to look at the fashions myself, so you can imagine my dismay at this little *mésaventure*. At any rate, I was just running a critical eye over the denizens of the quarter, wondering which of them was least likely to slide a cheerful stiletto into my innards if I dared approach to ask for directions, when I caught a glimpse of a face I thought I recognized. No doubt there are many other one-eyed men prowling the streets of Nice, chief inspector, but this one seemed familiar, so I set off in pursuit. I didn't have anything more in mind than following him to his hiding-place, but he led me in and out of the streets for a good way, and after a while I began to suspect that he'd spotted me and was pulling my leg. I wasn't about to let him go by that time, though, and I kept up the chase like a good 'un. Eventually I cornered him down a dead-end, which I really oughtn't to have done, because he bared his teeth like a ferret and sprang at me. There was something of a set-to, and he got me one on the jaw—' (here he rubbed the site of the supposed blow) '—then ran off. However, in the scuffle this fell out of his pocket.'

He was about to weave into the story a fortuitous meeting with a poor but honest girl of great beauty, wearing a shawl over her head and carrying a basket of fruit, who had led him out through the alleyways to safety, when he saw Guichard's face.

'So I brought it back and here I am,' he finished hurriedly. 'I wasn't certain it was the missing brooch, but it looked enough like it that I thought I'd better bring it to you as quickly as possible.'

'You dear boy!' said Jessie Weeks. 'How can I ever thank you?'

'Did you notice which way the man went?' asked Guichard.

'I'm afraid not. I was seeing stars for a minute or two, and in any case I thought the most important thing was to get the diamond back as soon as possible, to relieve Mrs. Weeks's mind.'

'Is this your diamond, Mme. Weeks?' asked Guichard.

'It certainly looks like it. Oh, Garnet, can it be? Your father will be so relieved!'

Guichard took the brooch and examined it non-committally.

'We must have an expert look at it, to be sure it is the real one,' he said. 'M. Pilkington-Soames, I shall want to speak to you later.'

'I'll be here whenever you want me, chief inspector,' Freddy assured him.

'Oh, but it must be the real one!' said Jessie. Her effusive thanks and exclamations had begun to draw people from across the room, and she now began to receive congratulations from fellow-guests upon the recovery of the diamond. Freddy was pleased, for he was convinced the news would have spread all over Villefranche by the end of the evening, given the way it was already spreading through the hotel. He was not certain Guichard had believed him; moreover, he felt slightly guilty about pulling the wool over the Weekses' eyes, and for the disappointment that lay in store for them once the brooch had been examined properly. Still, he consoled himself with the thought that his motives were pure, and that his aim was to find the real diamond, so a little deception could not really do any harm. In that regard, he could not have wished for his plan to go better. If the news reached La Duchessa, he was sure she would show herself, if only out of curiosity as to how the fake jewel had been recovered. If she did, then perhaps she would lead them to the Mariensee diamond.

---

FREDDY HAD half-agreed to meet his grandfather at the casino that evening, so after dinner he betook himself to Beaulieu in a taxi. He was feeling rather pleased about the outcome of his efforts with the fake jewel, and on the strength of it had fortified himself with plenty of Montrachet at dinner, followed by three large glasses of excellent Cognac. As a result he arrived at the casino with the glassy-eyed smile and swaying step which causes casino doormen to salute with more than usual alacrity, for it assuredly betokens a good evening for the house. The place was busy again, but Freddy soon found Nugs, who had requisitioned a bottle or two of Great-Aunt Ernestine's best whisky when her back was turned, and was in a similar condition to himself, and the two proceeded to the Baccarat table and engaged in an enthusiastic contest to see which of them could lose his money the fastest.

After a while, Freddy tired of the game and decided to try his luck at the roulette instead. All the tables were crowded, and as he stood there, observing the play and waiting his turn, he noticed his grandmother and the Comte de Langlois standing in a corner, engaged in animated conversation. Baba seemed upset about something. At length the Comte made a remark which was evidently intended to put an end to the discussion, and stalked off haughtily. Baba gazed around wildly, then burst into tears. Freddy tottered over to her, with some vague idea of handing her a handkerchief.

'Oh, Freddy!' she sobbed, when she saw him. 'Whatever shall I do? Yves has thrown me over!'

'I say, not really? What the devil for?'

'He said I'd deceived him because I'd told him—because he'd been under the impression that Nugs and I were already divorced, but then Nugs turned up and told him it wasn't the case at all. Yves accused me of lying to him about it—but it was *nearly* true, wasn't it? After all, separation is almost the same thing. He said he hadn't expected to have to stand up in court just to get married. Then he said—he said—'

Here her sobs became heavier and her speech almost unintelligible, but Freddy gathered someone had given a hint to the Comte as to Baba's true age, and he had not taken the news well. Freddy had done little more than utter a few vague words of sympathy when Nugs turned up, demanding to know what the fuss was about. Freddy enlightened him as best he could.

'He said he couldn't possibly marry an *elderly* woman,' burst out Baba. 'Elderly! How could he? Oh, Nugs!'

She threw herself into his arms, and he patted her back awkwardly.

'There, there, my dear. Don't you fret. I'll take a horse-whip to the blackguard, see if I don't! Now, come and sit down.'

'Look here, I think you were right,' whispered Freddy to Nugs over Baba's head. 'He thought she was easy pickings, and he's been put off by your presence. You've got what you wanted and frightened him away. Stay in Villefranche a few more days and he'll take himself off altogether.'

But Nugs's chivalrous instincts had been aroused.

'I won't stand for anyone insulting my own wife in this way, d'you hear?' he said sternly. 'Where is the fellow now?'

'Over there,' replied Freddy. 'But—'

Nugs was not listening. He drew his brows together and stamped off purposefully in the direction indicated, hampered only slightly by his inability to walk in a straight line. He stopped at the table at which the Comte was sitting. After a few moments the Comte appeared to become aware of someone breathing down his neck, and turned.

'Sir, I should like a word,' said Nugs.

'What do you want?' replied the Comte. 'I have nothing to say to you.'

He turned back to the table, but Nugs was having none of it. Warmed by Great-Aunt Ernestine's whisky, he gave the Comte a sharp slap on the shoulder with the back of his hand. The Comte whirled round again, throwing Nugs off balance. He staggered back a little and was righted by Freddy, who had followed. The other card players were watching the scene with great interest. Nugs drew himself up and addressed the Comte with as much dignity as he could muster.

'I say, I should like a word,' he repeated.

'Then you may have it here,' replied the Comte. After his initial surprise he seemed more amused than anything.

'Very well, if you insist. Sir, I demand you marry my wife.'

There were several giggles from the people sitting around the table, which only served to exacerbate Nugs's ire. He went on:

'You have given her to understand you would marry her, and have gone back upon your word. Furthermore, you have insulted a lady, and I won't stand for it. I demand you keep your promise, or I shall have satisfaction. In my father's day one chose swords or pistols, but I suppose swords are old hat now, so pistols it will have to be. Choose your spot and a time and I'll be there.'

The laughter grew louder. The Comte regarded Nugs disdainfully.

'I think you are mad,' he said. 'Please go away.'

He turned his back ostentatiously and motioned to the dealer to continue.

'Oh, no you don't,' said Nugs, enraged. 'Stand up and face me like a man, you lily-livered blighter.'

He slapped the Comte on the shoulder again. The Comte stood up and turned. He was at least six inches taller than Nugs, and towered over him. He poked Nugs gently in the chest.

'Go home, old man,' he said.

It was perfectly obvious he did not consider Nugs a worthy opponent, and so his astonishment was no doubt all the more acute five seconds later when he found himself flat on his back, trapped under the not inconsiderable weight of a seventy-five-year-old man who was making the most strenuous attempts to modify the shape of his perfect Grecian nose. There were shrieks as everybody tried to get out of the way at once. One scream, louder than any of the others, came from Baba.

'Yves!' she cried. 'Nugs, leave him alone! How could you?'

A circle of interested observers had formed and begun cheering on the fight. Baba darted forward and began raining blows onto her husband's back as the cheers grew louder. Although his assailant had the advantage of blind drunken fury, once the Comte had recovered his faculties the altercation could have ended only one way. However, perhaps fortunately, Nugs was very swiftly dragged off his opponent by two dealers and invited in the most pressing terms to vacate the premises at his earliest convenience, much to the disappointment of those of the spectators who had already begun to place bets upon the outcome of the contest. The last thing Freddy saw as he followed his grandfather out of the casino was Baba dabbing anxiously at the Comte's bleeding nose with a handkerchief.

After some little ado a taxi was found and they got in.

'How much will you pay me not to tell Mother about this?' said Freddy, who had enjoyed the whole thing immensely.

'Hmph,' replied Nugs, from under the handkerchief he was holding against a rapidly developing black eye.

'I don't know if that's what you were intending, but you certainly seem to have reconciled them,' Freddy went on.

'The man's a scoundrel and I'll prove it,' was the only answer.

# Chapter Nineteen

Freddy was woken the next morning by a loud knocking at his door. It was Nugs. Freddy regarded him with a bleary eye.

'Is there to be no peace?' he said.

'It's almost nine o'clock. I've got the car. If we hurry we ought to be there in an hour or so.'

'Which car? Ought to be where?'

'Sospel, of course.'

'Why do you want to go to Sospel?'

'Because that's where the Comte lives. I found out from his tailor—rather a clever piece of detection on my part, if I do say so myself. Did you know he's never told Baba his address? Highly suspicious if you ask me.'

'But why do you want to see him again? I thought you'd said everything you had to say to him on the floor last night.'

'Hmph. I didn't intend to fight. It was your fault for plying me with drink.'

'I did no such thing!'

Nugs paid him no attention.

'Still, never mind. Have you seen my black eye?' He examined himself complacently in the glass. 'I haven't had such a splendid shiner in forty years at least. There's life in the old dog yet.'

'But why do you want to go to Sospel and see the Comte?'

'I don't want to see him particularly. But I do want to find out what he's hiding, show the evidence to Baba and convince her once and for all that the man's a bounder. The more I reflect on it the more certain I am that he must have had something to do with the theft of this diamond everyone's talking about, and since the Sûreté aren't doing anything about it, it's up to me to expose him.'

'This is pure guess-work on your part, based on nothing but your dislike of him. You have no evidence at all that he stole the diamond, other than the fact that he danced with Mrs. Dragusha at Benjamin Roche's party.'

Nugs waved a dismissive hand.

'Well, if he didn't steal the diamond, I'm sure he's hiding some other skeleton in his cupboard, and I mean to find out what it is.'

'I thought we'd agreed that Baba wouldn't care even if you presented her with fifty skeletons wearing top hats and dancing a polka.'

'She was slobbering all over him when we left last night,' went on Nugs, ignoring him, 'but I'm certain he only let her do it because it was one in the eye for me. After all, he'd only just given her the boot five minutes earlier, and I don't believe he really wants her at all. We'll go up to Sospel, get the goods on him and send him about his business.'

'But what if he's there? You can't just walk into his house and start rifling through his personals.'

'We'll think of that when we get there. If he turns up then we shall talk, man to man, in a civilized fashion—although if he won't play ball then I might still need you as my second. Where can we get a gun? Do you suppose those antique pistols on the wall at the Villa des Fleurs still work?'

'Listen, you old ruffian—' began Freddy, then thought

better of it. Why not go to Sospel? It was unlikely that the Comte had been concerned in the disappearance of the Mariensee diamond, but it was as well to make certain. After all, he had been standing near Jessie Weeks when the lights went off, and Baba herself had said that he had been absent for several minutes during that period. They were still waiting for La Duchessa to show herself—if she ever did—but in the meantime it could do no harm to go up and see the Comte's house, and perhaps get an idea of what sort of man he was, or even find some evidence that pointed to his having been part of the plot. Quite apart from any other consideration, it was vitally important to keep Nugs out of further trouble in case word ever reached Cynthia of what had been going on, for it was certain that whoever was at fault, Freddy would get the blame for it. He made up his mind.

'Very well, but I'm not going until I've had breakfast,' he said. 'Give me half an hour.'

On the terrace Freddy found Angela sipping tea and reading a newspaper. She raised her eyebrows at the sight of him.

'Late night?' she inquired.

'Not as late as it might have been, thanks to Nugs. He'll be *persona non grata* at the casino for a while.'

He sat down and ordered coffee.

'They've found Rolf, by the way,' she said.

'I say, have they? Where?'

'He drifted across the bay and washed up on the private beach of a hotel on Cap Ferrat—much to the consternation of the guests, no doubt. I heard the maids talking about it this morning.'

'They'll have no choice but to believe us now. Let's just hope they don't suspect us of having killed him. Any other news?'

'Not that I've heard. I suppose you mean the diamond. The police haven't been here today as far as I'm aware, but they must know by now that the thing is a fake, and I imagine they'll want a word with you.'

'Almost certainly, but they can't prove my story isn't true, so I'll just have to cling to it unto death. After all, it's not as though I've thrown the blame on the wrong person.'

'Better avoid the police altogether, I should say, if we're to get any detecting done today,' said Angela. 'So, then, what is our plan, Mr. Holmes?'

'First of all I am going up to Sospel with Nugs.'

He related the events of the night before.

'And you say you have nothing in common with him,' she remarked dryly.

'We're not in the least alike,' said Freddy with dignity. 'I'd never dream of challenging anyone to a duel. And I've never been thrown out of a casino—or not lately, anyway. At any rate, it can't hurt to go with him. I'll keep the old reprobate out of trouble and take the opportunity to do a little investigating while I'm there, just in case it turns out that the Comte is mixed up in this business after all.'

'I'd forgotten we'd put him down as a suspect, but of course you're right. Then may I come with you?'

'You'd be better off staying here and looking out for La Duchessa, since the whole point of handing over the fake diamond was to draw her out, and we don't want to miss her if she does turn up.'

Angela sighed.

'I suppose so. Very well, I shall do as you suggest. Sitting about waiting isn't exactly exciting, but somebody has to do it, and it may as well be me.'

'If she doesn't show her face you can have a nice, relaxing time of it and pretend it's the last day of your holiday, but I'm almost certain she will. I have an odd sort of hunch about it. She's here somewhere, I can feel it.'

'All right, then, I'll stay and watch out for developments on the home front.' She regarded him earnestly. 'Just promise me you'll be careful in Sospel. If the Comte is mixed up in it all then he may be dangerous. How long will you be? At what time ought I to start worrying?'

Freddy consulted his watch.

'Let's say three o'clock. That ought to be plenty of time to get there, scout around and get back. If you haven't seen me by then, either the Comte has taken me prisoner or I've thrown Nugs off a mountainside from sheer exasperation and been arrested.'

'What fun. Off you go, then. I expect things will be very dull here by comparison,' she said mournfully.

When Freddy had finished his breakfast he went outside to find Nugs waiting for him in Great-Aunt Ernestine's venerable Armstrong-Siddeley.

'You'll drive, won't you?' he said as Freddy got in. 'I'm not feeling quite up to it this morning.'

'I'm not surprised. Doesn't the Great-Aunt mind your sailing around the countryside in her car?'

'She might if I'd told her I was taking it,' replied Nugs.

Freddy opened his mouth, ran through the likely course of the conversation in his mind, and shut it again.

'Very well, let's get this over with,' he said.

The road up to Sospel was not busy, and they made good time. It was a pleasant drive through the mountains, and ordinarily Freddy would have enjoyed the scenery, but he was distracted by the car, whose steering was temperamental, and by Nugs, who had fallen asleep and was snoring loudly. As they approached the outskirts of the town Freddy prodded him and he awoke with a start.

'We're nearly there,' said Freddy. 'Now, where is this place?'

They stopped the car and Nugs peered at a crumpled scrap of paper on which he had written the Comte de Langlois' address.

'I don't know where this is,' he said.

'Fortunately for you, I thought to ask at the hotel for a map,' replied Freddy, bringing the article in question out of his pocket. He consulted for a moment. 'Hmm. It ought to be to the left just up here.'

After one or two wrong turnings they eventually found the place, which turned out to be a dilapidated building on the edge of the town which was little more than a cottage. In front of the house was a yard, bounded by a fence that was in a state of some disrepair, in which one or two threadbare chickens scratched around disconsolately.

'This can't be the place,' said Nugs, perplexed.

Freddy looked about him. There was no other building nearby.

'There's no other house it could be. Perhaps the tailor gave you the wrong address.'

'I don't see why he would. How odd.'

'Well, we're here now,' said Freddy. 'Let's go and have a look.'

They walked through the yard and up to the front door. Freddy knocked and they waited. Nobody answered. He knocked again, with no result.

'Bah, let's go,' said Nugs at last. 'There's no use in our wasting any more time here.'

'But I thought you wanted to discuss things with him, man to man,' said Freddy absently as he peered through one of the front windows.

'It's perfectly obvious this isn't his house. The tailor must have made a mistake.'

Freddy was unwilling to give it up just yet.

'I'd just like to be sure.' He disappeared around the side of the building. 'I say,' he said, when he returned. 'There's an open window at the back.'

'I want to talk to the man, not burgle his house,' replied Nugs.

'I thought you wanted to find proof of his ghastly character,' said Freddy.

'Well, yes, but—'

But Freddy had already disappeared around to the back garden again. Here, the ground sloped steeply downwards, making it impossible to see into the lower floor rooms at the back. Above their heads, as Freddy had said, a window was open.

'You're not really going to break in, are you?' said Nugs, who seemed to have changed his mind about investigating and was looking around nervously.

'Not if I don't have to,' replied Freddy. 'Give me a leg up, will you?'

Nugs obliged, muttering, and with his assistance Freddy succeeded in grasping the high window-sill. He stuck his head through the window and craned his neck, looking for any signs that might indicate the Comte de Langlois lived there.

'What are you doing?' rapped out a voice in French.

Freddy started and bumped his head on the window frame, and they both turned to see a woman standing there. She was about forty years of age, with wispy hair under a straw hat and an air of long suffering. She was carrying a heavy string bag and had obviously just returned from buying groceries. At the sight of her Freddy, who was perched precariously on Nugs's hands, overbalanced and fell on top of his grandfather, and they both toppled to the ground in an undignified tangle of arms and legs. This spectacle ought to have been enough to tell any surprised householder that her valuables were in no serious danger, and the woman's startled expression cleared, to be replaced by one of wary resignation as the two strange Englishmen disentangled themselves and stood up.

Nugs dusted his hat, which had fallen off, and replaced it.

'*Madame*,' he said, removing his hat again and accompanying the gesture with a courtly bow. 'Please accept the compliments of two humble travellers to your admirable land on your most sublime and magnificent residence. It is rare that one sees such a combination of utility and symmetry framed so harmoniously within such a glorious landscape.' He threw out an arm to indicate the mountains all around them. 'Why, not even in Italy, where the lofty peaks of the Apennines swoop down to the Tuscan plain, have I drawn into my nostrils air of such an ineffable freshness. It is quite invigorating.'

Nugs had learnt his French during the time of Napoleon III, and his blandishments were of the most grandiloquently rhetorical. He went on for some time in this vein, and she stared at him as though he were mad, then turned to Freddy.

'I'm very sorry,' he said. 'We're looking for the Comte de Langlois.'

At that her brows drew together.

'The Comte de what? Langlois? Is that what he's calling himself now?'

'Isn't that his name?'

She gave a humourless bark of laughter.

'Who knows? Perhaps it is. But it's not the name he was using when he married me.'

'Married you? You're his wife?' asked Freddy in astonishment.

She pulled off her thin glove and showed him a wedding ring.

'He gave me this, for all it means anything. I'd have thrown it down the well long before now if it weren't for the fact that I might need to sell it one day. So, what is it this time? Has he been up to his tricks again? Last time it was a woman, but it might be anything.' She threw up her hands. 'Every day is a surprise. Does he owe you money too?'

'Not exactly,' replied Freddy.

'Last week it was a visit from a tailor, the week before it was a wine-merchant. Each time I tell them I don't know where he is, and I'm telling you the same thing. He's not here, and if you see him just you tell him that if he dares show his face here again I'll take a hatchet to him.'

Freddy could not quite believe what she was telling him. It seemed impossible that the urbane and handsome Comte de Langlois could have any connection with this tired housewife.

'Pardon me,' he said. 'But are you sure we're talking about the same person?'

In reply she went into the house and came out a minute later with a snapshot.

'That's him. And that was me a few years ago before he wore me down.'

Freddy and Nugs peered at the photograph. It showed a couple in wedding dress of the style of fifteen or twenty years earlier. The groom was clearly the man who called himself the Comte de Langlois, while the bride was a pretty girl who was just recognizable in the face of the woman who stood before them, although time had not been kind to her.

'That's the one, yes?' she said. 'René Cardot is his name, not—whatever you said. So what has he been up to this time? Is he in England now?'

'No,' replied Freddy. 'We've come from Nice.'

'Oh, Nice. Plenty of women with money there. He likes them rich and stupid.'

'Now look here,' began Nugs, but Freddy shot him a warning glance.

'Might I ask when you saw him last?' he said.

'A few months ago, it must have been. He turns up now and again when he likes—although you can be sure his bills arrive as regularly as clockwork,' she added dryly. 'So he's back down here now, is he? The last I heard he was in Paris, living in a fancy apartment full of expensive furniture, paid for by some fool of a film actress.'

Freddy hesitated. It was obvious the woman had been

sorely tested by her husband. He decided to lay his cards upon the table.

'We're terribly sorry to trouble you with all this,' he said. 'But there was something in particular I wanted to speak to your husband about. There was a robbery the other night, and something very important was taken—a diamond. Your husband was there at the time, and we think he might have witnessed something.'

She was not fooled for an instant.

'You mean you think he stole it.' She looked doubtful. 'He might have, although it doesn't seem like him. He prefers an easy life. Likes to keep his hands soft, you see. At the first sign of difficulty he tends to run off.' She indicated the impoverished surroundings Nugs had praised so fulsomely. 'As you can see, we're not exactly living in luxury here—I suppose I can't wonder that he decided it would be easier to live by his looks. But if you've come in search of a stolen jewel it's certainly not here. If it was I don't mind saying I'd have taken the thing myself. Lord knows I need the money.'

There was little more to be said. If this woman was telling the truth—and Freddy had no reason to doubt her—then they would find no evidence in Sospel that the Comte had had anything to do with the theft of the Mariensee diamond, or with the murder of Rolf Boehler. Whether he had been mixed up in the plot was still uncertain, but it was perfectly clear that he could never marry Baba.

They took their leave of the woman, with many more flowery compliments on the part of Nugs, and returned to the car. Nugs was frowning and fidgeting.

'You ought to be happy,' said Freddy.

'Hmph,' replied Nugs. 'That's easy enough for you to say. I'm the one who has to break the news to your grandmother.'

They set off and made the return journey to Nice in silence, mainly because Nugs fell asleep again.

# Chapter Twenty

ONCE FREDDY HAD LEFT, Angela felt herself at a loose end. It was all very well having laid a trap for La Duchessa, but the waiting was tedious, and she was acutely conscious of the fact that she had promised Edgar they would go home the next day whether the real diamond had turned up by then or not. But what if more time were needed? Angela was beginning to regret not having extorted an extra day or two's grace from him. She was also not a little fearful that he would become bored with his enforced concealment in Nice and would decide to show his face in public. He was a man who liked to take risks—after all, he had worked the Riviera and other places as a thief for many years without bothering to hide himself, and although he had a remarkable talent for blending into the background when necessary, there must surely be some sharp-eyed people—possibly even the police—who would recognize him from the old days. Angela sighed. Being in love with a man who was supposedly dead, and who would be arrested if it were known he was not, was most inconvenient at times. Perhaps it would be safer to go back to America after all, and return to their ordinary state of unsatisfactory anonymity. She wanted the Mariensee diamond to be recovered, but not at the expense of Edgar's safety.

Still, there was the best part of a day left in which to find the thing, and the weather was much too nice to remain in the hotel, so after lunch Angela decided to take a walk into town, with some thought of returning to the café at which they had first seen La Duchessa. Perhaps it was a frequent haunt of hers. If it was, Angela would watch her from a safe distance then follow her to see where she went.

She wandered up and down the promenade several times, surveying the customers sitting in the cafés as she passed, but saw no sign of La Duchessa. It was too much to have hoped for, really. She hung about for a while, then decided to walk up into the old town, for she had one or two things she needed to buy. There, in one of the narrow alleys close to the church of Saint-Michel, she saw Garnet Weeks, who was staring very hard into a shop window. Angela was wondering what was so interesting about the display, since the place seemed to sell nothing but fishing equipment, when she realized that Garnet was crying. She had not quite made up her mind whether or not to leave the girl alone to enjoy her misery in peace when Garnet turned and saw her.

'Is there anything I can do?' asked Angela.

'No, there's nothing! Everything is terrible!' Garnet burst out, and began sobbing uncontrollably. Angela glanced about in slight embarrassment, patted Garnet uncertainly on the shoulder in a general gesture of sympathy, and eventually thought to offer her a handkerchief. Garnet took it, then gulped and calmed herself a little.

'Suppose you sit down somewhere,' Angela suggested.

Garnet made no objection, and Angela, seeing she was expected to take charge, led the girl to the nearest café, sat her down and ordered tea as the quickest and easiest restorative. The drink worked its charm and Garnet was soon almost herself again.

'I'm sorry, I didn't mean to make such a display of myself,' she said. 'What you must think of me!'

'I don't wonder you're upset,' replied Angela. 'You and your mother must have had a trying time of it over the past few days.'

'Oh, but you don't know the half of it. I don't suppose you've heard, but the diamond that was returned last night is a fake.'

'Indeed? Goodness me. How unfortunate,' said Angela.

'Yes. Poor Freddy—he was so pleased when he thought he'd recovered it, but it looks like the thieves have been too clever for us. They've fooled us, and now we're back where we're started—only it's worse this time.'

She gave a little sob. Angela was puzzled for a moment. Garnet seemed unduly upset about the theft of an object that was not even hers. Then enlightenment dawned: only one thing could cause this sort of anguish.

'Has something else happened?' she asked gently.

The tears began rolling down the girl's face again.

'Jacques—' she began, but was unable to go on.

'I thought so. You've had a row?'

'Not exactly, but I found out something awful this morning. It's the most dreadful thing, and I don't know what to do about it. When it all comes out there'll be so much trouble. How shall I tell Mother? And then there's the police—oh, it's all too much!'

Angela, whose mind had been running along other lines entirely, paused at the mention of the police. She looked at Garnet in mystification, then a sudden memory came back to her and she frowned. Surely it was not possible, was it?

'He doesn't know something about the diamond, does he?' she asked hesitantly. 'Did he—did he see what happened?'

The girl stared down at her hands and said nothing. Angela eyed her in dawning astonishment.

'Garnet, you're not telling me Jacques took it, are you?'

Garnet looked up and gasped.

'How did you know?'

'I didn't until now. But I've just remembered what happened on the night of the party. You and Jacques were standing next to your mother when the lights went off, and when they came on again you were still there but he wasn't. I don't know why it didn't occur to me before, except that it seems so unlikely. Then he's the one who tore it off her dress?'

'Yes. We were standing next to Mother, and I'd just put my hand on his arm when the lights went off and he pulled away from me suddenly as if he'd been burned. I thought I must have done something to upset him, and even more so when the lights went back on and he'd gone. But he turned up again shortly after you fainted, and wouldn't speak to me for the rest of the night or all yesterday. I was frantic, racking my brains to remember whether I'd done anything to offend him, but I couldn't think of anything. Then this morning the news came that the diamond Freddy handed in was a fake, and Jacques came to me and said he was ending things. I demanded to know why, and he said it was because he wasn't worthy of me.' Here her manner changed and she looked at Angela dryly. 'Well, that was nonsense. I've had lots of boys in love with me before, and none of them have ever worried about whether they were worthy of me. Men don't, do they? But eventually I got the true story out of him.'

'But why on earth did he do it?' asked Angela. 'It seems incredible.'

'He said it all started out as a joke. You see, he's been a little wild in the past—getting into bad company and giving his father a few grey hairs—so when Mother and I came to Europe with Daddy for the talks, Mr. Fournier thought it would be a good thing if Jacques were to look after us and take us about. It would help us and keep Jacques out of trouble, he said.

'The night before we arrived in The Hague Jacques was in

a bar with some men he knew—they were bad people, he said, but that didn't worry him any at the time, because he didn't know me then. They had too much to drink, and Jacques must have let it slip that he was to act as escort to Mother and me. The men he was with knew who we were, he said, and they all had more to drink, and everything got a little out of hand, and by the end of the evening Jacques found somehow that he'd agreed to steal Mother's diamond for a bet. It was a joke, he said—he'd never have dreamed of doing it, and by the next day he'd practically forgotten it anyway, so he thought no more about it.

'Then we arrived in The Hague and Mr. Fournier introduced us to Jacques, and he and I hit it off right away, and I was so happy.' She flushed miserably. 'Well, never mind that. He took us about as agreed, but after a few days we'd seen all there was to see in The Hague and the talks were dragging on, so Mr. Fournier suggested we come down to the Riviera and wait there.

'So we came here, and everything was wonderful—for me, at any rate. Not for Jacques. It turned out these friends of his had followed us down here and were expecting him to honour his promise to steal Mother's brooch. He laughed at them at first, and told them not to be ridiculous. Then one of them—Fritz, I think he was called—took Jacques aside and said he had a photograph that would cause all kinds of trouble, and Jacques had better take the brooch as he'd promised or Fritz would make it public.'

'Goodness!' exclaimed Angela. 'What was the photograph?'

'Not the kind of thing I was thinking of when Jacques first mentioned it. As a matter of fact, that would have been preferable. No, it was a picture of Jacques sitting at a table with a man called Théodore Archambault.'

'Oh, I see,' said Angela in sudden understanding. 'Yes, that explains a lot.'

'I don't really understand the story myself,' went on Garnet. 'But Jacques said it would be terrible for his father and for the government if the photograph came to light. I guess this Archambault means trouble.'

'Yes,' replied Angela. 'There was an enormous to-do about it. Archambault was the head of a savings bank, and after he died in a train accident it turned out he'd been embezzling the funds for years and the bank was insolvent. It very quickly collapsed, taking with it the savings of thousands of honest working people. But Archambault had been very well connected, and it was suspected that many important people—including the Prime Minister—had known what he was up to and had been protecting him from prosecution. The Prime Minister denied ever having met Archambault, but his government was very nearly brought down because of the scandal. Many people were not satisfied that Mr. Fournier was telling the truth, and if there really exists proof that Archambault had been associating with Fournier's own son, and the photograph were to be made public, then that would be a very grave matter indeed, for both the French government and the reparations conference.'

Garnet looked aghast.

'Oh, heavens! I had no idea it was so serious. Jacques said he only met this Archambault once or twice. Archambault was trying to butter him up because of who his father was, but Jacques wasn't interested in that kind of thing and shook him off as soon as he could. But the photograph made it look as though they were close friends. The worst thing is that there had been rumours they knew each other, and Jacques denied it at the time for the sake of his father. I can see why he thought he had no choice but to take the diamond, but why did they make him do it so publicly? After all, he was spending most of his time with us. He could easily have found a way to take it without anybody knowing. Then perhaps he could have convinced Mother that it was just lost, or something of the kind.'

'I expect the thieves had their own particular plans,' replied Angela, thinking of Edgar.

'I guess they did. Anyway, he agonized over it but couldn't see any way out of it without getting his father into terrible trouble. So he took the brooch when the lights went out then went into the garden as he'd been told to do and handed it to a man who was waiting for him.'

'Do you happen to know whether he saw anyone else while he was out there?' asked Angela.

If Garnet saw anything odd in the question she made no mention of it.

'Not as far as I'm aware,' she replied. 'He just said he couldn't find the man he was supposed to meet at first, so he stumbled around the garden for a few minutes, terrified that he would be caught. He found the man at last, handed him Mother's brooch then went back inside. He was frantic about the whole thing, because by that time he wanted—well, he'd been thinking of asking me to marry him. I know it was a little rash, but we met and it just all happened so quickly. Then for a while last night, when we thought the brooch had been recovered, he hoped that everything was all right again, and that nobody need ever know the part he'd played in the theft. But this morning we found out the diamond Freddy handed in was a fake, and now Jacques has confessed to what he did and I don't know what we'll do.' She looked down. 'It's a good thing he didn't get a chance to propose, given what's happened.'

'Have you told your mother or Chief Inspector Guichard about this?' asked Angela.

'Not yet. I've been worrying all morning about what I ought to do. What if Daddy pulls out of the talks because of it? It could cause all kinds of international trouble.'

'Where is Jacques now?'

'I don't know—that's the worst of it. He said he was going to do the honourable thing and put it right. I took it to mean he was going to speak to his father and confess, but what if that's not what he meant at all? I'm terrified he's going to do something silly.'

'Has the Prime Minister arrived?'

'He and Daddy are expected any time now. Perhaps they're already here.' Garnet glanced up at the clock on the building opposite. 'I ought to go, just in case Daddy has arrived at the hotel. I guess I'll have to tell him and Mother what happened.'

'I'll come back with you,' said Angela.

At the hotel they found Mrs. Weeks in the lounge, gazing at the fake brooch and bewailing the fact that her diamond had not been recovered as she had believed.

'But it looks so real!' she said mournfully, holding it up to the light. 'The man who examined it said it was one of the best fakes he'd ever seen, but it's certainly not the real thing.' She held it out to Angela. 'Can you tell the difference, Mrs. Marchmont?'

Angela could hardly mention that she had already examined it the day before, so she took it and peered dutifully at it.

'Not at all,' she replied.

'Has Daddy arrived?' Garnet asked her mother.

'No, he's not here yet. Where is Jacques? Isn't he with you? I passed him in the hall this morning and he looked almost ill. He didn't reply when I said hallo but left the hotel in an awful hurry. Have you two been quarrelling?'

'Not exactly,' said Garnet. 'Listen, there's something I have to tell you, but not here.'

'Of course, dear,' replied Mrs. Weeks. 'You will excuse us, won't you, Mrs. Marchmont?'

The Weekses went off, leaving Angela to sit and stare in vexation at the brooch in her hand. She was coming to the conclusion that it had been a mistake to give it to the police at all. La Duchessa had not risen to the bait as they had hoped, and all they had to show for their efforts was a fake diamond which was not likely to do anything but draw attention to Edgar and the original plan for the robbery which had not gone ahead.

Angela was still contemplating the brooch when a note was brought across to her. She opened it quickly and was surprised to find it was not from Freddy, as she had supposed, but from Benjamin Roche. He presented his compliments and apologized for the late notice, but he was holding a little tea-party for a group of English women that afternoon—quite a last-minute thing—and he hoped Mrs. Marchmont would grace it with her presence. Some of the ladies—here he mentioned one or two well-known titles—were particularly anxious to be introduced to her, he said. In addition, Mr. Roche confided that he hoped to consult her about something which had occurred to him regarding the unfortunate events of the other night. It was quite a small thing, but he could not get it out of his mind, and before he troubled Chief Inspector Guichard with it he would very much like to hear her opinion on the matter. He ended by pressing her in the most friendly terms to come up to La Falaise on receipt of the note.

Formal tea-parties did not appeal to Angela as a rule, and she had no interest in titles; besides, she was supposed to be waiting for news of La Duchessa, and she would have declined with thanks had it not been for Roche's hint about the Mariensee diamond. Had he remembered something about the men who had attacked him? There could be no harm in going to find out. Roche might have some useful information, and she need not stay long once he had told her what it was.

It was already three o'clock, but there was no sign of Freddy yet. Angela went to request a taxi, then scribbled a note and handed it to the man at the reception desk, asking him to deliver it to Mr. Pilkington-Soames as soon as he returned. At La Falaise she was admitted by Werner, who informed her that she was the first to arrive and led her upstairs to a small sitting-room on one of the upper floors, a comfortable and informal apartment which stood in stark contrast to the grandeur of the downstairs rooms. Werner murmured something about fetching her host, and went off. Angela walked across to the window, which afforded views of the terrace below and the sea beyond. She was contemplating the scenery when she heard a sound like a click behind her. She did not realize what it was at first and continued gazing out to sea. After a few seconds it suddenly occurred to her that the noise had sounded exactly like a key turning in a lock. She went across to the door and tried the handle. It did not open. She tried it again. It was certainly locked.

'Bother,' said Angela.

# Chapter Twenty-One

FREDDY RETURNED to the Hotel Bellevue later than intended, for he and Nugs had been required to provide an explanation to Great-Aunt Ernestine as to why they had abstracted her motor-car. Eventually Freddy managed to tear himself away (although his great-aunt was still scolding Nugs as he left) and returned to the Hotel Bellevue, to be greeted by a note from Angela which said that she had gone to La Falaise for tea and would be back by six o'clock or so. But by dinner-time there was still no sign of her, and Freddy began to feel a vague sense of unease. He inquired at the reception desk, but all they could tell him was that Mrs. Marchmont had received a note earlier that day and had departed for La Falaise in a taxi. He came away and ate a solitary dinner, still feeling a little unsettled. At ten o'clock she still had not returned, so he telephoned La Falaise, but received no answer. By this time he was feeling really worried, and was wondering what to do, when it occurred to him that after she had left Roche's house she might have gone into Nice to see Valencourt, and had simply forgotten to let him know. It could not do any harm to call and find out. He telephoned the hotel in Nice, and eventually Valencourt's voice came on the line.

'No, I haven't seen her,' he answered sharply in reply to Freddy's inquiry. 'I thought she was with you.'

'I went to Sospel, and when I came back I got a note to say she'd gone up to La Falaise. She said she'd be back by six, but it's getting late now and there's been no sign of her.'

Valencourt said scathingly:

'You went to Sospel? You were *supposed* to be keeping an eye on her.'

'I know,' said Freddy uncomfortably. 'I'm awfully sorry, I didn't think.'

'That's obvious.'

'Surely it's you they want, though? Shouldn't we have heard something by now if they've taken her?'

'They don't know where I am, so they have no choice but to wait until I turn up.'

'But are you sure she's in danger? I've tried the house and nobody's answering, but she might be back soon. Perhaps we ought to wait a little longer.'

'No,' replied Valencourt. 'If she's not back by now then something's happened to her.' He gave a weary sigh. 'I suppose I shall have to go and get her. Are you coming with me?'

'Of course I am.'

'Then stay where you are, and I'll be there in twenty minutes—no, better still, meet me at the look-out point on the road above La Falaise. And for God's sake show me you have more sense than you've demonstrated so far by wearing dark clothes.'

He put the telephone down with a clatter and Freddy winced. He went upstairs to change as instructed, came downstairs and was about to leave the hotel when he saw Chief Inspector Guichard coming towards him with a purposeful look in his eye. Freddy's heart sank.

'M. Pilkington-Soames, I should like to speak to you about this story of the man you followed yesterday in Nice,' said the chief inspector. 'It seems the brooch he dropped was a fake.'

'Oh dear, was it really?' replied Freddy. 'I'm terribly sorry to hear that. Listen, I'd love to stop and chat, but I'm afraid I'm in rather a hurry.'

He made as if to pass Guichard, who put out a hand to stop him.

'I should like to speak to you *now*,' he said. 'I have reason to believe that you know more about this business than you have told me so far, and I should like to hear the rest of the story.'

'But I say, can't it wait until tomorrow? I've promised to meet a chap in a few minutes.'

'I am afraid not,' replied Guichard. 'This is a very serious case. Your friend must wait.'

Guichard obviously meant business. Freddy's mind began to work rapidly. He could not afford to spend time answering questions about the fake jewel—not least because he had no good story to offer, and would merely have to tell more lies on top of the ones he had already told. He had no wish to confuse the investigation even further; moreover, Angela might even now be in danger, and since he could hardly confess that he was about to search for her in company with a wanted criminal, there was no alternative but to take desperate action.

'Oh, very well,' he said. 'Perhaps we might go into the lounge.'

He led the way through the reception hall, the chief inspector following. Two elderly ladies were just coming out of the lounge, and as Chief Inspector Guichard stepped back and held the door for them politely Freddy took advantage of his momentary lapse in attention to dart through a door to the right which led to the kitchens. Ignoring Guichard's shout of 'Stop!', he shot down the corridor, upsetting a tray of drinks carried by a waiter as he passed, barrelled out through a side door, up some steps and out into the street. Guichard was not a small man, and since Freddy could get up quite a turn of speed when he liked, he did not have to run for more than a minute or two before he judged it was safe to stop and go in search of a taxi.

Twenty minutes later he was standing in the shadow of a large bougainvillea on the road above La Falaise, avoiding the light of the moon, which was nearly full and uncomfortably bright. There was the slightest rustle of leaves and then Edgar Valencourt was standing by him.

'You're late,' said Valencourt.

'I had to take the long way round after the police decided they wanted a word,' replied Freddy. 'I say, I really am dreadfully sorry. If I'd had the faintest idea Angela was going to take herself off like that I'd never have dreamed of leaving her today.'

'Yes, well, we'll pick that bone later—although it's hard to see how the two of you could have made more of a mess of things if you'd tried.' He eyed Freddy dubiously. 'I'm wondering whether it mightn't be better if I did this alone.'

'I'm not quite as idiotic as you seem to think,' said Freddy, stung.

'That remains to be seen.' He sighed crossly. 'Drat the woman! Has she no sense? All she had to do was keep out of trouble for *one* day. Was that too much to ask? This isn't exactly how I intended to spend the evening.'

'How are we to get in? I suppose we're not planning to knock on the door?'

'That would be rash,' agreed Valencourt. 'No, we won't be announcing our presence, but before we do anything at all we must find out where we need to get in *to*.'

'Isn't she in the house?'

'She might be, or she might be in the villa next door. That's where Fritz and his pals have been staying, as I expect you've deduced by now.'

'Oh, quite, what?' said Freddy, who had not deduced anything of the sort.

'I don't know whether they're still there. We know from Bruno that they planned to leave the place as soon as they had the diamond, but since they didn't get it there's a good chance they're still hanging around. If she's not there we'll try La Falaise. I dare say we can get in through the French windows or the roof terrace.' He grimaced. 'It's a pity I don't have any lock-picks with me, but I didn't expect to be doing this sort of thing when I came over here.'

'I have some,' ventured Freddy, who felt as though he needed to make amends.

Valencourt threw him a look of surprise.

'Do you, indeed? What the devil are you doing with lock-picks?'

'As a matter of fact, your friend Miss Sangiacomo gave them to me—*and* taught me how to use them. Although I'm not especially good at it,' he added honestly. 'Have you brought Bruno's gun, by the way?'

'Yes—although if Angela had agreed to take it in the first place as I suggested we wouldn't be standing here now.' Valencourt glanced around. 'Very well, it looks as though we're all set. Now, stay close to me and don't make a sound.'

The way to the villa next to La Falaise was down a curved drive which was almost concealed from the main road by vegetation. The narrow road wound down to a flat area evidently used for the parking of cars, and thence to a flight of steps leading down to the garden of the house, which was not so much a garden as a series of three or four small terraces, one below the other, connected by short flights of steps.

The house was in darkness and it looked as though nobody was at home. They crept around the outside of the building, looking for a way in, and came to a wooden veranda onto which a pair of French windows opened. Valencourt tried one of the doors quietly and found it unlocked. Throwing a warning glance at Freddy, he drew Bruno's revolver and slipped inside. Freddy followed. It took no more than a minute to go over the house and establish that it was empty, although there were clear signs of recent habitation, and a smell of cigarette smoke hung in the air.

'They've gone,' said Valencourt. 'And not long ago.'

'What about Angela? Do you think she was here?'

'Not that I can see. If I know her, she'd have left a sign of some sort—if she was capable of it, at least.'

The implication was not a pleasant one. There was nothing to do here, so they left the house and passed through the garden, avoiding the moonlight and keeping to the shadows. At the end of the last terrace was the iron gate which Freddy had seen and looked through from the cliff path on the day after the party, but where before it had been locked, now it stood wide open, propped in place by a large stone. Valencourt put a finger over his lips, and they proceeded cautiously through it and down towards the fork in the path, intending to take the branch that led back up to La Falaise.

As they approached the place where it divided, however, they both stiffened as their attention was caught by a scene below them: thrown into sharp relief by the moonlight, two men were making their way down the cliff path towards the *Neptune*, carrying something heavy between them. It was not possible to see their burden clearly, but the form was unmistakably human—and, from the fact that it was motionless, presumably either unconscious or dead. Freddy's blood ran cold at the sight.

'Angela!' he breathed.

Valencourt swore violently under his breath.

'Gaston and Bruno. Damn it all! I knew I ought to have shot Bruno while I had the chance.'

He set his jaw grimly, and once again Freddy noticed the ruthless streak in the older man which had struck him before. Valencourt turned to him.

'We've only got the one gun,' said Freddy, in answer to his unspoken question.

'Can you fight?'

'Yes.'

'Good. We have the advantage of surprise so if we act fast we might not have to.'

'Where's Fritz?'

'I don't know. Let's hope he's already on the boat, out of the way. If he's not then it can't be helped—we've no time to worry about him. Now, I'll cover them and you disarm them. I'll shoot if I have to.'

He set off down the path without waiting for a reply, and Freddy followed. He was not in the slightest bit nervous, only filled with an unshakable sense of purpose. If the bundle the men were carrying was Angela, then they might be too late, but they had to try.

They ran swiftly down the path, making as little sound as possible. Valencourt was a little way ahead, much more sure-footed in the darkness than Freddy, who was less used to this sort of thing and found that the uneven surface underfoot tended to slow him down. As a result he had fallen a short distance behind by the time Valencourt reached the last flight of steps that led down to the cove. Gaston and Bruno had already reached the boat and were preparing to load their burden on board. In a moment it would be too late to attempt a rescue. The men were not paying attention to anything except their task, so without stopping to wait for Freddy, Valencourt ran swiftly and quietly down the last few steps, intending to catch them by surprise. Freddy hurried to catch up—then stopped dead and ducked down behind a rock as a familiar figure detached itself from the darkness ahead of him and stepped in front of Valencourt. It was Fritz Boehler, and he was pointing a gun straight at Valencourt's heart.

## Chapter Twenty-Two

'DROP THE GUN!' snapped Fritz.

Freddy's heart, which had leapt into his mouth, sank again, and he kicked himself for the haste which had made them careless. They had known Fritz would be somewhere about, but had disregarded the fact in their race to rescue Angela. Freddy watched, crouching, from the darkness as Valencourt held out his hands. Instead of dropping the revolver, however, he paused a second, then with a flick of the wrist tossed it into some scrubby bushes to the side of the steps. Fritz swore, but evidently he was in a hurry and had no time to look for it. He glanced round as Freddy crouched further into the shadows and held his breath, then searched Valencourt's pockets quickly and efficiently.

'Get moving,' he hissed, and gave Valencourt a shove.

Valencourt had no choice but to comply as Fritz marched him to the *Neptune*. Freddy watched helplessly from a distance as Gaston and Bruno emerged from the cabin and saw the newcomer. He could not hear what they were saying, but at an instruction from Fritz, Bruno pinioned Valencourt's arms behind his back and pushed him roughly down into the cabin. Fritz and Gaston remained on deck, Fritz glancing around.

Freddy guessed that whatever they were planning to do they did not want to do it here close to land where they would be visible to any watchers. At length Fritz, too, disappeared below deck, and Gaston busied himself at the bows of the boat.

Nobody was looking back towards the cliff path. There was not an instant to lose. As quick as lightning, Freddy darted out to the place towards which he thought Valencourt had thrown the gun and began scrabbling about in the bushes. Any minute now the Boehler gang would be casting off, taking with them Valencourt and perhaps Angela too, and once they got out to sea there was little doubt as to what would happen. But the gun was nowhere to be found. Freddy's search became increasingly frantic. Where had it gone? Without it he could not hope to be of any use. He was formulating wild plans in his head about creeping aboard the *Neptune*, somehow taking three violent men unawares and single-handedly disarming them, when his heel knocked against the missing gun, causing it to skitter away from him. He pounced on it thankfully and glanced towards the boat. Had they seen him?

But it seemed they were too intent on their business to have noticed Freddy. Gaston and Bruno were now both on deck, and as he watched, Fritz emerged from the cabin and went to speak to his men, who had stopped to light cigarettes. Freddy heard Fritz snapping at them for wasting time, and as they argued Freddy took his chance. Fortified by the comforting presence of the gun in his hand, he crept down the last few steps and moved silently across to the *Neptune*. The men were not facing his way, but any second now one of them might turn and see him. He took a deep breath, sprang lightly onto the boat and slipped into the tiny cabin.

Inside it was pitch dark, and he bumped his head painfully on the ceiling when he tried to straighten up. He swallowed his exclamation of pain, but before he could do anything else he felt the floor beneath him lift and swoop, and he realized he had come aboard just in time, for the boat had cast off from the shore. As it rocked, Freddy stumbled against something on the floor which felt unpleasantly human against his shoe and caused him to overbalance and drop the gun, but before he had time to pick it up there came the sound of footsteps overhead and a voice approaching.

Freddy had only a few seconds to make a decision. There was nothing he could do by himself—everything depended upon his having Valencourt's help, and if he were found now, he would be swiftly overpowered. It was idiotic to think he could conceal himself in a place this small, but Freddy had no choice. He remembered the tiny berth with the pile of rough blankets on it which he had seen on his previous examination of the boat, and groped towards the place where he recalled having seen it. His hand met the familiar scratchy feeling of rough wool, and he had just managed to wriggle under the pile of blankets and curl up when there was the creak of footsteps coming down into the cabin.

There came the sound of a match striking, and the blackness in front of Freddy's eyes gradually thinned and became a dim glow. Whoever it was had lit a lamp. Freddy curled himself up so as to occupy as little space as possible, and hoped against hope that no part of him was protruding from the blankets. His heart was thumping almost painfully in his chest. There was a silence, and his imagination filled him with the fear that whoever had just come in had seen the disarrangement of the blankets as soon as he came into the cabin, and was perfectly aware of his presence. The silence went on for so long that the suspense became almost unbearable, and Freddy began to entertain mad thoughts of bursting out from his hiding-place and attempting to take the man by surprise. Then a voice spoke, and he recognized it as that of Fritz Boehler.

'What have we got here?' said Fritz. 'Two pretty birds all trussed up. The other one's no good for anything now, but I guess you can tell me what I want to know.'

There was a rustle. Freddy, half-suffocated under the blankets, thought that if he shifted just a little, he might be able to breathe slightly better and see what was happening. Cautiously, moving inch by inch, he moved a hand and lifted his coverings just a fraction. Before him he saw Fritz Boehler, crouching down by Edgar Valencourt, who was lying on the floor, his hands tied behind him and a makeshift gag around his mouth. Freddy's eyes moved to the other bound figure lying next to Valencourt—the body he had seen Bruno and Gaston carrying down to the cove. To his enormous relief he saw that it was not Angela at all, and was even more astonished to recognize the bound figure as Jacques Fournier. The Prime Minister's son had been badly beaten and was unconscious or possibly even dead, as far as Freddy could observe through the tiny chink in his blanket. He could not see the gun, but from the sound it had made when it fell Freddy judged it had landed directly on the floor of the cabin rather than on either of its human occupants. He was certain Fritz would spot it at any moment. If he did, he would turn his attention to the cabin and immediately discover Freddy, hiding not two feet behind him under a heap of blankets. But Fritz seemed to have other things on his mind.

'Where is the diamond?' he said to Valencourt.

Valencourt did not reply—not surprising, given the gag in his mouth. Fritz hauled him up roughly to a sitting position and took off the gag.

'Where is the diamond?' he repeated.

'If I knew that why would I be here?' answered Valencourt with some difficulty.

'I guess you came to rescue this little pal of yours. You double-crossed us, didn't you? You two and Bettina. The boy here wouldn't speak—he was tougher than I expected, but you will. Where is the diamond?'

As he rapped it out a third time, he hit his prisoner hard

across the face. Valencourt flinched but said nothing, and Fritz hit him again.

'I've had enough of you,' he said. 'You've crossed me too many times now. Rolf might be dead but I'm still here and I don't forget. You'll talk or regret it.'

Valencourt was bleeding from a cut at the side of his head, but still he clamped his mouth shut and refused to reply. Freddy was in an agony of indecision. He could not bear to hide here like a coward while Fritz beat a bound man. He must do something, but what? Fritz was unaware of Freddy's presence, but the advantage of surprise would be nothing without the gun. Would it be better to move cautiously forward under the blankets and attempt to see where the gun had fallen while Fritz's back was turned? The cabin was so cramped that he could not hope to do it without being spotted. The only alternative was to burst out from his place of concealment and create as much confusion as he could, hoping to find the gun quickly. But if he did not succeed, Fritz and his men would overpower him in an instant, and then it would be all over. Either way it was obvious he might have no choice but to shoot Fritz, but the cabin was so small that if he did that then there was the danger that somebody else might be caught accidentally.

The situation was difficult, but to do nothing was impossible. Freddy held his breath, wriggled forward an inch or two and adjusted the blankets as quietly as possible to give him a view of the floor. He saw the gun immediately, not six inches from Fritz's foot. Fritz was concentrating his attention on Valencourt and had not seen it, but if he turned his head he could not miss it. If Freddy did not get hold of it first then all was lost. Cautiously he poked out an arm and extended it towards the gun, but it was just beyond the reach of his hand. Fritz was too busy concentrating on Valencourt to pay attention to what was going on behind him. It was now or never. Freddy lifted the blanket and was just about to lean out of the berth and pick up the gun when there was a clatter of feet and Gaston descended the steps into the cabin. Freddy retreated hurriedly back under the blanket, cursing to himself.

'We're far enough out now,' said Gaston to Fritz. 'We'd better get this over and done with. We want to be well away before they get the search-parties out. Are we getting rid of both of them?'

'We've no use for the boy—we've got nothing out of him. If you ask me he doesn't know where the jewel is. But this one —' Fritz indicated Valencourt, and an ugly smile spread across his face. 'I'm going to take my time with him.' He brought out a lethal-looking knife and tested its blade with great deliberation. 'We're going to have a bit of fun, aren't we?' he said, and laughed unpleasantly. He stood up and put the knife away, then aimed a kick at Jacques Fournier. 'Bring the boy out, then. Bruno can help you.'

Fritz left the cabin, then Bruno came in and together he and Gaston hauled Jacques Fournier to his feet. The young man had begun to regain consciousness and was groaning softly. He began to struggle and protest a little as they bundled him up the steps and onto the deck.

'Fritz will be back for you in a minute,' said Bruno maliciously to Valencourt as he left.

As soon as they had gone Freddy shot out from under the blankets and was fumbling in his pocket for a pen-knife.

'I'm so glad you didn't come earlier,' said Valencourt as Freddy cut through the ropes. 'I should hate you to have interrupted the party.'

'I'm awfully sorry—I dropped the gun when I tripped over you. Are you all right?'

'I've been better.'

Valencourt got stiffly to his feet and dabbed at the blood which was running down the side of his face. An ugly bruise was already forming over his eye. But there was not an instant to lose. Above them on deck came the sounds of a struggle.

'Sounds like he's not going quietly,' said Valencourt grimly. 'Now, it all depends on whether Bruno has found himself another gun since yesterday. If he has then I don't think much of our chances.' He picked up the revolver. 'I'll take this. Can you swim?'

'Of course I can,' said Freddy.

'Good, because you might have to. I'll go first. Now, quiet—and don't hesitate to hit below the belt or chuck somebody overboard if you have to. This is no time to play the sportsman.'

They emerged cautiously from the cabin to find that the three remaining members of the Boehler gang were concentrating far too much on what they were doing to notice what was happening behind them. Fritz and Bruno were at the forward end of the deck, struggling with Jacques Fournier, who had somehow managed to free one arm from his bindings and was fighting back with everything he had. Although he was a well-built young man, he was badly injured and it was an unequal struggle that could have only one conclusion. As they watched, Fournier managed to put a well-placed elbow into Bruno's stomach. Bruno doubled up in pain and collapsed in a heap, wheezing, while Fritz and Gaston roared with laughter.

'So there is still some life left in you, is there?' said Fritz. 'I was beginning to doubt it. Now, if you've finished having your fun with Bruno, come here and let's get this done. Don't worry, we'll weigh you down—it'll all be over in a couple of minutes.'

But Fournier was not laughing. He was fighting for his life and he knew it. He lumbered forward, aimed a blow at Fritz and missed. Fritz laughed even more. He was enjoying himself immensely.

'Come on then,' he taunted. 'Show me what you're made of!'

With the last of his strength, Fournier threw a kick and caught Fritz a glancing blow on the leg.

'Hey!' snapped Fritz, finally losing his patience. He shoved the boy, who stumbled backwards and fell across the deck, exhausted. Fritz raised his gun and pointed it at the young man, ready to finish him off. Watching helplessly from ten feet away, Freddy closed his eyes for an instant, preparing for the inevitable.

There came the sound of a shot, and it took Freddy a second or two to realize that it was not Fritz who had fired at all, but Valencourt. Fritz staggered back and raised his head in astonishment to stare at the man he had very nearly killed less than two years before, and who was now standing before him, aiming a deadly weapon at him, a hard look in his eyes. Barely hesitating, Valencourt fired again, and Fritz, still wearing the look of surprise, spun sideways, tipped and fell over the rail. He was already dead when he hit the water.

'Goodbye, Fritz,' said Valencourt coolly.

Gaston, meanwhile, had finally realized what was happening. As Valencourt lifted the gun to fire for a second time at Fritz he let out a shout and reached into his pocket for his own gun, but Freddy was too quick for him. He took a mighty leap forward and brought Gaston down to the deck between the cabin and the rail. Gaston was thick-set and much bulkier than Freddy, but the immediate thing was to stop him shooting, and Freddy in his time had found himself in the middle of enough fights with men bigger than Gaston to know that catching someone unawares was the thing. Before Gaston could gather his wits together to push him off, Freddy had delivered several smart blows and had pinned Gaston's right arm, which was holding the gun, to the deck. It is not to be supposed that Freddy would have prevailed in normal circumstances, but the space between the rail and the cabin roof was a cramped one, which prevented Gaston from gaining much purchase with his hands. Even so, he managed to deliver a sideways swipe to Freddy's face with his left hand, which hurt, but also had the happy effect of exasperating Freddy into a final burst of effort. He stuck a knee hard into Gaston's midriff, slammed his hand against the deck, and with one last wrench got the revolver from him. He leapt to his feet, levelling the weapon at his foe.

'Up you get,' he commanded breathlessly. 'And don't think I won't shoot if you try anything funny.'

Gaston struggled to his feet, glowering, and Freddy risked a glance across at Valencourt, who seemed to have had less difficulty in subduing Bruno, and was in the process of tying his hands behind his back. In a very few minutes, the two remaining members of the Boehler gang were sitting, tied up and sullen, on the deck.

'It seems Bruno didn't have time to get another gun after all,' remarked Valencourt, as he and Freddy looked down at the two men. 'Lucky for us. Now, we'd better get back to shore and find this fellow a doctor. Think yourselves lucky we don't dump you overboard,' he said to Gaston and Bruno.

'Now all we have to do is find Angela,' said Freddy. 'If Fritz didn't have her then it must have been Bettina who took her. I only hope she's all right.'

'It's not Bettina I'm worried about,' muttered Valencourt.

'What do you mean?'

Valencourt did not reply. Freddy looked at him searchingly.

'I think you'd better tell me what you know, old chap,' he said.

# Chapter Twenty-Three

When Angela discovered she was a prisoner at La Falaise, several thoughts crossed her mind in quick succession. The first was that she had been dreadfully stupid and Edgar would be very cross with her. The second was to take some small satisfaction in her own perspicacity with respect to Werner. She had thought there was something suspicious about him, and she had been right—although the knowledge was of little practical use, given that she had failed signally to act on her suspicion. The third was that she was not in any immediate danger, for if anybody had been planning to kill her then surely they would have done it as soon as she arrived. The fourth was that there had been no reason for anyone to take her prisoner at all except for the purposes of luring Edgar here—and that in turn led her full circle back to the first thought that he really *would* be very cross with her.

There was no sense in wasting time in useless self-recrimination, however; the important thing was to find a way out. She waited a few minutes to make quite sure that nobody was coming, and that Werner had not locked her in by accident, then set to exploring. In the wall to her left was another door. She tried it and found it open. It gave on to a passage ending in a door which was also locked, as she had expected. There were two more doors in the passage, one each to the left and right. Behind the one to the right was a lavatory, while behind the one to the left was a large cupboard containing various odds and ends and assorted cleaning things.

She returned to the sitting-room and inspected the windows, but they were too high, and escape this way was impossible without risking a drop of fifty feet and a broken neck at the end of it. After pondering a while she went back into the passage and rummaged around in the cleaning cupboard, in the forlorn hope that she might find a tool-box containing something that would help—although what sort of tool that might be she had no idea—but found nothing. Short of attempting to break the door down, then, it seemed she was stuck here for the present.

She turned up her eyes, looking for inspiration, and saw in the ceiling of the cupboard a wooden hatch. Angela considered it with interest. Where there was a hatch there was undoubtedly a space beyond—perhaps an attic, or even a way to the roof. And in a house as big as this one, surely this was not the only such hatch. No doubt there would be other hatches in other rooms, and if she could get up through this one, perhaps she could come down through another and make her escape that way.

The hatch was too high to reach, even if she stood on tiptoe, but there might be something she could stand on. She returned to the sitting-room and cogitated upon the chairs therein. The only one that might do was standing in front of an elegant writing-desk under the window. It was an antique with spindly legs, and it looked a little rickety for her purposes, but she tested it and thought it might hold her weight. She carried it through to the cupboard, set it down under the hatch and stood on it. It creaked and swayed slightly, but held. The ceiling was within reach now; the hatch-cover pushed up easily enough and she slid it sideways. Beyond it was darkness.

This was a start. Alas, the chair on which she stood did not bring her near enough to the ceiling to allow her to climb through. Had William, her driver and man-of-all-work, been in the same predicament, he would have pulled himself up through the hole with ease, for he had once performed acrobatic tricks in a music-hall act. Angela was not an acrobat, however, and must look for some other solution that did not require her to swing from the ceiling like a monkey.

Perhaps she might stand the chair upon a table. That ought to bring her close enough—although it would have to be a small enough table to fit in the cupboard. She thought she remembered seeing one or two such in the sitting-room, and had just emerged from the passage to fetch one when there came the sound of a key in the lock. Quick as a flash, Angela pushed the door to the passage closed, and was already standing well away from it when the door opened and someone came in.

'Good afternoon,' said La Duchessa.

Angela was not sure whom she had been expecting, but La Duchessa had certainly been on the list of possibilities. Bettina was wearing a frothy confection of deep orange silk which on anyone else would have been rather too showy for the time of day, but which somehow suited her perfectly. Angela was not looking at her dress, however, but at the gun she was holding in her right hand. Bettina looked her up and down with unconcealed interest, and Angela assumed an expression of polite puzzlement.

'I was expecting Mr. Roche,' she said, 'but he doesn't seem to be here, and then I couldn't open the door. Where is he?'

'He has gone away until tomorrow,' replied Bettina, still studying her closely.

'But he sent me a note,' said Angela, although she knew full well by now that he had done no such thing. 'He invited me to tea.'

'I wrote the note.'

'But why? And who are you, might I ask?'

Bettina uttered a sound indicative of impatience.

'You know who I am. And I know who you are, Mrs. Marchmont. I recognized you immediately in the casino the other night. We met before, in Italy, and you remember it as well as I do, so you may as well stop pretending.'

This was a surprise, for Angela had been sure La Duchessa had been much too wrapped up in her own concerns in Stresa to have even noticed her. But it appeared Angela was not as anonymous as she had supposed—and if La Duchessa remembered her, then she also knew of Angela's connection with Valencourt, since she had interrupted them at a most inconvenient moment to try and kill him.

'Very well, then, yes I know who you are,' she said. 'But I'd still like to know why you brought me up here under false pretences.'

'I want to find Edgar. Where is he?'

'I haven't the faintest idea.'

'That is not true. The whole town is talking of this fake diamond, so I know he is still here. You must know where he is staying.'

'If I do why should I tell you? What do you want with him?'

'We had an agreement, but he disappeared before I could speak to him.'

'He disappeared because if he hadn't then he would have been found in possession of the fake jewel and arrested,' Angela pointed out.

'He was in no danger—we would have seen to that.'

'We? You and Fritz, do you mean?'

'Fritz! What has he to do with it? Fritz had better not come here, or I will know how to deal with him.'

'Did you know the Boehlers were planning to snatch the brooch before Edgar could take it?'

'They are men with very loud voices, and they did not

think to speak quietly when I was near,' replied Bettina. 'I was very stupid to trust them. I found out what they were planning almost too late and had to think quickly. I was lucky this time, but I shall not rely on luck again.'

'Did you kill Rolf for the diamond, then?'

'Perhaps—but he will never tell,' replied La Duchessa, and let out a harsh laugh.

'Who has the diamond now?'

La Duchessa held out her hands with a smirk.

'As you can see, I have no diamond with me. Where do you suppose I would keep it? In my shoe?'

Angela was finding the woman most irritating, but refused to be drawn into a petty squabble with her. She said coolly:

'Well, I'm afraid I can't help you. If you want Edgar you may go and find him yourself, but in the meantime I should be obliged if you'd let me out of here.'

'I have no time to look for him. He must come, and quickly. I must be in Paris by tomorrow evening, and I need his help.'

'In Paris? What's happening in Paris? Another job, is that it? But what has Edgar to do with it? He did what you wanted the other night at the party, but it was meant to be the last time. Why do you need him now? He's retired. Why can't you leave him alone?'

'Because we work well together and we could be useful to each other. Besides, I like him.'

'You shot him,' said Angela in disbelief. 'Is that what you do to people you like?'

La Duchessa made a dismissive gesture.

'It was a long time ago. I did not hurt him very badly. And you don't really think he will retire, do you? Men of his sort do not retire. They do not like to go to work every day, and have a wife and children, and grow old and fat. Life is nothing to them without danger and excitement.'

She looked Angela up and down again, and her face said

clearly that in her view Angela could provide neither of those things. It was all Angela could do not to toss her head. She returned the other woman's stare haughtily.

'You will write him a note and tell him to come here,' went on Bettina.

'I most certainly will not,' said Angela firmly.

La Duchessa's face flushed with anger. It was evident that people did not often say no to her.

'You will,' she said, and showed the gun.

'What are you going to do? Shoot me as you did Edgar? What a marvellous idea! I'm sure he'll be overjoyed when he finds out what you've done, and only too pleased to join you on your next job. Murder is such an effective means of persuasion, don't you think?'

'You think you are funny,' said Bettina.

'I don't think I'm anything. But perhaps I'm not quite as stupid as you believe. Freddy Pilkington-Soames knows where I am, and the police know who *you* are, and if I disappear he'll lead them straight to you.'

'That foolish boy? He can do as he likes, but they will find nothing if they come here. There are many places to hide you so that nobody will ever find you. Now, I am in a hurry. There is some paper over there at that writing-table. Write and tell Edgar that he must come to La Falaise. I could write it myself and tell him you are here but I imagine he is more likely to come if it is in your handwriting.'

Angela's heart gave a sudden thud as she realized that the desk Bettina was indicating was the very one from which she had taken the chair. On the rug in front of the desk were four tell-tale imprints which showed it had been there a little time before, and if Bettina noticed them and put two and two together then all would be lost. She walked deliberately away so that her captor was forced to turn her head away from the writing-desk.

'I'm not going to write him a note,' she said. 'You can't

always get your way by waving a gun at people, you know. Shoot me if you like, but it won't do you any good. You'll have nothing to bargain with, Edgar still won't be here and you'll have another murder on your head, as well as Rolf. If you want Edgar go and find him yourself and leave me out of it, but if he's as keen to go back to the old life as you seem to think then I dare say he'll turn up looking for you sooner or later. And if he's not, then he'll turn up looking for *me*. Either way, you don't need my help.'

Angela held her breath, willing herself to show no trepidation, for La Duchessa was mercurial and unpredictable. Who knew how she would react to a flat refusal? A few years ago Edgar had offended her and she had shot him, while only two days ago Rolf had tried to take the Mariensee diamond and she had dispatched him ruthlessly. Would she do the same to Angela now?

But it seemed Bettina had recognized the force of her argument: there was nothing to be gained from killing Angela —for now, at least. La Duchessa glanced at the gun in her hand and gave Angela a calculating stare.

'Very well,' she said at last. 'Refuse if you wish. But you are only harming yourself, because now you will have to wait here until he comes.'

And with that she left the room. Angela let out a thankful breath. One thing she was sure of was that it would be highly unwise of her to write that note, for once La Duchessa had it and knew where Edgar was, there was no reason why she should keep Angela alive, and Angela was not in a mood to die that day. Nor was she in a mood to wait for Edgar to turn up—on the contrary, she had every intention of getting out of the house as soon as she could by her own efforts. She turned her attention once more to the matter of the hatch, but she had barely taken two steps towards the little table she hoped to stand on when Werner came in with tea, just as though she were any other guest. His manners were impassive and impeccably polite, but he made it clear that he had been given orders not to let her leave. He refused to engage in conversation on any subject other than that of milk and sugar, and merely ignored the questions Angela put to him about the whereabouts of Benjamin Roche.

As soon as Werner at last went away with the tea things she went to examine the table in the corner. It was heavy and awkward, but it might just fit—but only if the cupboard were completely empty. With a sigh Angela returned to the cupboard and began lifting things out, but had barely removed a pail or two when Werner came in again to find out if there was anything she needed, and she was forced to come out of the passage again and reply. A few minutes later he was in again. She could hardly claim she was visiting the lavatory each time, and since she did not wish him to become suspicious about her continued absence from the sitting-room, she gave it up for the present.

It seemed like endless hours of frustration. Werner came in at frequent intervals, while she read books from the bookshelf and thought about the hatch in the cupboard. As darkness fell Werner brought her some food on a tray, which she regarded with distaste.

'Am I to stay here all night?' she asked.

'No, *madame*, you are to be accommodated in one of the bedrooms once you have finished your meal,' he replied.

Angela was horror-struck. If they took her to a different room then all her plans would come to naught. She cast around wildly for an excuse.

'That's very kind of you,' she said. 'But it's rather too early to be going to bed. You wouldn't mind if I stayed here a little longer, would you? I don't suppose there's much to do in the bedroom, whereas here I have plenty of books to keep me entertained.'

She indicated the bookshelf.

Werner hesitated.

'Very well, *madame*, it makes no difference. I shall come and fetch you at ten o'clock.'

She hid her relief and thanked him graciously, and at length he departed with the tray containing the remains of her supper.

As he had promised, he returned at ten o'clock to find her apparently sound asleep on a divan. He coughed delicately, then called her name, but she did not respond. He hovered, and seemed to be debating with himself as to what to do. At last he left, turning the light off as he went out, and Angela heard the key turn in the lock. With any luck he had decided to leave her there for the night. At last she was alone. She would give it ten minutes and then make her escape.

## Chapter Twenty-Four

ANGELA OPENED her eyes and wondered why she was feeling so cold, and why her bed felt so hard. After a second she remembered where she was and why, and to her great disgust realized that she had fallen asleep. A beam of moonlight shone brightly in through the window, and she looked at her watch and found it was just after midnight. At least she had not slept the whole night through, and need not call herself a total disgrace. Besides, she could be reasonably sure that Werner had gone to bed by now and would not disturb her.

There was no time to lose, so she stood up and set to work. After a very few minutes she had cleared the things out from the cupboard, and had found among them a torch, which she took. Then she carried the little table through from the sitting-room, set it on the floor under the hatch and placed the chair on top, observing with annoyance as she did so that her smart trousers, which she had bought only a few weeks earlier, were not fit to be seen. Dressing to the latest fashion was all very well for the social whirl of the Riviera, but white was not the best colour for emptying cupboards and clambering through trapdoors into dusty attics; nor were heels the most practical choice of footwear for creeping quietly around a house at night. Still, it could not be helped.

With the added height she had no difficulty in pulling herself through the hatch. It was pitch dark up here, and she switched on the torch. As she had expected, she found herself in a sort of attic space under the flat roof. It was bare, and obviously unused. She crept forward, taking care to make as little sound as possible in case somebody in a room below heard her footsteps. Ahead of her was a door which led to another attic space—a much larger one, this time. From there another door led to another room, then another, and she began to be afraid she would get lost and be unable to find her way back. In the fourth room, however, she spied another hatch in the floor and pounced upon it. To her frustration she could not lift it; it must be fastened on the other side. She grimaced and carried on. She was just beginning to think that she would never find another way down when she emerged through a door and into a kind of box-room that was evidently much more frequented than any of the rooms she had passed through previously. From here a flight of stairs led down to a door. Angela's heart leapt, but sank again when she found it was locked.

But the same stairs also led upwards to another door. This one was unlocked. There was no other way to go, so Angela went through it and found herself on the roof, under the stars. It was boarded underfoot, and furnished as a terrace, with deck-chairs and tables positioned in such a way as to afford the best view. It was a fine night and the moon cast a silvery glow over the scene, but Angela had no time to appreciate the sight. She must find a way out. She knew from their investigations of the day before that from here a flight of steps led down to the garden, and she found them and hurried down them. The gate to the stairs had been locked yesterday, and there was not much hope that someone had opened it in the meantime, but she had to try.

As she had expected, the gate was still locked. Undaunted, she returned to the roof and looked about her. This part of the terrace, overlooking the sea, was surrounded by a wall, but at the rear an opening in the wall led to that section of the roof which covered the back of the house. This area was not set out as a terrace, and was evidently not intended to be used as such. It was dirty and unswept, and looked as though it were never used. At the far end of it was another door. Angela tried it, expecting it to be locked, but to her surprise and relief she found it was not. She went in and down several flights of stairs, and at length found herself on a landing in a part of the house she did not recognize. It was unexpectedly dark here, and Angela realized that this side of the house must get little light as a rule—either from the sun or the moon—backing on to the cliff as it did. She switched on the torch cautiously and stood a moment to get her bearings. The big entrance-hall through which they had entered on the night of the party was on the cliff side of the house, and must be a floor or two down. The front door seemed as good a way as any to leave, but how to get there? Cautiously she pushed open a door and was pleased to find another flight of stairs leading downwards.

At the bottom was another passage, this one dimly lit. By now she was rather lost, but as far as she could tell, it led towards the entrance-hall. She was just about to enter the passage when a door at the end of it opened and La Duchessa came through. Instantly Angela retreated into the darkness of the stairs, hoping against hope that she would not come this way. But La Duchessa passed the entrance to the stairs without so much as looking up, then disappeared. Quickly and silently Angela slipped out and went the way Bettina had come. La Duchessa had left the door ajar, but as Angela passed she noticed it was furnished with several locks, one of which had a key protruding from it. Presumably the door was not left open as a rule, and Angela guessed that La Duchessa would be back soon, if only to lock it again.

The door did not lead to the entrance-hall at all, but into a room. At first Angela thought it was the room that held Benjamin Roche's collection of historic jewellery, and from which the necklace that had belonged to the lady-in-waiting of the Empress Joséphine had been stolen. But the impression was only momentary, for this was not the same room: the ceiling was much lower, for a start, and it was laid out differently. Just as in the other room, however, the furnishings were antique, and there were paintings on the walls, as well as many display cabinets containing *objets d'art* of various description. In the centre of the room a comfortable chair and a low table had been set in such a position as to afford the best view of everything.

There was no way out, except by the door through which she had just come, and Angela was just about to leave quickly before La Duchessa came back, when her attention was arrested by something. A large painting on the wall in front of her seemed familiar to her, and her mouth fell open as she remembered what it was. A year or two ago there had been a daring robbery from an art gallery, during which many valuable paintings had been stolen. The most mourned loss had been a battle scene by the French master Delacroix, and photographs of it had appeared in all the newspapers at the time. This was the very same painting, Angela was almost sure of it.

She looked about her, observing more closely this time, and saw a vase that resembled one of the objects from a collection of Chinese porcelain that she had read about as having been stolen from an auction house in New York earlier that year, although she could not be certain. Were all these things stolen, then? Angela stepped further into the room and surveyed it carefully. Around the walls, just as in the room she had seen the other day, were glass cases containing necklaces, diadems, bracelets and other articles of jewellery that were obviously extremely valuable. By this time her suspicions were coalescing rapidly into certainties. She walked along the row of cases and stopped in front of one of them. Inside it, she was not at all surprised to see something which was wholly familiar to her. There it sat in pride of place on a bed of dark blue velvet, where it had no doubt been ever since the night of Benjamin Roche's party. The low light of the room had dimmed its sparkle, but there was no mistaking it.

'The Mariensee diamond,' Angela murmured to herself.

She stared at it thoughtfully. The many hours which she had spent at La Falaise had given her plenty of time to ruminate on things and come to certain conclusions—one of which was that Mr. Roche would not be especially astonished to find Bettina in his house—and now here was proof that her surmise was correct.

Benjamin Roche was the buyer whose name La Duchessa had guarded so jealously. He had concealed himself well, in among the highest circles of society, and his connections with the rich and aristocratic had brought him into contact with many objects of value from which to pick and choose. La Duchessa could not possibly be the only thief of his acquaintance, for his tastes were clearly not confined to valuable jewellery. Presumably he had only to see something he wanted, and with a word in the right ear it would be his.

Everything was explained now. Bettina had been intending to have Edgar exchange the Mariensee diamond for a fake at the party then pass it on to Roche, but she had found out at the last minute that the Boehlers were planning to snatch the jewel from under her nose. She had acted swiftly, intercepting Rolf as he tried to escape down the cliff path, silencing him ruthlessly and taking the diamond back from him. She could not dispose of Rolf herself so had hurried back indoors to fetch help—presumably from Werner—but in the meantime Angela and Freddy had stumbled upon the body, disrupting her quick-thinking attempts to salvage the situation. The reason for the theft of Roche's necklace was also clear now:

Roche had faked the robbery and the attack in order to divert suspicion away from himself. Had the original plan worked then nobody would have known even that the jewel had been stolen, but the Boehlers in their greed had spoilt everything.

Angela walked slowly from case to case, marvelling at all the beautiful things which Roche had hidden away in this secret room to gloat over privately. Then a creak of floorboards under her feet brought her to herself, and she remembered why she was here and what she was supposed to be doing. There was no time to waste: she must get out of here before anybody found out she had discovered the room. She was halfway to the door when she thought of the diamond and stopped. She really ought not to leave the house without it. But if she were caught while trying to get out, they would certainly discover what she had done, and she did not give much for her chances of staying alive if they did. However, if she *did* get out and went to the police without the diamond, would they believe her story of Benjamin Roche and his collection of stolen goods? He was a well-respected newspaper proprietor with an unassailable position in society, and it was by no means certain that anybody would listen to her extraordinary tale.

Angela was about to give it up and leave when she suddenly remembered something and almost laughed out loud. She put a hand into her pocket and brought out the paste diamond, which she had taken earlier, intending to give it back to Mrs. Weeks. Could she get away with it? There was no harm in trying. After all, the most important thing was the recovery of the jewel. Bringing the thieves to justice was a merely secondary consideration.

She turned back to the case in which Roche had placed the real Mariensee diamond, and to her relief found it was not locked—presumably there was no need, since this room was secret and usually fastened securely. Angela gave the fake diamond a quick polish and made the substitution, then, just to be on the safe side, pinned the real diamond to the inside of her waist-band. She had just closed the lid of the case when she heard footsteps approaching along the corridor and almost jumped out of her skin. Any second now whoever it was would come in and discover her. Glancing about for a hiding-place, she slipped behind the large wooden case housing the Chinese porcelain just as La Duchessa entered and went straight to a cabinet at the far corner of the room. Quickly, while her back was turned, Angela slipped out then bolted down the corridor and through a door at the other end. To her enormous relief she at last found the entrance-hall and made a dart for the front door. She was just struggling with the bolts when her run of good luck came to an end.

'There is no use in trying to get out that way,' came Werner's voice. 'The key is not in the lock.'

She started and whirled round, and saw him standing before her. He approached the door and fastened the bolts again.

'It is a good thing I thought to come and see whether you required anything,' he went on. 'I did not expect you to try and escape through the attic. Now, you will come with me and we will put you in one of the spare bedrooms, as I had intended earlier. Please.'

He indicated to her to go ahead of him, and she had no choice but to comply.

## Chapter Twenty-Five

WHEN VALENCOURT TURNED up very early the next morning he found Angela calmly having breakfast with La Duchessa in the dining-room.

'We have another visitor,' announced Werner as he brought Valencourt in. 'I have taken his gun. It is rude when the ladies are eating,' he added.

A complacent look spread across Bettina's face.

'I knew you would come sooner or later,' she said.

Valencourt had cleaned off the blood as best he could, but several nasty bruises were forming around his eye and down the side of his face. Angela gasped at the sight of him.

'Oh, goodness me!'

He favoured her with a hard stare.

'I want a word with you,' he said. 'What the devil possessed you to come here? Are you quite mad?'

'It wasn't—I didn't mean—I was invited to *tea*!' she exclaimed, flustered.

'Why did you take so long?' asked La Duchessa.

'I had an appointment with Fritz,' he replied.

Angela had come towards him and was staring in horror at his injuries.

'With Fritz? I thought you were supposed to be keeping away from him. Why in heaven's name did you go looking for him?'

'Because I thought he had you. But it seems he didn't, and you were here all along having *tea*,' he said pointedly.

'But are you all right?'

'As it happens, yes—no thanks to you.'

She bridled.

'How is it my fault? I didn't ask you to—do whatever it is you've been doing. And I didn't tell anyone where you were, either, so why did you come here? There was no need—I was managing perfectly well without you.'

His eyes took in her appearance. She was grubby and dishevelled from her adventure in the attic, with streaks of dirt on her face and a tear in the knee of her trousers. The corners of his mouth twitched slightly.

'So I see,' he said.

She scrubbed at her face self-consciously.

'But what happened? Where is Fritz now?' she asked.

'He's dead.'

'That is good,' said Bettina with satisfaction. 'Now I will not have to kill him.'

Valencourt strode across to her.

'Listen, Bettina, what's the meaning of all this?' he said. 'Why did you bring Angela here?'

'I was waiting for you but you did not come, so I had to take certain measures, that is all. It was most inconvenient. You ought to have told me where you had gone.'

'What was it to you where I went? I told you this was the last time and I wasn't going to do any more. It wasn't my fault things went wrong, but you could hardly expect me to stick around and wait while you put them right. After all, it wasn't my job—I was only doing it on sufferance.'

'That is not true,' said La Duchessa. 'That is what you said, but I could see you were eager to do it. It made you alive again, did it not?' She approached him and stood before him, her eyes glittering. 'But why stop now? Why live in dullness and quiet when there is excitement to be had? It is a sport, a game. You may think you have given it up, but that is impossible, because it will never give *you* up. Do not think you can escape it, because it will run in your blood forever.' She eyed him, looking to see the effect of her words. 'Now, I have a little idea up my sleeve for the next few days, but it is in Paris and we must leave today, or it will be too late. What do you say? It will be very easy and very fun.'

He said nothing, and she went on, speaking to him in a language Angela did not recognize. He replied in the same tongue and they fell into animated discussion. Angela did not know what they were saying, but from Bettina's gestures it was obvious they were talking about her, and it did not take any great perception to deduce that Bettina was urging him to leave her and come to Paris instead. Angela could not contribute to the conversation, and since they had ceased to pay any attention to her and her breakfast was getting cold, she went to sit down again. Bettina had begun a long diatribe, but eventually she was forced to pause for breath, and subsided into a temporary silence.

'So, then,' said Angela sweetly to Valencourt, as she spread butter on a croissant. 'Have you decided whether or not to run off together without me? Ought I to leave you discreetly alone? One doesn't wish to play gooseberry.'

'Don't be ridiculous,' he replied. 'Bettina, there's no use in continuing this. I told you before, that was the last one. If you have a job arranged in Paris I suggest you go and find someone else to help you. Now, I have things to do so if it's all the same to you I'll be off.' He turned to Angela. 'Are you coming? Or would you prefer to stay and finish your *tea*?'

Angela abandoned the croissant and stood up, a sensation of triumph swelling secretly in her breast.

'Of course I'm coming,' she said, as though it did not much matter one way or the other.

But La Duchessa was not about to let them go as easily as that.

'Stop!' she snapped, and Angela saw she had brought the gun out again and was pointing it at them both. Now she was angry, and Angela was reminded vividly of a similar scene in Italy some two years earlier, which had ended badly. But she had no time to react when there was an interruption.

'Bettina!' came a voice, and they all whirled round to see Benjamin Roche standing with Werner by the door. He had obviously just returned from somewhere, for he was still wearing his hat. He handed it to Werner, who took it and retreated silently. Angela noticed that Edgar had stiffened, and that the temperature seemed to have dropped by one or two degrees. Roche ignored both of them and directed his attention at Bettina.

'What do you think you are doing? What kind of behaviour is this in my house? Did I not tell you to keep out of sight and make yourself inconspicuous?'

'This is my own business,' she replied. 'If you had come back this afternoon as you were supposed to, you would have known nothing of it.'

'And you think that is an excuse?'

Gone was his usual genial manner; now his eyes were cold and hard. He walked slowly across to La Duchessa.

'Upon my word, Bettina, you have already displeased me with the fiasco of the diamond, but now you add this to it?'

She was unapologetic and defiant.

'You know very well the diamond was not my fault. The plan was perfectly good.'

'Perhaps so—if it had gone ahead. But it did not. It is of the utmost importance that attention should not be brought down upon my house. It was already a great risk to do the job here, but I allowed it on the condition that there should be a quiet exchange, and that nobody should know it had been taken until no suspicion could possibly fall upon me.' He shook his head in disbelief. 'But instead you allied yourself with those imbeciles, who decided to take matters into their own hands and make a big noise by snatching the jewel before the eyes of three hundred people.'

'And what if they did? I got it for you in the end, as I promised.'

He stared at her coldly.

'You did, but at what cost? Murder? In my own garden? The last thing I wanted to do at my own party was to waste time in instructing my servants to dispose of dead men—especially since Werner was not quick enough, and the body was seen before he could get rid of it. And then I had to make a big show of myself by pretending I had been robbed too, just to make sure that nobody suspected I had anything to do with it. And now the police are here every day, asking stupid questions, and instead of remaining quiet and out of sight you bring people here and threaten them loudly like some common street criminal. You,' he snapped, turning to Werner, who had just come back in. 'My house is not to be used for this kind of thing. Why did you allow it to happen?'

Werner looked uncomfortable.

'I beg your pardon, *monsieur*,' he replied. 'I thought—'

'You did not think, that is the trouble. Bettina is excitable and headstrong, but that is no reason to allow yourself to be swept along by her ill-considered schemes. You will not do this again.'

'No, *monsieur*,' said Werner.

Roche turned his attention to Angela, and resumed his old, courteous manner.

'I am deeply sorry you had to see all this, Mrs. Marchmont. A little domestic disarrangement, shall we say?'

'Oh, quite,' replied Angela, nonplussed. 'May we go now?'

She was not very hopeful that he would say yes, and he did not.

'No, my dear,' he answered. 'I'm afraid there's the little matter of the diamond, which must remain a secret.'

'Look here, Roche,' said Edgar. 'Leave Angela alone—she's with me and won't talk. The police think the Boehlers took the jewel, and there's nothing to connect you with the job at all. It's perfectly safe to let her go.'

Roche pursed his lips in a negative.

'I cannot risk it. I am sorry.' He regarded Valencourt thoughtfully. 'By the way, I understand you have retired. Perhaps that means you are no longer to be trusted either. Yes, perhaps it is as well to be on the safe side. I regret it, since you have brought me some very pretty things in the past.'

'You said you didn't know who he was. Oh, Edgar,' said Angela, looking at Valencourt reproachfully.

'One doesn't snitch,' he replied stiffly.

'But if you'd told me in the first place, I'd never have come here.'

'You ought to have had the sense not to anyway.'

'I don't think the way you do. When anyone invites me to their house it's generally because they want to give me nice things to eat and drink, and play music on the gramophone, and talk about the theatre. I can't remember the last time one of my friends pointed a gun at me.'

'Werner,' said Roche with a nod, as Angela and Valencourt glared at one another. 'Take them away. Do not make a mess and make sure they are not found.'

Angela looked round and saw that Werner had also furnished himself with a revolver. It was clear their captors meant business. She glanced at Valencourt, who was not looking at her now, but at La Duchessa.

'Bettina,' he said. But she was not to be won over.

'Goodbye,' she replied composedly. 'It is a pity. I liked you very much, once. I wish you well of him,' she said, addressing Angela. 'Even if it will not be for very long.'

'Please.' Werner indicated towards the door with the gun.

Angela was thinking rapidly, and regretting not having made a grab for Bettina's gun when she had had the chance. They would have to act fast, but what could they do?

At that moment the doorbell rang. Roche darted a glance at his manservant.

'Give me the gun, and answer it,' he said. 'Do not let them in.'

Angela held her breath, listening. Roche would not shoot them while there were people at the door, for the sound would be heard. Then came voices, one in particular raised above all the others, and at the familiar sound she felt a wave of relief rushing over her.

'What the devil took him so long?' murmured Valencourt, who did not seem surprised at the interruption.

Werner returned, looking taken aback.

'It is the Prime Minister, with the police and M. Pilkington-Soames,' he said.

Freddy was already talking as he entered. He, too, looked as though he had been in a fight. He waggled his eyebrows at Angela and Valencourt as he strolled into the room.

'Terribly sorry to barge in, old bean. Werner didn't want to let us in but I felt the case was urgent enough to require an elbow in the ribs. Good news! We've found the men who took the Mariensee diamond and your necklace, and we thought we'd better let you know. It's been an eventful night, all told. Poor old Jacques Fournier had an unfortunate lapse of judgment and nearly found himself at one with the Mediterranean trying to put it right. He's sleeping it off now, but the doctors say he'll get over it. His governor here has had rather a shock and wants a word with you, Mr. Roche.'

Roche had slipped the gun smoothly into his pocket at the visitors' entrance, and he stepped forward to shake the hand of the Prime Minister, who looked tired and drawn, and as though he had had a trying night of it.

'You have caught the thieves who stole the Mariensee diamond, you say?' inquired Roche. 'I am very pleased to hear it. Who are they?'

'A gang called the Boehlers,' replied Freddy. 'The ring-leaders are dead now, and Chief Inspector Guichard here has another two in custody. Desperate fellows, they were—put up no end of a fight, I can tell you, but I was lucky enough to wrestle a gun off one of them, and after that the thing could go only one way.'

'My son has been very foolish,' said Fournier, 'but I have this brave young man to thank for the fact that he is still alive. M. Pilkington-Soames single-handedly rescued him, dispatched one member of a very violent and dangerous gang, and captured another two.'

'It was nothing,' said Freddy modestly.

Chief Inspector Guichard looked as though he did not believe a word of it, but maintained a judicious silence.

'Oh, Freddy!' exclaimed Angela. 'I'm so terribly pleased you're safe. Why, you might have been killed!'

She flew at him as she spoke and flung her arms around him. Freddy looked somewhat startled.

'Steady on, old girl, there's no need for that, I'm quite all right.'

She disentangled herself, looking slightly embarrassed.

'Yes, of course. It's been a long night, and I was a little overcome, that's all.'

She turned away, ignoring Valencourt's surprised look at the display, which was most unlike her.

'My friend,' said the Prime Minister to Roche. 'This comes at a most delicate time, and we must find a way to keep the real story out of the papers. Jacques has been extraordinarily stupid, and I shall deal with him, but in the meantime it is of the utmost importance that the reparations conference continues. Nothing else matters. The men who stole the Mariensee diamond have been apprehended, yes, but the jewel has still not been found, and M. Weeks is most upset. Together you and I must persuade him that the talks are more important than his wife's brooch. I rely on your diplomacy. My wife is with my son now, as is the young lady Miss Weeks, who fortunately seems inclined to forgive his mistake. Perhaps her influence and ours together will help convince M. Weeks not to pull out of the talks.'

Freddy, who had been looking at Angela thoughtfully, gave a theatrical start.

'Good Lord—I'd completely forgotten! I'm most awfully sorry.' He stepped forward and produced something from his pocket. It was the brooch which Angela had pressed into his hand only moments before. 'I don't know what I was thinking, only I got so distracted with making sure that young Fournier was safe that it must have quite slipped my mind.' He handed the brooch to Chief Inspector Guichard. 'I got it off Fritz Boehler in my last struggle with him on the boat. A stroke of luck, eh? But for the grace of God it might be at the bottom of the sea by now.'

Guichard looked down at the brooch in his hand, then up at Freddy, a suspicious expression dawning on his face.

'You say you got this from Fritz Boehler in a fight? You told me something similar not two days ago. But the diamond you gave us then was a fake.'

'It does seem rather odd that the same thing should happen twice, doesn't it? I had no idea the other one wasn't real when I gave it to you. Let's just hope we've got the right one this time.'

'I'm sure you have,' said Angela, nodding vigorously.

Fournier's face had lit up at the sight of the diamond in the chief inspector's hand.

'Can it be true?' he said. 'This is the Mariensee diamond, you say?'

'If it is the real one,' replied Guichard.

'But how can we tell?'

Roche was staring at the diamond in some perplexity.

'If I might take a look,' he suggested. 'I have some little expertise in these things. Werner, fetch me my eye-glass.'

Werner departed immediately and returned with the requested article. Roche applied it to his eye and examined the brooch, as Angela very carefully avoided looking at anyone. There was a silence as everybody waited for Roche's conclusion. At last he removed the eye-glass.

'It appears this is the real jewel,' he said in a level tone.

'*Mon dieu*!' cried Fournier. 'You have saved the diamond! This is of the most wonderful news! Guichard, we must go at once and give it back to Mme. Weeks, and let M. Weeks know that his jewel has been found.'

He seized Freddy and kissed him resoundingly on both cheeks, much to Freddy's dismay.

'My dear young man, I do not think it is too much to say that you have saved these most important talks—and perhaps also the honour of France.'

'Oh, I say, what?' said Freddy.

'My friend Roche, I implore your help,' went on Fournier. 'I have heard that some of the foreign newspapers have got hold of the story and are about to publish it. You must make a big sensation in *Le Moniteur* and let the world know that the diamond is safe and that the talks will be a success. Young man, I thank you from the bottom of my heart.'

'It was my pleasure,' said Freddy, slightly guiltily.

'I do not suppose you also have the necklace of the lady-in-waiting of the Empress Joséphine in your pocket?' inquired Chief Inspector Guichard.

'I'm afraid not.'

'Then we shall continue to search for it.'

Benjamin Roche waved a hand.

'My necklace is of little importance. The diamond was the vital thing, and I am overjoyed that you have found it.'

Fournier just then spotted La Duchessa, who had been observing events in silence.

'I beg your pardon for the interruption, *madame*,' he said.

Bettina was nothing if not shameless.

'Not *madame*,' she said. 'I am La Duchessa di Alassio. I am charmed to meet you, M. Fournier.'

She held out her hand and he bent over it. Chief Inspector Guichard, who had glanced up suddenly at the mention of the name, looked as though he were about to say something, but thought better of it.

Angela and Valencourt had begun edging towards the door.

'Ah, but do not let me spoil your little party,' said M. Fournier. 'You must not go now.'

'It's quite all right, M. Fournier,' replied Angela. 'We were about to leave anyway.'

'I'll come with you,' said Freddy. 'It's been a long night, and a few hours' shut-eye wouldn't go amiss.'

The Prime Minister waved his hand.

'Yes, yes, you deserve a rest. But please let me know where to find you, M. Pilkington-Soames, for we must speak of this again.'

'Oh, certainly. You'll find me at the Hotel Bellevue for the next few days,' replied Freddy. He looked at Angela and Valencourt. 'Shall we go?'

'I do hope you enjoy your trip to Paris, Your Excellency,' said Angela to Bettina. It was a low shot, but she could not help herself.

La Duchessa made no reply, but watched them inscrutably through half-closed eyes as they went out.

## Chapter Twenty-Six

FREDDY SLEPT until half past eleven, then got up and went downstairs to find Angela reading a book on the terrace in the sunshine. She looked up and smiled as he approached.

'I didn't expect to see you until two o'clock at the earliest,' she said.

'Someone woke me up rattling about outside in the corridor. Where's Valencourt?'

'Exhausted and fast asleep in my room.'

'So much for discretion.'

'Hang discretion. I was hardly going to pack him off back to Nice in his state. He needed cleaning up at the very least, so I did that and put him to bed and told him to sleep it off. I expect he'll be rather sore and grumpy when he wakes up, but it won't last long, because I've some good news for him—William has found Nightshade!'

'By Jove, has he really?' said Freddy, who had thought that of all recent events this was the least likely to be resolved satisfactorily.

'Yes. I had a very long and slightly incomprehensible conversation with him this morning, after he'd just got back from wherever it was he'd been. As I suspected, the temptation was too much for Gino, and instead of holding onto the horse for the Boehlers, he sold it to a trainer of dubious reputation. William had to threaten him with who knows what to get the information out of him, then he took some of Edgar's men and went to get it back. They had to bribe some people and thump some others, but Nightshade is back home now, safe and sound. From what William told me it sounds as though he'd been brawling his way across New York State. He has two black eyes and what sounds to me like a broken rib, but that's just his sort of adventure. I'm sure he had a marvellous time.'

'It sounds like it,' replied Freddy.

'So, how do you like being a hero?' she inquired. 'The news is all over the hotel about how you defeated Fritz and got the Mariensee diamond back.'

'I say,' said Freddy uncomfortably. 'I don't like taking the credit for all this, you know.'

'You're more than welcome to it. It's much better if Edgar and I stay out of it. He's not exactly anxious to spend time in the company of the police, which is what he'd have to do if it were known he was there on the boat with you.'

'Still, though, it doesn't sit well with me. I didn't do anything, really.'

'Nonsense. You saved Edgar's life—and mine. If you hadn't turned up at La Falaise when you did I dare say we'd have gone over the balustrade just like Rolf. Why did you bring the Prime Minister, incidentally?'

'Well, by the time we got young Fournier back to shore it was getting late—or early, rather. We brought him back to the hotel and got him a doctor, and were just about to let the Weekses know what had happened when as luck would have it his father turned up with R. G. Weeks himself and Guichard. Naturally, explanations had to be made, but Valencourt couldn't very well appear in the story, and besides he was still frantic about you. He was pretty sure Roche was behind the theft of the diamond and knew he was more dangerous than he looked, so he hared off to get you while I did all the talking. As soon as I could I made my excuses, and was going to scoot along to La Falaise brandishing Gaston's revolver to do my bit, but the P. M. was so fearfully keen to come and speak to Roche himself that I thought, why not? Guns are all very well, but sometimes it's better to use the old noodle. Besides, I'd had enough of the rough stuff for one night, and I'm no sort of shot anyway, so there's every chance I'd have done nothing but bring down a chandelier if I'd started firing at people.'

'As it turns out, you did exactly the right thing,' said Angela. 'And so did the Prime Minister, with all his flattery. If there's anything Roche cares about more than his collection of stolen objects it's his reputation. He does like to be thought influential.'

'I wonder how long he's been doing all this shady stuff.'

'To judge by his secret room, many years. Edgar told me once about a mysterious rich collector and buyer of stolen goods, and I suspect he was referring to Roche, although he claimed at the time he didn't know the man's identity.'

'La Duchessa will have some explaining to do,' said Freddy. 'My word—I shouldn't like to have been in her shoes after we all left La Falaise and she had to tell Roche exactly how she lost the diamond they both went to such trouble to get their mitts on—especially after she'd already offended him by letting the Boehlers get out of hand. I wonder whether she and Roche have worked out what happened yet. They can't possibly believe the story that I got the thing in my deadly struggle with Fritz.'

'I imagine they went straight into his secret room after we left and put two and two together. Werner knows I was wandering around the house in the middle of the night, so they must have realized by now what I was doing.'

'That was quick thinking with the diamond on your part,

by the way. I didn't know what you were playing at for a moment.'

'Nor did I, really—I thought of it quite on the spur of the moment. When you turned up with the police and Mr. Fournier I was going to hand it over to Guichard immediately, but then I saw the Prime Minister fawning all over Roche while Edgar stood there, covered in bruises and looking particularly disreputable. It was perfectly obvious which one of them would end up getting the blame if I handed it over, so I decided the safest thing all round was to give it to you instead and let everyone think Fritz had taken it.'

A dissatisfied expression fleetingly crossed her face. Freddy thought he understood it. At one time she would have insisted on doing everything she could to bring Roche and La Duchessa to justice, but now she could not risk it without bringing Valencourt into it. No, the world must be allowed to believe that the Boehlers had been wholly responsible for the theft of the Mariensee diamond, and Angela and Valencourt must fade into the background as soon as possible, while Roche and La Duchessa would get off scot-free. It was hardly satisfactory, but what choice did they have?

They were interrupted just then by Jessie Weeks, who wanted to thank Freddy for restoring her diamond to her.

'I could hardly believe it when Garnet told me what the silly boy had done,' she said. 'Allowing himself to be blackmailed like that. Why, it hardly bears thinking about! It wasn't his fault at all—it seems this Archambault had manoeuvred him into a difficult position, and when it looked like coming out into the open Jacques was forced to lie about it publicly to protect his father. But of course if the papers had found out about the lie then the whole scandal would have started up again, and for it to happen just at this time, with the talks and everything, would have been terrible.'

'I gather he was trying to put things right when the gang got hold of him,' said Freddy.

'Yes—he went to their hide-out to tell them he wouldn't be part of it any more, but I guess they were scared he would talk so they roughed him up and kidnapped him. Mr. Fournier is saying he ought to be punished for what he did, but if you ask me he's already been punished enough. They hurt him so badly, I was shocked to see it! I know I ought to be angry, but the poor boy is in such a state and so sorry for what he did that I can't find it in my heart to stay mad at him. Garnet, poor dear, declares she won't leave his bedside. She's trying to persuade Randall not to make a fuss about it now that the diamond has been returned.'

It looked as though Mrs. Weeks and her daughter had already decided to forgive Jacques Fournier, and Freddy suspected the matter would never be made public, since everything had been resolved to the satisfaction of all. Benjamin Roche in particular had every reason to keep the truth quiet, and to publish only a version of the story that kept him well out of it, while it would benefit no-one to reveal young Fournier's rôle in the affair.

Freddy escaped Mrs. Weeks at last and went up to the Villa des Fleurs. He was greeted by Great-Aunt Ernestine, who could talk of nothing else but the news of the diamond, which was currently spreading throughout the town.

'My dear boy!' she cried. 'I always knew you would be a credit to the family one day. I did not think you could possibly be the disappointment your mother has always claimed. "Cynthia," I told her, "you mark my words—Freddy may be frittering his time away in useless idleness just now, but one must make allowances for youth. You will see: one day that young man will come to good." And I have been proved right. But this is no time to rest. I understand there is an important conference going on—I don't understand politics myself, but I always rather hoped your Great-Uncle Algernon would take an interest in that sort of thing. Alas, he did not, but here is a good chance for you. I hear the French Prime Minister himself regards you with high favour, and perhaps this would be an opportunity for you to begin to make your own mark in the political sphere. Strike while the iron is hot, as the old proverb has it.'

'That's very kind of you, Aunt E, but I don't think it's quite my sort of thing,' said Freddy. 'Where are Nugs and Baba?'

'In the garden.' She lowered her voice. 'I think we may have good news at last. It appears there has been a cooling of relations with the Comte de Langlois. Cecily does not tell me anything, but he did not come here at all yesterday, or the day before, and rumours have reached me that he is nowhere to be found—in short, has vanished without a trace. I should be delighted to hear the thing has come to an end. As a matter of fact, there seems to have been a rapprochement between Cecily and Lucian, too. You know how I disapprove of Lucian, but at least he is family. Now, go and see what you can find out, and tell me.'

Nugs and Baba were walking around the garden together, arm in arm.

'Hallo, Baba,' said Freddy, eyeing Nugs to see which way the wind was blowing. Nugs gave him a brief nod, and he judged it was safe to proceed. 'I'm sorry your Comte turned out to be a wrong 'un.'

Baba gave a sniff.

'Thank you. Of course, I'd already realized he wasn't quite—quite, you know. There were certain things about his behaviour which I won't mention, but which didn't sit very well with me. And he was disgracefully rude to me at the casino the other night.'

'The damned effrontery of it,' growled Nugs. 'I ought to have horsewhipped him when I had the chance.'

Baba went on:

'I know I got a little caught up in the moment when you made his nose bleed, Nugs, but that was only out of womanly sympathy. Once I'd had a chance to think about things it was obvious that it could never have worked anyway, even if he had been—who he said he was.'

'He was a swindler and a parasite, my dear, and that's the long and short of it. I hope you didn't give him any money.'

'Oh dear, I'm afraid I may have given him just a little—just to defray current expenses, you know. He never asked for much, and he was awfully charming about it. A problem with his bankers, he said. There was some misunderstanding about a cheque once, and some other things. But let's not talk about it any more. I won't waste another thought on him. Men of his sort are dreadfully immature and don't understand the wisdom of a woman who has lived in the world.'

'They most certainly don't,' said Nugs gruffly. 'These whipper-snappers know nothing, Baba.'

She turned to him. In the sunlight she looked rather like a delicate, glittering butterfly, and it was easy to see why he had first fallen in love with her.

'Thank you for defending me the other night, Nugs,' she said. 'It's so nice to have someone on whom one can really rely.'

In reply Nugs took her hand and kissed it, and she fluttered a little.

Freddy judged this a good moment to depart. He bade goodbye to his Great-Aunt Ernestine and returned to the hotel, reflecting with satisfaction on how things had turned out. It was all very well helping to return a priceless jewel and saving the future of France, but there was still his mother to face, and he could now return to London and tell her that thanks to his efforts in Sospel the divorce was off—at least for now.

# Chapter Twenty-Seven

There was a more than usually gay atmosphere in the Hotel Bellevue that evening, for everyone was talking about the extraordinary events of the past few days, and Freddy was in great demand to recount the story of how he had defeated the Boehler gang, returned the Mariensee diamond and saved France. Ordinarily he would have relished all the attention, and would have seized with alacrity the opportunity to hold forth upon his own ingenuity and resourcefulness, but his sense of fairness protested at the fact that he should receive all the praise while others should receive none. He understood the reasons for it, but it felt awkward nonetheless.

Still more awkward was the atmosphere hovering over Angela and Valencourt, who were sitting with Freddy at dinner. A coolness had descended between them, and they spent most of the meal having a complicated and silent conversation with their eyes. Freddy sensed he was surplus to requirements and excused himself as soon as was decently possible, but some time later he found Angela sitting alone in the lounge, looking pensive, and went to join her.

'All set?' he said. 'When do you sail?'

'Tomorrow,' she replied.

'I expect you'll be glad to get away now that everything has been resolved to your satisfaction.'

'Yes.'

She appeared distracted and only half-listening. There was obviously something on her mind. Freddy regarded her keenly.

'What is it, old girl? You both seemed a trifle glum at dinner. Is he still peeved at you for going up to La Falaise?'

'No, it's not that.' She sighed. 'He wants to get married.'

'Congratulations.'

'I've said no.'

'Oh.'

She gave an exasperated shake of the shoulders.

'How can I marry him? It would never work. For a while I thought perhaps it could, because he was living quietly and nobody knew who he was, and I'd half-convinced myself that there wouldn't be any trouble. But Gino has made me realize that he'll never be safe—there'll always be the danger that someone will recognize him. And then what? If he doesn't want to be arrested he'll have to run again, and I can't run with him. I have a daughter to think of now, and I can't just abandon her. I haven't even plucked up the courage yet to tell her he's still alive.'

'Barbara doesn't know?' said Freddy disbelievingly. 'Good God!'

Angela looked defensive.

'She's only just turned sixteen! How can I ask a sixteen-year-old to keep that sort of secret from the police? It's hardly setting a fine moral example, especially when I'm trying to make up to her for everything. But even if Barbara weren't a consideration, what if Edgar has to spend the rest of his life in hiding? What kind of marriage would that be? Always sneaking from place to place, and changing our names, and pretending we're something we're not. I hate all the pretence, and all the lying. You were there this morning—you saw what happened. In the old days I'd have told the truth to Chief Inspector Guichard without a second thought, but I had to keep quiet—and so did you—and so a guilty man goes free. I hate this furtive, secretive life that isn't a life at all. I'd like to be seen with Edgar in public without forever looking over my shoulder for the police. I've had a lifetime of keeping uncomfortable secrets, and I'm tired of it.'

'I say, I'm sorry. I had no idea,' said Freddy.

'But it's not just that,' she went on. 'However you look at it, there's no getting around the fact that he hasn't paid for any of his crimes. For myself I can forgive him—I do forgive him, twenty times over—but they aren't my crimes to forgive. The law is rather stricter about things than I am, and I can't say I disagree. We can't just let criminals wander around unpunished.'

'But you wouldn't like him to go to gaol, surely?'

'No—yes—no, of course not. I'd like him to pay his debt to society, but I don't want him to be arrested. I don't know exactly how many things he's stolen, but I'm sure he'd get at least ten years, if not more, and I might never see him again.'

'Would you marry him, though?' asked Freddy. 'I mean, if he were one of those bankers or farmers you talked about, and if he didn't have an interesting array of criminal charges hanging over his head. Would you say yes?'

'Of course I would, like a shot. You know I would.' She sighed again and looked forlorn. 'But it simply can't be done.'

---

VALENCOURT WAS OUTSIDE, leaning on the terrace rail and smoking. He glanced up as Freddy joined him.

'Would you go to gaol for Angela?' asked Freddy without preamble.

'What?'

'She's rather down in the dumps, and I gather it's over

you. I know it isn't any of my business, of course—'

'No, it isn't,' said Valencourt, eyeing him with disfavour. 'And I'll thank you to keep out of it.'

'I can't, though. I feel responsible for all this, since I was the one who suggested you follow her to America in the first place. Angela's my friend, you see. She's been through a lot, one way or another, and I'd like to see her happy, but the thing standing in the way of that is your unfortunate history.'

'Well, there's not much I can do about that now. She knew what I was when she took up with me—it's not as though I've ever kept it a secret. But I'm not doing it any more. Isn't that enough?'

'If only it were, but you must have realized by now that yours isn't the sort of profession one can simply retire from—at least, not safely. You might have got away with it when everyone thought you were dead, but the cat's out of the bag now and there's no use in pretending things can go back to normal. You know how news gets about, and it's only a matter of time before Gaston or Bruno say something and the police come sniffing after you. I don't know how strongly you feel about Angela, old chap, but you're likely to lose her if you don't do something about it.'

'Did she say that?'

'Not in so many words, but that's the impression I got.'

Valencourt turned to stare moodily out to sea.

'Women bring nothing but trouble,' he said at last. 'By "do something about it" I suppose you mean "give myself up." It's all very well saying I'll lose her if I don't, but she'll lose *me* if I do. I hate to think how many years they'll give me.'

'What if you could get off with a light sentence? I don't know how things work in France, but if you got a good lawyer and confessed to everything you've done like a good boy, then perhaps they might not put you away for too long. After all, it's not as though you're not familiar with the inside of a cell already, is it? Six months would be doable, don't you think?'

'Six months? He'd have to be a *very* good lawyer,' replied Valencourt dryly.

'But would you be prepared to serve a short sentence? If Angela agreed to marry you, I mean?'

'Did she put you up to this?'

'Good Lord, no! She's far too sensible to come up with such an idiotic idea. No, she doesn't know anything about it. I speak as a friend, and entirely off my own bat.'

'Well, then, you're not really serious, are you?'

'I'm never serious except on special occasions, of which this is one. What do you say?'

Valencourt gave it some thought.

'Why, I don't know,' he said finally. 'I suppose I might be prepared to do a short stretch if it would keep her happy and remove the threat of future action against me. But there's no use in asking me, because the idea is ridiculous. It simply can't be done.'

'Funny—that's exactly what Angela said,' said Freddy.

---

NEXT MORNING FREDDY, scrubbed and smartly dressed, presented himself at a grand hotel in Nice, having been summoned to the presence of Michel Fournier, who had much more to say to him on the subject of his daring exploits. After the greetings had been said Freddy inquired after Jacques Fournier.

'He is much better today, I thank you,' replied Fournier. 'Those miscreants treated him very harshly, but I believe he will make a full recovery. And in future I hope he will choose better companions. As for you, M. Pilkington-Soames, there is something I would ask of you. I understand from my friend Roche that you are a reporter for a great and most esteemed publication in London.'

'Oh—er—' said Freddy, who thought this was carrying the

description of the *Clarion* a little too far. 'You might say that.'

'You will understand of course,' went on the Prime Minister, 'that the situation is still somewhat delicate. I have succeeded in persuading M. Weeks not to withdraw from the reparations talks, and we are to return to The Hague soon, but this whole episode has discomposed him greatly, and I believe if any unfavourable stories about my son's involvement in the theft of the jewel were to get into the newspapers, he might decide that the whole thing is too much trouble for him and withdraw.'

'You can rely on my secrecy, sir. I promise I won't breathe a word about your son.'

'Thank you. You will not find me ungrateful for your forbearance. And now we must talk about your actions of the other night. It cannot be that such heroism should go unrewarded. If there is any favour...'

He gestured expansively, as though to indicate that Freddy had only to name his wish.

'As a matter of fact, there *is* something,' said Freddy. 'But first of all I have a confession to make.'

---

'Is this really the only way, my darling?' asked Edgar.

'I'm afraid it is,' replied Angela sadly. 'I've tried to think of another answer but I can't. I can't live like this any more, keeping things secret in this guilty sort of way. I have to think of Barbara.'

'But what if they give me a long spell in prison? There's only so much Fournier can do.'

'We must trust Freddy. He says Mr. Fournier has given him an undertaking that he'll press for leniency. He's awfully grateful to you for what you did, and he'd be giving you and Freddy an award for bravery if it weren't for the need to be discreet about things.'

'Hmph. I'd have been happier if Freddy had taken all the credit and left me out of it.'

'It couldn't have stayed a secret for long—it was only a matter of time before Jacques Fournier remembered there were two of you on the boat and started asking questions. Besides, Freddy was uncomfortable about it. He's not nearly as conceited as he'd have us believe, you know. Underneath it all he's a dear. And as to whether he can get you off lightly—well, if anybody can he can. As a matter of fact, I do believe Freddy can achieve anything he puts his mind to. After all, we wouldn't be here now if it weren't for him. We wouldn't have had this past year. And we've been happy, haven't we?'

'Yes—for the first time in years in my case. I'd forgotten what it was to live a normal life. But it could all end so easily if I agree to this.'

'You don't have to do it,' said Angela. 'I won't make you. If you want to leave me and go somewhere that's safer for you we'll say goodbye now and you can disappear wherever you like and live the life you want, and I'll never think badly of you or tell a soul what I know of you.'

She took a deep breath.

'But if you choose to stay I'll stand by you and wait for you, and if anybody says anything bad about you, or—or about how I feel for you, then I shall have something to say about it. And when you come out I'll be waiting for you as your wife, and I'll hold my head up in public and be proud to be married to the fine man I know you are, whatever people might say about us.'

He looked at her wordlessly, and she went on:

'It's a lot to ask of you, I know. If you don't want to do it, I'll understand. I won't be selfish; I'll let you go.'

She did her best to keep her voice steady as she said it, but could not quite manage it.

'My dearest girl, you don't have to,' he said, as he drew her to him. 'I don't want to run any more.'

# Chapter Twenty-Eight

It was not exactly a romantic or conventional wedding day. The bride wore a pretty, pale blue number she had previously worn to two other weddings and appeared somewhat preoccupied, while the groom looked altogether as though he were in two minds about the whole thing, but since this is a not uncommon state of affairs among bridegrooms, nobody noticed anything particularly unusual in his manner. The ceremony was duly performed—although in the circumstances it was doubtful whether either of the principals were paying much attention, or could remember afterwards what they had vowed to do. Then the groom kissed the bride in a distracted sort of way and they came out of the town hall to find two very smart policemen waiting for them. The final formalities of the day were about to be concluded.

Angela and Edgar glanced at one another, then Angela lifted her chin and said in a clear voice, 'I'd like you to arrest this man. I believe you've been looking for him.'

'Edgar Valencourt de Lisle,' said one of the policemen. 'I arrest you on a charge of theft.'

Valencourt's eyes darted around wildly and he looked for a second as though he were about to make a bolt for it. Then he saw Angela gazing at him fearfully and thought better of it. He gave a sigh.

'Oh, very well, if you must,' he said resignedly. The policemen stepped forward.

'Please don't put him in handcuffs,' begged Angela.

Valencourt held up his hands to indicate that he would go quietly.

'You'd better go now,' he said to her.

'Certainly not! I'm coming to see they treat you nicely. You'd better, or I shall complain to the Prime Minister himself,' she said fiercely to the policemen.

They went off, Angela clasping her new husband's hand tightly and refusing absolutely to let go even when they got into the car. After more than a year of resisting his proposals, now that she had finally given in it seemed she was determined to do the thing properly.

Freddy, who had given the bride away, watched them go then returned to the hotel, for he had one or two things to do: the first being to telegraph his editor at the *Clarion*. He had been away from the office for much longer than a mere attack of German measles warranted, and he was beginning to worry that Mr. Bickerstaffe might have sacked him in his absence. He would have to confess all when he returned, for word of his adventures was bound to filter through to the London newspapers. However, he was confident that Mr. Bickerstaffe would overlook the offence, since Freddy was by way of being hero of the hour, and was bringing home enough material to furnish several days' worth of stories.

He sent his telegram, then went to book his tickets home. He would be travelling alone, for Nugs had decided to remain a few weeks. There had been a reconciliation of sorts with Baba, and they had decided to try again after many years apart. Freddy suspected their current amity was due mainly to the formation of a temporary alliance against Great-Aunt Ernestine, and would last only as long as there was any fun to be had from it, but they seemed happy for now.

The business of the tickets done, he returned to the hotel and went onto the terrace. The Weekses were there with the Prime Minister and his son, who, with the resilience of youth, had insisted on getting out of bed. Jacques and Garnet were sitting next to one another, both looking slightly sheepish. A tall man was sitting with his back to the door, and to his surprise Freddy recognized him as Benjamin Roche.

'Ah, it is you,' said a voice at his side. It was Chief Inspector Guichard. 'May I have a word?'

'Certainly,' replied Freddy. 'Which one would you like? You're not still irked with me about the other night, are you? Sorry and all that, but I really was in rather a hurry. Besides, all's well that ends well, what? The Mariensee diamond has been returned, the talks have been a success, and all the criminals have been brought to justice one way or another.'

'Not all the criminals. You have forgotten the woman who calls herself La Duchessa. And there is the small matter of a dead body which washed up on Cap Ferrat the other day.'

'Ah, yes—Rolf Boehler. Not exactly a loss to the world.'

'Still, I cannot permit that people should go around committing murder,' said Guichard.

'No, I suppose not.'

'Do you know who did it?'

'I rather think it was La Duchessa herself, but I doubt you'll ever get proof of it,' replied Freddy. 'Still, you could try asking her. She's pretty full of herself, so she might even admit to it.'

'I wanted to speak to her yesterday and went up to La Falaise for the purpose, but M. Roche told me she had left suddenly and without telling him where she was going.'

'Women!' said Freddy, shaking his head in mock disapproval. 'They're a law unto themselves.'

'I do not know what M. Roche was thinking, having this

woman under his roof.' Guichard eyed Freddy, who said nothing, then went on:

'Incidentally, I understand there was also a wedding this afternoon between two of the guests at this hotel.'

'Yes, I was there myself. It was all very affecting.'

'I saw their names. Strange—one of them is that of a man who was thought to have died last year.'

'Well, dead men don't tend to get married, so I expect someone typed the wrong word on a report, or something of the kind.'

'Perhaps. At any rate, it is clear that he is still alive. But this man, he was somewhat notorious at one time.'

'Yes, he was a bad lot and no mistake. Reformed now, of course.'

Guichard gave a grunt of disbelief.

'What, Chief Inspector—don't you believe in redemption?'

'Perhaps. But I should not like to be his wife.'

'Oh, she has the measure of him all right, and I dare say she'll keep him straight.'

Guichard hesitated, then lowered his voice.

'You understand it is out of my hands now that the Prime Minister has interested himself in the case. But I should like very much to know: did this Valencourt have something to do with the theft of the jewel?'

'Not exactly,' replied Freddy. 'He was caught up in it accidentally and as far as I know never touched the thing.' He considered a moment, then decided it was time to say something. 'If you really want to know who was behind the whole business, Chief Inspector, you ought to be looking higher up.'

He nodded significantly towards Benjamin Roche, who was at that moment laughing at a joke the Prime Minister had made. Guichard glanced across at Roche and gave a huff of resigned amusement. He did not seem surprised.

'It is known.' He shrugged and held his hands out. 'I hear

stories, many stories. But you see the company he keeps. There is nothing that can be done. Perhaps one day.'

'Perhaps one day,' repeated Freddy.

Across the terrace, Benjamin Roche could be heard taking his leave of the little group. He stood up, and the Prime Minister stood up likewise, then the two men shook hands and Roche prepared to depart. As he went out he saw Freddy and paused for a second, then gave him a gracious nod. Freddy nodded in reply, and he and Guichard watched Roche's retreating figure as he left the hotel.

---

LATE IN THE afternoon Angela returned and came to find Freddy on the terrace. She was still wearing her wedding frock and looked slightly dazed by the whole thing.

'All serene?' asked Freddy.

'As much as one can expect,' she replied. 'The lawyer was there—very old and dignified, and wearing lots of medals. He took charge and told me not to worry and said they'd do the best they could.'

'I didn't expect you to turn him in yourself.'

'It was Edgar's idea. Now nobody can accuse me of having harboured him.'

'How long do you think they'll give him?'

'I don't know. Mr. Fournier says there's only so much he can do, but he's pulling as many diplomatic strings as possible and saying Edgar is a credit to France. If he admits to everything and promises to be good from now on they're hoping he'll be out in less than a year. A year! What have I done?'

She looked stricken.

'It might have been so much longer,' said Freddy.

'I know, but this is the second time I've sent him to gaol, and I'm awfully afraid it's going to become a habit. He didn't just steal things in France, you see. There were other countries, too. Mr. Fournier made noises about diplomatic protection, but I think that might be stretching things a little too far.'

'You'd better start making a list of countries to avoid, then.'

'I would, but I have the dreadful suspicion that he likes the excitement of being in danger of arrest.'

'Rather like La Duchessa,' said Freddy. 'She's scarpered, by the way.'

'Has she?'

'Yes, I just heard it from Guichard. It seems he also knows all about Roche, but doesn't think there's anything he can do.'

'You've told him, then?'

'I thought I'd better, now that Valencourt's safe—in a manner of speaking.'

'I'm glad you did. That's a weight off my mind. Roche might never be arrested, but at least it won't be because we kept quiet about him.'

'My thoughts exactly. Everything has been put in its proper place and I can return home with a clear conscience—which is not something I say often.' A shade of regret crossed his face. 'It would have been fun to get the Legion of Honour and rub Corky Beckwith's nose in it, but I think this way is better. I mean to say, it would be awfully churlish of them to hand Valencourt the whole book now, after what he did for his country.'

'I hope the judge sees it like that,' she said dolefully.

'Of course he will. So, then, now that you've delivered your husband into the hands of the law, what shall you do next? Are you staying in France to wait for him?'

'No, I must go back to the States soon. I've promised to go and see to things up in Saratoga—and besides, I can't abandon Barbara forever. She's at school, of course, but she does like to come home once in a while.' She wrung her hands. 'Oh dear, how do I tell her about all this? Now I have to confess to her that not only is Edgar not dead, I married him and didn't invite her to the wedding, then promptly sent him to prison. She'll never speak to me again. I shall have to buy her a pony.'

They fell silent for a few minutes. Angela was looking out to sea, her eyes suspiciously bright.

'Don't cry, old thing,' said Freddy.

'I'm not crying,' she replied with dignity. 'The sun's dazzling me and making my eyes water. And anyway, even if I were,' she added after a minute, 'I understand it's the done thing to cry at weddings.'

'What you need is some champagne. Just because the groom can't be here doesn't mean we oughtn't to celebrate.'

'I do believe you're right,' said Angela.

A bottle was brought and Freddy raised his glass, preparing to make a toast. Angela had quite recovered from her momentary lapse of composure and held up her glass likewise.

'To the new Mr. and Mrs.—er—' began Freddy, then lowered the glass and looked inquiringly at Angela. There was still some doubt as to what name they would be using. It might be any one of several.

'Don't look at me—I'm sure I don't know,' said Angela, then laughed suddenly. 'Oh dear, it's all quite absurd, isn't it?'

'What's life without a little absurdity?' said Freddy. He lifted his glass again.

'To new beginnings, then,' he said.

---

## Books by Clara Benson

### THE ANGELA MARCHMONT MYSTERIES

1. The Murder at Sissingham Hall
2. The Mystery at Underwood House
3. The Treasure at Poldarrow Point
4. The Riddle at Gipsy's Mile
5. The Incident at Fives Castle
6. The Imbroglio at the Villa Pozzi
7. The Problem at Two Tithes
8. The Trouble at Wakeley Court
9. The Scandal at 23 Mount Street
10. The Shadow at Greystone Chase

### THE FREDDY PILKINGTON-SOAMES ADVENTURES

1. A Case of Blackmail in Belgravia
2. A Case of Murder in Mayfair
3. A Case of Conspiracy in Clerkenwell
4. A Case of Duplicity in Dorset
5. A Case of Suicide in St. James's
6. A Case of Robbery on the Riviera

### SHORT STORIES

Angela's Christmas Adventure

The Man on the Train

A Question of Hats

## COLLECTIONS

Angela Marchmont Mysteries Books 1-3

Angela Marchmont Mysteries Books 4-6

## OTHER

The Lucases of Lucas Lodge

CPSIA information can be obtained
at www.ICGtesting.com
Printed in the USA
LVHW050416280423
745506LV00003B/407